LONGINGS

LONGINGS

TRACY STERN

Michael Joseph
London

MICHAEL JOSEPH LTD
Published by the Penguin Group
27 Wrights Lane, London W8 5TZ, England
Viking Penguin Inc., 40 West 23rd Street, New York, New York 10010, USA
Penguin Books Australia Ltd, Ringwood, Victoria, Australia
Penguin Books Canada Ltd, 2801 John Street, Markham, Ontario, Canada L3R 1B4
Penguin Books (NZ) Ltd, 182–190 Wairau Road, Auckland 10, New Zealand

Penguin Books Ltd, Registered Offices: Harmondsworth, Middlesex, England

First published in the USA by
Simon and Schuster Inc. 1988
and first published in Great Britain
by Michael Joseph Ltd 1989
Copyright © Tracy Stern 1988

Made and printed in Great Britain by
Richard Clay Ltd, Bungay, Suffolk

Filmset in 11 on 13pt Sabon by
Cambrian Typesetters, Frimley, Surrey

A CIP catalogue record for this book is available from the British Library

ISBN 0 7181 3240 8

For B. B.
With boundless affection

All is available to everyone, in a universe that calls for happy boldness, that waits to give, to take, and to multiply the abundance brought to it.

Mireille Johnston, *Central Park Country*

1

ALL the taxis seemed to have disappeared. It was one of those midsummer days that even the most seasoned New Yorkers found hard to cope with. There were usually five or six of them during the summer, but they generally came during August, when one could rationalise, 'Oh, there's only another five or six weeks of this, and then it will be autumn in New York, and you know how fantastic that is. No city in the world like New York in the fall – crisp, clear days with a super blue sky to outline the beauty of the buildings; cool comfortable nights when apartment windows can finally be opened.' It was difficult for Jennifer Martin even to imagine making it through the next few hours, her interview, and then the seemingly endless trip back to the comfort of the air-conditioned studio.

A haze hung over the island of Manhattan that made it impossible to see across town from one river to the other. It reminded her of those cheap folding nets that her grandmother would put over food when the family had gathered for a meal outdoors. One of those things that looked like an umbrella without a handle that was supposed to protect the food from insects and anything else that wanted to intrude on a perfectly iced cake or a platter of fried chicken. It seemed that some perverse individual had created a giant version of that net, and had placed it over the city, not to keep things out but to keep the inhabitants of the city in.

On the corner of 57th Street and Sixth Avenue, Jennifer approached the cart with the man selling hot dogs, pretzels, and, most appealing to her, ice-cold drinks. She surveyed the selection – all the variations of Coke, Tab, Sprite and Pepsi. She would bet that if someone had a stand with an equally expansive selection of mineral waters, instead of all these syrupy liquids, they would make a fortune.

'I'll have a Diet Coke, please,' she said, her mouth beginning to water at the thought. The man looked at her grudgingly, and didn't move. 'Please, a Diet Coke,' she repeated, a little more slowly, thinking that his English was not too good or perhaps he was just interested in a bigger sale, like a Coke, a hot dog, and maybe two pretzels. Finally, he got up and opened the refrigerator compartment of his travelling food show and produced a dripping can. Jennifer could see that the New York humidity had overpowered the refrigerator's ability to keep anything cold, and the can he was handing her was lukewarm at best. Oh well, at least it would be wet. Perhaps that was all she could expect on this exceptional day.

She had three or four swallows of the sickeningly sweet liquid and discarded the can at the basket ten feet from the vending cart. No matter how hot it was, she hated to be seen eating or drinking on the streets of New York City. When she had first moved to New York, a little over two years ago, she had been appalled at the number of people who walked down the street with pretzels dangling from their mouths, or with a mustard-encrusted chin from the hot dog they had just swallowed. Maybe it was the year she had spent studying in France that had instilled in her a respect for food and a desire to see people dressed and well-mannered on city streets.

She had the same strong feelings about all those women who wore tennis shoes with mink coats in the winter, but she didn't concern herself too much with them. Jennifer had always felt that there was too much competition in a city like New York for a woman ever to look less than her very best. Even today, on one of the most humid, miserable days of the year, Jennifer was wearing Charles Jourdan summer pumps, with two-and-a-half-inch heels, and stockings. That was another thing she could never adjust to – women with untanned, bare legs walking the streets. OK, maybe that was her Midwest upbringing and *not* the year in France, where no one wears stockings from May to September. Of course, nothing looked better than long, bronzed, well-defined legs, with beautifully pedicured toes, striding gracefully down Madison or Fifth Avenue. But that look was for ladies who lunched, not someone who was committed to making history in her profession.

Jennifer looked around at the other women on the streets; only a few looked comfortable and well put together; the majority looked, she decided, like unmade beds. She felt very pleased with her appearance, smart white gabardine straight skirt that hit just above her knees and a collarless white silk Giorgio Armani shirt covered with her new blazer. Under her shirt she was wearing a lacy camisole instead of a bra, and she noticed men's eyes glancing at her with interested looks of approval. She knew the importance of looking professional and serious in order to get the attention of the people she interviewed, yet she was adamant that she never wanted to trade her femininity for those masculine suits and bow ties that she saw being worn by so many 'New York career women' – matching jackets and skirts, the ill-fitting jackets never allowing a woman to show off her figure. Boring, boring, boring! No, Jennifer had decided long ago that she would continue to spend a large percentage of her income on stylish, elegant, classically tailored clothing that would show off the terrific body that she worked so hard three mornings a week to keep in prime shape. Clothes couldn't make the woman, but they certainly helped.

She had six blocks to go – but four of them were the long, cross-town ones, she reminded herself. She walked east across 57th Street – Sixth Avenue to Fifth, past the luscious windows of Tiffany & Co. and the cool grey granite of the IBM building to Madison, Madison to Park Avenue and finally to Lexington. Then just two more lights – 57th, 58th, and finally 59th – where her meeting was scheduled for three p.m.

*   *   *

3

Jennifer had gone home to see her family the weekend before, just to have a friendly visit and escape the heat for a couple of days. But as it turned out, the heat at home, of an entirely different nature, was more intolerable and oppressive than the heat in the city. The plane had been full, and, as was not unusual on Friday nights during the summer, it had been number fourteen for takeoff from La Guardia. So they sat on the runway in unairconditioned splendour for almost an hour. Because of the heavy air traffic and scattered thunder-showers, the pilot was unable to make up the time in the air, and they arrived in Minneapolis at seven-thirty instead of six-thirty that evening.

'How can you tolerate a country where nothing runs on schedule?' asked her mother as she kissed Jennifer lightly on the cheek, assessing her outfit, shoes, the condition of her nails and hair – all in one thorough glance. 'We've already had to reschedule dinner, and Susan had to feed Jason already and put him to bed. He's been cranky all day. I wish that just once you could take an earlier plane. Louise Eden's daughter works in New York and her office is closed in the afternoon on Fridays during the summer. She leaves with her boyfriend for their house in the Hamptons right after that. They've probably already had drinks and a nice walk on the beach by this time.'

'Hello, Mom,' Jennifer said, trying to hold her tongue and not get the weekend off to a rotten start. She knew from experience that if she said what she really wanted to say, her days at home would be damaged beyond repair before they even started. Christ, they weren't even out of the airport yet, and the barrage of complaints had already begun. Louise Eden's daughter, the fabulous Julia, she smiled to herself. She worked as a secretary for some no-name cosmetic house, earning about thirteen thousand dollars a year, most of which she put up her nose in the form of cocaine. The last time they had met for drinks, precipitated by a phone call from Julia, Jennifer had been amazed at the stories she had told her about her life in New York. She was twenty-five, a year younger than Jennifer's youngest sister, Christie, and attractive in a wild, unkempt way. Her hair was dyed a deep cherry red, permed and heavily moussed, and when she met Jennifer after work one night she wore a chartreuse leather miniskirt and a T-shirt about three sizes too small for her more-than-full-breasted chest. She had eyed Jennifer's conservative dress warily.

'I saw you on TV the other night, you were interviewing that guy about the condom machines in the bathroom in his new restaurant. I think it's a hoot that he gets more sales from the women's machines than the men's, don't you?'

The conversation went downhill from there, with Julia doing most of the talking. She had told Jennifer many of the intimate details of her life – the drugs, the sex, the abortion last month, the late nights at the newest hot clubs. It came as no surprise that she didn't have much time to devote to work. Jennifer wondered if her mother would enjoy hearing about their conversation. Maybe she'd like Jennifer to be more like Julia. She decided against mentioning it.

'Welcome home, Miss Jennifer.' It was John, the Martins' driver and houseman for many years. He took her luggage and the presents she had brought for her nephew, Jason. 'You sure look like a sophisticated city girl, but prettier every time you come back. There must be someone special up there keeping you looking great.'

Not him, too, she thought, but she knew John didn't mean any harm. In fact, she wished John had met her alone, without bringing her mother.

'Thanks, John. I'm afraid it's not someone but some*thing* special. I love my new assignment.'

'Working eighteen hours a day suits her,' added her mother. 'Wait until she's forty and starts to lose her looks from all this work.'

'Barbara Walters looks pretty terrific and she's over fifty. No one puts a bag over Diane Sawyer's head, and she turned forty a couple of years ago,' Jennifer commented, mostly for her own satisfaction, since she knew better than to try to change Marion Martin's mind.

The thirty-minute drive to Jennifer's parents' home passed

without any additional confrontations. Jennifer and her mother talked about Jennifer's apartment and whether or not she was finally getting it furnished; next season's clothing; and new restaurants. Marion graciously refrained from asking about Jennifer's social life, or lack of it. She figured she'd hear if there was anything to tell. Jennifer asked about her sisters. She knew that two of them, Susan and Pat, the twins, were also going to be at the house that weekend.

'How's Pat doing?' she asked, knowing her mother would have the up-to-the-minute report on her condition.

'She's fine now. She had a little trouble last week with those Braxton-Hicks contractions. Dr Jacobs put her in the hospital for two days, just to make sure she was all right. With twins, you know, they can never be too careful. Even though she's only twenty-eight, it could be a difficult birth – you know, even ordinary pregnancies are much more difficult, much more dangerous with every passing year.'

Dig, dig, dig. A constant reminder of her disapproval of the way of life Jennifer had chosen.

'Yes, I know, I spoke with her in the hospital. She was pretty frightened. I wonder if she ever imagined that marrying a man whose mother was a twin would impact her life so dramatically!'

She looked forward to seeing Pat. She had always been her favourite sister; even though her relationships with Susan, the other twin, and Christie, the youngest, were always good, it was Pat who had become her closest friend over the past few years. She was now pregnant and the babies were due in late August. She was having a difficult time and had revealed to Jennifer the last time she was home that the experience wouldn't be over a minute too soon for her. Peter, her husband, had been so supportive and loving during the pregnancy. He had encouraged her to stop working full-time almost as soon as she found out. She had continued in her job as the fashion director at Dayton's, the area's most stylish speciality store, until her continuing morning sickness caused her to miss too many early meetings. It really wasn't a problem though. They would hold her position until she could return. No one else could replace Pat's exquisite taste and unerring eye for the fashions that would appeal to the women in one of America's most conservative, wealthy suburbs.

'Jason's just fine,' her mother continued, moving on to Susan's son, her only grandchild so far. 'We had a party for his third birthday at the house last week. Thirteen children, from six months to five years, all in the pool at once. What a show! The mothers reported that they all went home and slept the rest of the afternoon. They wanted to know if we could do it more often.'

'I brought a present from F.A.O. Schwarz for him. It's the cutest stuffed animal, a polar bear, all cosy and cuddly like the one I used to have. The one Aunt Emily gave me when I was about his age. I was late getting up there, so there was no time to mail it. I don't think he'll mind, though. It'll just be an extension of his celebration.'

'Believe me, he'll love it! He got so many things at the party I don't think he's had enough time to play with all of them.'

'Here we are,' John announced as he turned into the Martin property, which was marked by two white marble columns. For as long as she could remember, John had always said 'Here we are' as he turned the car in through the columns.

The drive was in full bloom, the trees at their peak of greenness. She could see her father's wildflower garden in front of the house. He had created it thirty years ago in celebration of the birth of his first daughter, Jennifer. With the birth of each of the other children, he had doubled the size of the garden, so it now covered almost three-quarters of an acre. Kenneth Martin had studied English wildflower gardens at great length before starting his, and Jennifer was never disappointed at its beauty and gracefulness. He laboured over the land, weekend after weekend, and the result was a magnificent profusion of colour, textures, and heights.

Jennifer always marvelled at the transition the garden made from season to season. The snowdrops with their milky white buds were the first to blossom in the early spring. A profusion of daffodils, both yellow and white, followed within days. She knew it had to be June when the campanulas, and their glorious heart-shaped leaves, appeared. The metamorphosis continued all summer. Each week there was something new to see. By late October, only the hardiest plants survived. By the time of the first frost, all the summer varieties lay fallow, to make room for the flowering winter jasmine.

'The garden looks especially wonderful this summer,' Jennifer commented.

'Yes, I don't think your father could ever leave it. We really don't need all the space in the house, now that you're all gone, but I don't think he could ever part with his flowers.'

'Can't say that I blame him,' John added. He sometimes overstepped his role as employee, but, after thirty years, why shouldn't he?

As the car pulled into the circular drive, Jason was the first one out the front door. Susan had been unsuccessful at getting him to go to bed before his aunt arrived.

'Aunt Jennifer, hi!'

'Hi, giant one – boy, have you grown. Is this what a three-year-old looks like or are you an oversized specimen?'

'What's a specimen?' he shot back.

'Good question; an example, I guess,' she answered, not used to dealing with return questions.

'Jason, settle down honey. You'll have plenty of time to ask lots of questions,' Susan yelled, as she hugged Jennifer in greeting.

'You look great. New York OK?'

'Just fine. A little hot right now, but I'm not outside too much. Jason, how come you're still up? I thought you'd be in bed, fast asleep by this time.'

'I wanted to see you, Aunt Jennifer,' he answered.

'You're just waiting for your late birthday present, right? Let me see what I can do. John, do you have that green box with the ribbons on it?'

'Sure do, Miss Jennifer,' he said as he handed her the large, slightly smashed box.

'For you, Jason. Let's take it in the house and open it.'

He disappeared in a flash carrying the larger-than-child-size box with both hands.

'Sweetheart, welcome home,' said Kenneth Martin, warmly hugging his oldest daughter. He was fiercely proud of her and her progress toward the success they had spent hours discussing. They were very close, far closer and more intimate than she would ever be with her mother. Since she was a child, her father had been the one to share her dream with her. And the dream had always been the same. She wanted to be a newscaster. As she grew, the dream evolved while she studied the power of the press in America and the role of a journalist in the process of reporting the news to the public. She studied voraciously and became a near-expert on not only the writing and editing of a story but the technical aspects of the media as well. She spent her summers during high school working as part of the camera crew at the local TV station. She went on location in addition to mastering the studio work, and she never missed a big story, regardless of when or where it happened. Many nights she had left the house at three or four a.m. to cover whatever local story was breaking. She endeared herself to everyone on the crew; they admired her for her enthusiasm and thoroughly cooperative attitude. No job was beneath her. She was hungry for every detail, and she learned them all. She was as comfortable behind the camera, with lights and sound, as she was in front of it.

She was also pretty. When she returned to spend the summer in Wayzata after her first year at the University of Missouri, where she had begun her major in journalism, the producer asked her to fill in for their weatherman, who had had a heart attack after twenty years of reporting the Minnesota forecasts. She was thrilled. It wasn't exactly earth-shattering journalism, wind chill factors and barometric readings, but it was an outstanding opportunity for her to gain some valuable experience. She had happily accepted and been a great success. After so many years of seeing Tom Barton on the air, Jennifer's fresh face and beautiful blonde hair were a welcome change for the viewers. She brought an enthusiasm to the job that made a rainstorm an event to look forward to, and a sunny day something to shout about. Everyone was sorry when September came and she returned to school. They could only imagine what she could have done with a blizzard!

Through all of this, her father had been there for her. He became her chief critic, discussing with her every night after the broadcast how she could make it better, more eye contact, different voice intonation, every aspect of her performance. He was proud of her and understood and appreciated her need to be the very best. He had experienced the same kind of all-consuming drive when he had finally decided to pursue a law career. Nothing and no one could divert his attention from his goal. He saw that tenaciousness in his oldest daughter. It was a force that did not exist in the other girls, and his relationship with Jennifer had surpassed rather than made up for his unanswered prayers that Marion would deliver him a son.

'Hi, Daddy. You look terrific. I missed you,' she said as he picked her up in his arms and gave her a huge bear hug.

'I've missed you, too. Just looking at your tapes is not the same thing as having you here. Although, I must say I'm enjoying your reports. I loved your coverage of the Fourth of July behind-the-scenes events. You must have had a great time.'

'Yes, that one was fun. I met some great people and got to go to some of the parties in the harbour. It was very different from watching the celebration on TV all those years. You really get patriotic! Not to mention pretty drunk after being out on the water all day. Your garden looks so beautiful this year, Daddy, did you add some things?'

'Just a few, in anticipation of the arrival of Pat's twins. The dahlias we planted two years ago for Jason have been excellent, too. Go get settled and come down and have a drink. I want to catch up on the excitement in the big city.'

'John, please tell Doris we'll be ready to sit down in, what do you think Ken, thirty minutes?'

'Fine,' he replied, thinking that he never had enough time to just sit and talk with the girls when they were home. Maybe he'd plan a trip to New York to visit Jennifer.

Susan was upstairs in Pat's bedroom. Pat was lying in bed and Susan was sitting at the foot, her legs folded underneath her.

'Looks like old times,' said Jennifer, kissing and hugging both of them.

'Hi, hot-shot reporter,' Pat said, throwing off the quilt she had been using to cover her enormous tummy.

'My God, you're huge! Are you planning to deliver during dinner?'

'Fuck you, single, svelte one,' Pat joked. 'Wait until you're in this situation. It's no picnic. I wish I could deliver this minute. Who would ever believe that a twin is having another set of twins? Somehow I managed to overlook, or maybe I just ignored, the fact that Peter's mom is a twin, too. How's life in the fast lane?'

'It's very fast from about seven in the morning to eleven at night. From then on it's pretty quiet. I love my work, the people are great, but there's very little outside of that. Mother's already been on my case on the way in from the airport. Where are the men? Where are the babies? She'll never change, will she?'

'It only gets worse. Those of us who have chosen to live within driving distance of her, and in the same area code, get it more often. She's now become an expert on child-rearing and she challenges everything I've taught Jason.'

'I'm thinking of willing her the twins at birth, in an attempt to get even,' added Pat.

'Girls, dinner is about ready.' They heard their mother's voice shout from downstairs.

'I'm going to get into some jeans. I've been in this little costume since daybreak. I'll see you downstairs. Make the drinks potent,' Jennifer said as she went out of the bedroom and down the hall to the room where she had lived for the first eighteen years of her life.

11

The weekend passed without incident. Difficult as it was, Jennifer managed to hold her tongue as she was barraged with questions and concerns from her mother about why she hadn't married, settled down, had children – any or all of those things. As always, she hadn't had enough time to sit and talk with her father – between swimming, playing tennis doubles with Susan and her husband and an old schoolmate – it was time to go to the airport before she knew it. She promised to return as soon after the birth of Pat's and Peter's twins as possible. She missed them all already.

Turning north on Lexington Avenue, Jennifer started to review the questions for her upcoming interview. She had formulated them in her mind late last night and formalised them this morning with the producer.

Finally, the Bloomingdale's logo appeared through the haze. The revolving doors were turning briskly, the shoppers undeterred by the heat and humidity. Jennifer glanced in the windows, which were all done in the theme of their promotion – the United Kingdom. The ready-to-wear windows honoured the best of British designers – Jasper Conran, Katherine Hamnett, Jean Muir and the hottest new star, Rifat Ozbek, really a Turk but he made London his home. She thought the clothes looked a little far out, but London was always on the cutting edge. The trends that were happening there now wouldn't be seen on the streets of Manhattan for at least two years.

The entire main floor had been transformed to show off the merchandise that had been selected to represent the Best of Britain. From the exclusive 'Colours of the Thames' cosmetic collection by Estée Lauder, to the antique Burberry raincoat exhibit, the creative geniuses of the store had done justice to their advertising tag line – it was truly 'like no other store in the world'. Jennifer took a few minutes on each floor to familiarise herself with the merchandise and special exhibits. Hordes of people lined up to taste the special blends of English tea that were being served in the gourmet food section. The aroma of freshly baked scones filled the air. On the main floor attractive models in tartan skirts offered small samples of fragrant potpourri made from English wildflowers. The Ralph Lauren boutique was spectacular – to the tiniest detail his collection of sporting gear was more English than the Queen Mother herself. Upstairs, the model rooms were done completely in Laura Ashley fabric and furniture. Jennifer wanted to transport the entire look to her own bedroom uptown. Glancing at her watch, she pulled herself away from the array of wonderful English merchandise.

She arrived at the office of the chairman at five minutes before three.

'Jennifer Martin, Channel 7, to see Mr Traub, please,' she advised the receptionist.

'Oh yes, Ms Martin, your camera crew arrived a little while ago and they're setting up in the conference room. You're welcome to go in and check on them if you like. Mr Traub will be a few minutes. It's just through those double doors.'

'Thanks so much.'

The crew was almost set up. They greeted her warmly. Everyone always enjoyed working with her, mostly because, of all the reporters on the staff, Jennifer knew more about their jobs than anyone. She appreciated all the preparations and care they took to make her look good on film.

'Please tell Mr Traub we're ready for him as soon as it's convenient,' she went back out and told the receptionist. She hoped he wouldn't keep them waiting too long. Over the years, she had come to believe that truly effective, successful, powerful men had learned to control their time. The others, those who were faking it, were always late.

Marvin Traub, the invincible dynamo behind the legendary Bloomingdale's, entered the conference room at three minutes after three.

The crew was on their feet and in position by the time he had walked the length of the enormous mahogany table.

'Hello, Jennifer.' He shook her hand and kissed her cheek lightly. They had met several times before, most recently only a week earlier. Jennifer had made sure that she was invited to the preview showing of the new line of fabrics from Ralph Lauren. Lauren was an important account at the store and this was a high-roller event. She was almost certain that Traub would make a courtesy appearance. And she had been right. It always helped to establish some contact with anyone you were interviewing before the actual taping. Unless, of course, you were going to discuss a controversial topic. In that case, cross the street to avoid a preview confrontation! But there was nothing remotely controversial about today's subject. The fact that Sarah Ferguson, the Duchess of York, and her husband, Prince Andrew, had chosen to visit Bloomingdale's during their stay in New York next week was indeed a coup for the store.

'Mr Traub, it's so good to see you again. Thanks for your time. We'll try to move along as quickly as possible. But it would be helpful to know just how much time you can spare.'

'For you, as much as it takes to get the proper coverage. It's an honour for us to have the Royals visit, so we want everything to reflect that mood. If we can be finished by four-thirty, I'd be delighted.'

Fantastic, she thought, they could get enough for a good, thorough report in that amount of time.

'That's wonderful. If I can get you over here in front of this camera, we'll start right away.'

'Lights, OK, sound check, OK – Jennifer, whenever you're ready.'

'Good evening, I'm Jennifer Martin. Tonight we have the pleasure of being in the office of Mr Marvin Traub, chairman of Bloomingdale's. Next week, the store will be honoured with a visit from Prince Andrew and his wife, the lovely Sarah Ferguson. They are coming to the store as a goodwill gesture to celebrate the best of Britain promotion currently being held in all Bloomingdale's locations. We're delighted to have the opportunity to speak with Mr Traub about this exciting event. Mr Traub, could you begin by telling us who will be meeting the Duke and Duchess of York when they arrive at the store?'

'They will be greeted by myself and Mr Robert Tammero,

our store president. They will then be given a floor-by-floor tour of the entire store. We'll take as much time in each area as they desire, but they have made a special request to spend some extra time in the home furnishings departments, so we'll have all of our merchants in those categories, from buyers to divisional merchandise managers, available to answer any questions they may have.'

'What will security be like in the store?'

'Well, I'm not at liberty to discuss that, but believe me when I tell you that we are taking every precaution imaginable to ensure their safety.'

On and on, question after question, response after response. Jennifer could have stopped the interview earlier, and chatted casually with the chairman, for she knew they had more than enough material for the finished piece which would only run two or three minutes. But that was only one of her skills as a reporter – she pushed the person she was interviewing, she wanted even the minutest details. Later on, she and the producer could decide what would end up on the cutting-room floor.

Marvin was a professional, he was comfortable with the press as well as the cameras, and he had prepared for the interview. He knew exactly what he wanted to tell his customers and he told it with flair and efficiency.

They were both pleased.

'If only everyone were as organised as you, my job would be a piece of cake,' Jennifer told him as she walked with him back to his office. 'Thank you for everything, Mr Traub. We'll do a nice piece.'

'I've no doubt about that. I told Sidney I wouldn't do the interview with anyone but you. I knew you'd approach the visit with just the right style. He agreed. And today you proved it. I'm very pleased. How is everything going for you?'

'Just fine. I'm hoping for a permanent live spot soon, but for now I'm still scooping the Special Segments.'

'Well, you know I'm rooting for you. I'd trade your glorious face and charm for Dan Rather's any night.'

'Thanks, Marvin. We'll air the story on the seventh or

15

eighth. I'll let your secretary know. And we'll get a tape over right away.'

The crew gave her a ride back to the studio in their air-conditioned van. It was almost six-thirty by the time they made it across town.

2

SIDNEY Lachman, the executive producer of Channel 7, was in his cluttered, paper-strewn office reviewing the final rewrites for the ten o'clock edition of the news. He smiled when Jennifer entered.

'So, queen of the Special Segments, I hear you charmed the designer socks off of ol' Marvin.'

'How do you know? You have a hotline to the building?'

'No, he was so overwhelmed by your on-target questions he called to tell me. Seriously, you're to be congratulated. He's not always that receptive to the press.'

'We did fine, the crew was great. And what's the big deal? It's not a summit conference. Just a little shopping spree by Fergie and her husband.'

Jennifer stayed until ten, reviewing the tapes and making her comments for the editors. She thought it was good. Overall, she was pleased with the questions and more importantly, his responses.

The ten p.m. edition of the news was just starting when she entered the newsroom. She watched the broadcast with the late-night staff, then said good night.

The air outside had cooled slightly and taxis were plentiful. Their availability was always inversely related to the foulness of the weather. The better the weather, the more taxis on the street. God bless the new disco down the block on West 57th Street. Before it had opened, you had had to walk for ages to see a moving vehicle that was not occupied by a pimp. Now an influx of yellow cars was dropping off the night people, those who began their days in the clubs and discos around eleven o'clock in the evening.

'Seventy-seventh and Madison, please,' she told the driver.

'Whatever you'd like, beautiful. Hey, didn't I see you on the news last week? I forget the story, but I remember you.'

'Yes, it was probably me,' she answered, not wanting to continue the conversation. It was just another reminder of the work she had cut out for herself to get where she wanted to be. Sometimes she wished that she had been more ugly or, better yet, a boy. But those thoughts only lasted for a minute. If she had been ugly, she wouldn't even have reached her current position. Women in broadcasting, why were so few of them working the network news? She was painfully aware of how much harder she would have to work to prove to herself and to others that she was as capable as any man of handling the job of anchor. But how long would it take, and were all the sacrifices really going to be worth it in the end? She hoped so, with all her heart.

Bed, bed, the luxury of freshly starched linen sheets. Even the hum of the air conditioner was a welcome sound tonight. Jennifer threw off her clothes and stepped into the shower. She allowed the hot water to run forcefully over her body. Hair, face, breasts, all the way down to her toes, she scrubbed away the film of a miserable day in one of the world's dirtiest cities. Calèche, the beautiful Hermès fragrance, was the only scent she could tolerate in this heat. She took the bottle of body lotion into the bedroom and applied lavish quantities all over. Starting with her neck, she rubbed her hands gently down her well-shaped body, over her breasts, across the flatness of her stomach. Closing her eyes, she touched herself and was surprised to feel the wetness between her swollen lips. For some inexplicable reason, Jeffrey had been at the back of her thoughts all day. Maybe she was missing him more now after all her mother's gentle reminders during the past weekend of what could have been. Yes, she supposed, she could have stayed in Kansas City and continued as the women's reporter at the local station. It was a job that, at the time, two years after graduation, she had welcomed. It

18

offered an opportunity to fine tune her editorial skills, and it had been a very successful stint. But, a stint it was. She had learned more about cooking, birth control and housewives than she ever cared to know. She had always seen it as a stepping-stone in her career, which would reach its pinnacle in New York. Where else did they broadcast network news from?

Jeffrey's voice echoed in her mind, as if she had only left yesterday instead of two years ago.

'A stepping-stone? Is that what you considered me, too, a mere stepping-stone in your climb to the top? Just another rung on the ladder to success. Well, you certainly stayed on my rung a long time, didn't you? And now, you were planning to leave without saying goodbye. That's terrific, Jennifer – three years together aren't worth a few tears?'

He had come home early to the apartment they shared, unexpectedly, from the hospital one night to find her packing her belongings. At some point, she had really believed that the easiest way to leave was to make a clean break, no looking back. New York was out of the question for Jeffrey. He had established a strong private practice in Kansas City and was both unable and unwilling to move now. That she understood. Why was it so difficult for him to see her need to go?

They had not spoken since that night. He had stayed in touch with Pat; she had received a Christmas card from him that indicated he still lived in the apartment he had once shared with Jennifer. He had written a short note, with no mention of her – just an all encompassing 'Give my best to your family.' Jennifer supposed that included her. Occasionally she had considered contacting him, she would have loved to have spent a weekend with him in New York – he adored great restaurants and was a big theatre fan. But she supposed that would be too painful for him. How could she be so strong? Probably her feelings would be different if they made love again. No one had ever satisfied her the way Jeffrey had. The intensity, the variety of their lovemaking had been all-consuming. It was the hardest part to forget. They had touched each other in ways that Jennifer could never have imagined, and it was hard for her to think of ever being so free and open with someone again. Certainly not with the men she had dated since she had been in New York. Most of them fitted into one of two categories – half were not interested in discussing the variety of subjects in which Jennifer was interested, and just after the entrée was served the conversation became strained. They were one-dimensional – one career, one subject. The second group were immediately threatened by Jennifer's success and career goals. She enjoyed a certain amount of notoriety, even now, and there were lots of men who couldn't stand having anyone else in the limelight. Even if, especially if, it got them a better table at a restaurant.

God, how she missed Jeff's touch – the multiple-orgasm nights and the mornings when he had awakened her without words, merely by entering with his huge morning erection.

She fell into bed, exhausted. For now, she would have to be content with the memories.

3

S*IDNEY* stepped out of his limo in front of Mezzaluna on Third Avenue and 74th Street. He told his driver he wouldn't be too long, he just wanted a drink and one of their delicious, thin-crust pizzas with sun-dried tomatoes and fresh basil. From the number of people crowding the entrance, it might take longer than he expected. He made his way to the bar and ordered a Heineken and a pizza to be served there. Seated, he observed the crowd. Mezzaluna had been open about two years, and by all accounts it was a hot restaurant. Its regular clientele included some media and television producers and loads of fashion types. Often one could see Calvin and Kelly Klein sharing a late-night bowl of pasta, and always there was an attractive smattering of Euro-trash, plus many members of the Junior International Club. The crowd was always well dressed, and Sidney stopped here frequently if he had put in an especially long day. His apartment was just around the corner on 79th and Park.

Ever since he had lost his wife of twenty years to cancer eighteen months ago, Sidney had spent much more time at the television studio. He had been so devastated at the enormity of his loss that work seemed to be the only outlet into which he could channel his energies without incurring additional grief. During the last two painful months of her life, when Rita had drifted in and out of consciousness but was alert enough to insist on dying in her own apartment, Jennifer had been there with him whenever he needed her. Late nights, early mornings, weekends, whenever the pain became too overwhelming, he would call her. There was never a question, she was never too busy, she was never not in the mood to give support, she just came. Sometimes he would meet her at a coffee shop in their neighbourhood, many times they would just walk through Central Park or visit one of the museums. Often they didn't talk and, if they did, never about the illness and Rita's impending death. Jennifer was just there, like a solid, dependable rock. He could accept anything she said, and one evening when it became too much, he got drunk and spent the night in the second bedroom in her apartment. She was there in the morning with freshly brewed coffee and her continuing offer of friendship, nothing more, nothing less.

After Rita died, Jennifer continued her efforts to bring Sidney back to reality, to the normality he had missed ever since the heart-breaking diagnosis had been delivered. She had demanded nothing in return, and he had been too weak even to consider thinking of their relationship on any other terms. But that had not always been the case, nor was it the case now.

Ten years ago, Sidney had been invited to serve as a visiting professor at the University of Missouri's School of Journalism. His meteoric rise to being a top-flight executive producer was just beginning, and he was delighted to be honoured by the finest school of its kind in the nation. He requested and was granted a three-month leave of absence from the station where he was working, and he arrived on campus during the fall semester to teach a workshop course in broadcast journalism. Since it was a workshop and required role-playing and the set-up of a mock television station, only twenty-five students were allowed to participate.

The first day of class brought the usual teacher-student anxieties. Would they like him? Would he be able to communicate the things he had learned along his fast-paced career path clearly enough to make an impact on these eager young minds? How would a group of students at this Midwestern university respond to his slightly arrogant New

York style? And, most important, would the hard-on that had come to him and refused to subside after he had seen the blonde in the front row be discernible to the students?

Who was she? Shoulder-length blonde hair, vibrant, saucer-size blue eyes, and long, lovely legs that – how did they say it in Missouri? – would make you cry till the cows came home. Something like that. It didn't matter. She was sensational. Her body was tight and she was only using six of the many buttons on the front of the white shirtwaisted dress she was wearing. The top was open to reveal the beginning of her enormous breasts, and the skirt was unbuttoned almost to the point where her thighs met. There must be some mistake, he silently prayed, then immediately rescinded his wish. Surely she was an art history or better yet, a physical education major, not a student of the serious subject of journalism. Even more preposterous, one of the top twenty-five students to have been personally selected by the dean to attend his workshop.

He'd find out soon enough, but right now he'd have to open the class while seated behind the desk. He prayed the students would see it as an attempt to develop a cosy, congenial atmosphere right from the start, rather than an attempt to hide his bulging penis.

'Good morning, everyone. I'm Sidney Lachman, and I'm a visiting professor here to try to share some of my experiences in journalism with each of you in this workshop course. Is everyone here a selected student for this course? If not, now's your last chance to get out before we put you on the air.'

Not a movement. He quickly counted twenty-five eager faces, including the blonde beauty in row one.

'Well, then, let's get started. I suppose names could be a big plus since we'll be spending so much time together. Please let's go around the room – give me your name, and after that please tell the rest of the class what role you'd like to play as we start to assign positions to create the network. I'm sure there will be duplications, but in twelve weeks we'll have enough time to let everyone have their turn. Can we start in the back and work forward, please?'

He half listened as the rest of the students gave their names and desired roles. He checked their names off from the master list that had been delivered to his room in the faculty dorm the night before.

Finally, it was her turn.

'Jennifer Martin, sir. I'd like to be the anchor.'

He loved everything but the 'sir' part. Did he look that old to her? Her voice was not what he had expected. Blondes usually had a high, sing-song pitch, but not her. She had a solid, believable sound, controlled and serious. She had meant what she said, she wanted to be the anchor. It was clear from her tone.

The workshop had turned out to be a rewarding experience, both for Sidney and, he was confident, the students as well. Everyone had worked together beautifully, and the predictable personality and political conflicts usually prevalent in these situations never surfaced.

They assigned duties the first week, and during the following eleven weeks they produced a daily news broadcast. Just like all of the major networks, ABC, CBS, and NBC, their XYZ was ready with a twenty-two minute news programme every day at four-thirty. From nine in the morning, the team worked nonstop. Sidney served as the executive producer, giving support to the correspondents and pulling everyone together. Jennifer Martin had indeed been the anchor. This was not a decision that Sidney had made arbitrarily, just because she was one of the most glorious females he had ever seen. No, that had been determined by the rest of the students. At the end of the first week, ballots were passed out that indicated each individual's job preference. The other students could either tick the space next to the name of the person, thereby showing their support, or they could indicate another individual whom they thought would be more effective in that position. In case of a tie, Sidney would make the final decision, usually splitting the assignment – six weeks instead of twelve. In the case of anchor, Jennifer had her peers' approval hands down. There was only one dissenting vote for another student, a boy who had neither the desire nor the charisma to carry off the task. Sidney had assumed it was just a joke.

Jennifer's handling of the anchor position was one of the most important factors in the success of the workshop. She embraced the fantasy job with an all-consuming ambition. She was in the studio each morning before any of the others, pulling up research for new stories, working on her commentary (a portion of the show she had asked to add at the end of each week), or beginning the first rewrite of the day's programme.

Each evening, when the cameras started to roll, she delivered an informative, authoritative, and compelling programme. Sidney was highly impressed, and they became friends outside the classroom. Their relationship was closer than that which he had with any of the other students, mostly because of her tenacity and the amount of time she devoted to the class. He held himself back from even attempting to consummate his almost overwhelming physical desire for her. He had enjoyed many extracurricular dalliances during his marriage, and he would continue to do so until Rita's illness caused the guilt that forced him to stop. For what it was worth, he was faithful to her during the last year of her life. But after Rita had died, Sidney's indiscretions weighed heavily on his mind. He promised himself that should he ever marry again, he would never allow himself to stray.

In all these years, however, his desire for Jennifer had never lessened. Long after he awarded her an A plus in the workshop and returned to the frenetic pace of his life in New York, they kept in touch. During the first few years, when Jennifer was finishing school and deciding what her best bets were as a career pattern, Sidney would call every few weeks. They lost contact for a few months when she decided to go to Africa on a post-graduate safari. After her return and her decision to take the spot in Kansas City, he invited her to

New York for a weekend. He remembered it as if it were yesterday.

'Can we please go to the studio?' she had asked on the way in from the airport.

'Don't you want to check in at the hotel first? I've been promised that you'll have a suite at the Plaza facing Central Park.'

'Thanks, Sidney, you really are a sweetheart. But it would be so special for me to see a network show. You know, I've never been here at the right time, and if we don't go tonight, I'll miss it again. Please . . .'

How could he deny her? So even at four-thirty at the end of a working week, he had redirected the driver to Manhattan's West Side. With the Friday-night traffic it took ages. They arrived just as the broadcast was beginning. The camera crew was momentarily distracted as they watched Jennifer's outstanding body settle into a seat in the studio to watch the show. Sidney could hear murmurs of 'Who is *that*?' through his earphone.

The weekend had been wildly successful, in all aspects except Sidney's desire to take Jennifer to bed in her suite at the Plaza; Rita was conveniently out of town visiting her sister, but as it turned out his absence from their apartment for the entire night was never necessary.

'Jenn, you must know by now how I feel about you. I've felt that way since I first laid eyes on you in my class so long ago. Surely we can talk about this . . .' Sidney was trying to understand her reluctance to make love to him. 'Is there someone special in your life right now?'

'No, Sidney, that's not it at all. It's just that I respect you so much as a professional, as a friend – I'm trying not to jeopardise that even though this weekend wasn't a testament to that viewpoint. Besides, I do recall that gold band on your left hand has some sort of a story behind it.'

And that was that. He had tried a couple of other times, once when they had been in Los Angeles together and his desire for her had become unbearable, and another time when she had been in New York researching a story. But her

26

response had always been the same. It would probably be terrific, but no.

Once she had told him about Jeffrey, but after her move to New York, she had never mentioned him again. He assumed it was over.

It was an odd bit of fate that Sidney had been offered a remarkable position at Channel 7 just six months after Jennifer had joined the station in New York. He had accepted it because it was a spectacular opportunity, but the fact that Jennifer was there was not unimportant. They had become close, but, to this day, not in the way that Sidney still dreamt of.

'Is it you, Sidney?' He turned on his stool at the bar to see Alicia Clemson and her husband, David. Alicia was a stunning brunette, an attorney with a small real estate firm. David was a partner at Davis, Polk & Wardwell. She had been a childhood friend of Rita's, they had played countless sets of tennis together. Over the years the two couples used to see each other frequently, either in the city or on weekends at the Clemsons' home in Greenwich. But since Rita's death, Sidney found it too painful to spend any time with them. Still, he liked them, and he missed their company. He wondered silently to himself how long it would be before he would be able to contact old friends again.

'You look fantastic. All of that hard work is certainly not destroying your looks.' She kissed him warmly and moved aside so David could squeeze in to shake his hand.

'Hi, ol' buddy. You know, Alicia and I were just talking about you on the train home last week. We've been meaning to call, but that's really no excuse. How have you been?'

'Pretty good – the news goes on, nightly as you know. And you two – are you staying in town tonight?'

'No, David just finished a board meeting at the convenient hour of eleven p.m., so we decided to drop off some of the partners who live in town and continue on with the car to Connecticut. The trains are too infrequent at this hour – not like the morning schedule.'

'I don't know how you do it. Seventy-ninth and Park to 57th Street is a long commute for me most mornings. But it is beautiful up there. How are Eric and Rachel?'

'Just fine – both enjoying school – they find very few reasons to return home any more. Rachel is going to spend the next semester in Florence studying art and wild Italians. But we do miss them. It's a big house for just the two of us.'

Sidney felt a mild melancholy come over him. He wondered if his suffering would have been any less if Rita had been able to have a child. She had miscarried three times, twice at full term, and they had stopped trying many years ago. It had been one of her great regrets, which she mentioned repeatedly during the last days of her life.

'Are you going to eat, or did you just stop for a drink?' Sidney asked.

'We were going to eat, but Gina said it would be at least forty-five minutes for a table. We decided to head home. We only fought our way to the bar to say hello to you. Promise we'll see you soon. I know it's been hard, it's been tough for all of us, but maybe enough time has passed for us to be together again.'

'I think so. I'm feeling pretty good these days.'

'I've got an early meeting in the city tomorrow,' David shouted over the din, 'but I'll call you after that and we'll make a date. Great to see you.'

'I'll look forward to it.' He kissed Alicia and watched as they made their way through the crowd and outside to the waiting limo.

It would be good to see them again. He looked forward to David's call.

4

*T*HE following morning Jennifer was lying lazily in her bed, listening to the hum of the window air conditioner, hating it more every minute. She wanted to shut it off, but within minutes the apartment would become so humid, so stifling she wouldn't be able to get up. The telephone rang, and she answered in a clear, wide-awake voice, even though the clock by her bed indicated it was only six a.m.

'Do you always talk like that in the morning? What the hell are you doing up at this hour?' Sidney's mind was racing with visions of her lying naked in bed, long blonde hair gently draped over the pillow. He was sure she even smelled terrific in the morning. Oh, to turn over and see that face, to hold her in his arms and take her quickly but gently before getting out of bed. He forced himself to concentrate on the business in hand.

'Who can sleep in this weather? It's really not fit for human life. I was considering taking a flight to a cooler clime.'

'Not so fast. I may have a better idea for you.'

'Oh terrific, something like yesterday,' she said. 'That was really fun. Running around town in this steam oven, no taxis in sight – if it's any trip south of 56th Street I demand an air-conditioned limo. I'll even take yours.'

'Jenn, there's been a terrible accident, or maybe it was deliberate. I don't know. I don't have any details yet. A train, one of the earliest ones from Connecticut, blew up at Grand Central just minutes ago, about a half-hour by now, I guess. Apparently it's really a disaster, bodies everywhere, some

29

dead, lots of injuries. Stewart called me from there. He was hurt but sounded OK. He wanted to tell me what had happened and to get someone over there right away. We were talking and they cut the line for emergency use, so I couldn't find out exactly where he was. I assume still in the station somewhere, covering the story. I could hear sirens and people yelling in the background. I didn't even get a chance to ask him what he was doing on that train so early in the morning. Or even why he was on the train – he lives in the city, doesn't he?'

Stewart was Stewart Honwrath, the charismatic young rising star of the station. Sidney had been grooming him for the anchor job ever since he had brought him over from the competing station where they had both been before joining Channel 7. Replacing him, if he was going to be out for a while with his injuries, was no small task. Converting viewers was a long, tedious process. But something told Sidney his star newscaster would not be doing the news tonight.

'Yes, he does, but I can tell you why,' Jennifer replied. 'He stopped by my office on his way out last night. He said he was leaving early to go to his sister's house in Southport for dinner. It was her birthday and they were having some friends over to celebrate. He said he felt guilty for leaving so early because he still had lots of writing to do, but he planned to take an early train in and finish it this morning. Oh, how awful . . . Did you send someone over right away?'

'Yes, they should be there by now. But I need you to get up now and get over there to take a look. Don't push to get the story, I've got a crew on the way. Just try and get a good look, and be careful. Don't get too close and take any chance of getting hurt. I've got a strange feeling that Stewart won't be doing the programme tonight. I don't know, he sounded a little disoriented. How do you feel about filling in?'

'Me?' she asked incredulously. 'Sid, there must be four or five people in line before you get to me.'

'Right, but I've had Bruce checking, and everyone's on vacation or tied up. I can't say I'm too disappointed, I've never felt we spend enough time developing strong backups.

Anyway, I think you can handle it; in fact, I've every confidence in you. Just remember your workshop days. How do you feel about it?'

She hesitated for another moment, still uncertain that Sidney had considered all his options.

'What about Steve Wykowski?' she enquired about a newscaster she knew Sidney couldn't stand to be in the studio with.

'That arrogant SOB?' he replied immediately. 'Bruce tried him too, but he's in Alaska on some rafting expedition, and they'd have to send someone in on a donkey to get him. I think it's very appropriate, though, it takes a horse's ass to find one.'

They both enjoyed the brief moment of laughter.

Jennifer felt the excitement course through her. 'Of course I'll do it, and I'll be delighted. I'm only sorry the opportunity is coming just because someone is injured.'

'Timing is everything in life, Jenn. Sooner or later you'll realise the value of both timing and luck. They're a lethal combination. They outweigh brains ten to one.'

'OK, I'm up. I'll be dressed and at Grand Central in forty-five minutes. I'll try to call you from there. If I can't, I'll come straight to the studio and update you then. Sid, did you arrange for make-up and wardrobe?'

'Yes, my darling. We wouldn't put you on looking less than your very best, which I distinctly recall is pretty terrific.'

'Flirting only makes me nervous, you know that. I'll see you later.'

'OK.'

'Sid?' She caught him just before he hung up.

'Yes, Jenn.'

'Thanks for everything.'

5

*J*ENNIFER rocketed out of bed. She was so emotionally torn between her concern for Stewart and her delight at the chance to anchor the news in his place that for a few minutes she simply wandered around her apartment, not thinking clearly. Finally she pulled out her well-travelled Louis Vuitton duffel bag and stuffed it full of cosmetics – an Estée Lauder tightening mask, a greenish foundation that would take out the sallow tone of her skin, Erno Laszlo's Shake-it, which could conceal any slight imperfections in her nearly perfect skin, and an assortment of Chanel blushers, lipsticks, eye shadows and the all-important tube of Lancôme Maquicils black mascara. It was the one product she would kill for if stuck on a desert island. Sometimes the make-up people didn't have everything they needed, especially if they were only used to working on men. Today was no time for taking any chances. She packed it all. Next, accessories. The Chanel faux pearl earrings Sidney had given her for Christmas would be good, they'd probably dress her very traditionally, a brightly coloured blouse with a stock tie, maybe a jacket. Throw in the Butler & Wilson pearl-and-stone Victorian-era brooch Pat had made her buy over the weekend; it was certainly conservative enough. One last check – she had everything. Grabbing her handbag, she was out of her apartment.

A blast of humid air hit her as soon as the doorman opened the lobby door. She lumbered out with her bag.

'I'll pray for a taxi for you, Ms Martin. You deserve one in this weather.'

'Thanks, Henry. Be sure to watch Channel 7 tonight at six. I'll be on.'

'You're always on with those interesting reports. My wife and I try never to miss you.'

'No, tonight will be a little different. Don't forget.' She dashed out of the door.

A few hours from now, she'd realise how much truth there was in what she had just said.

There was an ample supply of available taxis on Fifth Avenue at 74th Street. She thanked heaven when she saw one with an air-conditioning unit perched on the bonnet.

'Don't tell me Grand Central, lady,' the driver growled before he even released the door locks. 'There's been a terrible accident there. Some wacko blew up a train. Dead bodies everywhere. I won't take the cab near there.'

'No problem, just take me down Fifth to 46th or so. I'll walk from there,' she said as she got in. 'Do you know any more about the accident? How many injuries? Was it really an accident or a bomb?' she asked, amazed at the speed with which the news of a calamity travelled.

'I don't know nothin' more. It's been on the radio for about an hour now. You a reporter or somethin'?'

'Yes, as a matter of fact, I am. I'm on my way to cover the story now.'

'You got a press card? If you do maybe we can show the cops and they'll let us get in a little closer.'

'I do, I have my card right here. I'd sure appreciate it if we could try.'

'I'll do my best. A pretty thing like you shouldn't have to walk too far on a day like this.'

There were many times in her life that she wished she weren't so attractive. This morning was not one of them.

Between Jennifer and the driver, they charmed the policeman blocking the corner of 46th Street and Vanderbilt into letting the car pass through to the main building. She thanked the man profusely and handed him a ten-dollar bill even though the meter only registered three dollars and forty cents. 'Have an ice-cold beer on me when you get off this afternoon. Thanks.'

He smiled at her, but horror struck his face as he looked in his rear-view mirror to see the ambulances lined up to receive the dead and wounded.

'Be careful, lady,' he called after her, 'It looks gruesome.' But she was already inside the terminal.

Nothing in her experience could have prepared her for the scene she saw from the top of the stairs. Looking down into the main terminal area, where she had so often walked, or even more often run madly to catch a train, she couldn't believe what lay before her. It looked like a war scene. The only memories she had of anything that looked remotely like this were some film clips from the bombings in London during World War II. Only this wasn't a battlefield, and the enemy, if there was one, had not yet been identified. No, this was Grand Central Station, one of the busiest cogs in the machine that was the most influential city in the world. Seeing the devastation on television in the comfort of one's home and being twenty yards away from the reality of it were two entirely different things. She could hear the screams of those still buried in the rubble. Occasionally one of the search dogs would bark violently, indicating a body nearby, and the rescue workers would move in to try and clear the area. Her mouth tasted smoky, her throat dry. She sensed an unfamiliar, acid smell in addition to the smoke from the fire. She feared it was the stench of burning flesh.

The bodies they had been able to recover so far were laid out on stretchers, row upon row. Some had IVs attached, others had their injuries bandaged. The paramedics were walking through the aisles, two by two, one holding a clipboard. Apparently they were deciding who could or should be moved first. Off to one side, there were ten or twenty stretchers, it was difficult to count. On each stretcher lay a body bag encasing a morning commuter. It would be hours before anyone could turn their attention to those stretchers.

Nausea began to overcome her. She turned and rested her bag on the marble steps. Get hold of yourself, Jennifer, not only do you have to find out what's going on here, you have to report it to a million people tonight. Pull yourself together! Now! Before it's too late.

'Excuse me, miss. Miss, please move. We must get through.' It took a few seconds before she realised that the voice was speaking to her. 'Please, please let us through now.'

She stepped to the side to allow more emergency service personnel to go down the stairs. They were carrying stretchers for the injured.

The enormous room began to spin. The larger-than-life-size Kodak transparency billboard, a pastoral scene somewhere in Switzerland, became distorted. Jennifer managed to move to the landing on the staircase just seconds before she fainted.

6

'HELLO there, pretty lady,' said a very comforting, very English voice.

Could she be in London? Was this all a terrible nightmare? No, if it were a nightmare, she'd be home in bed, with a soft pillow that had a freshly laundered pillow slip on it. But whatever had been placed under her head now was not soft at all, in fact it was quite bumpy and uncomfortable. She reached back to feel it. It was made of parachute nylon and contained lots of little round jars. Was it a paramedic's bag filled with medicines? A very organised cosmetics travel bag, with all the containers the same size? She couldn't tell.

'How are you feeling?' he continued in the most soothing manner. 'You really go out cold when you decide to faint. Can't say that I blame you. It's pretty awful here, the injuries are hideous. Why don't I help you up and get you into a cab outside? You should probably go home and rest for a while, or at least go to a quiet spot for a hot cup of tea. This is really a very shocking experience for someone who's not used to it. I was round this kind of thing in Southeast Asia for six years, and it still bothers me. Especially this sort of madness.'

Her head began to clear, and her eyes came into focus. She could now associate the voice with the man. His entire face matched his charming voice. Sparkling kind blue eyes. Dark hair, a little on the longish side, and a neatly trimmed beard. She couldn't tell about the body or his clothing because he was kneeling on the floor beside her. He had the relaxed, tanned look of a man who enjoyed whatever he did in life.

'You don't understand,' she said forcefully, 'I'm a reporter. The anchorman for Channel 7 was on that train this morning. He got through to our producer before they cut the lines. He's here somewhere. I've got to find him and the rest of our camera crew. Are you with the press too?'

'Well, yes, I suppose so. I'm a photojournalist. Mostly, I cover events in Europe and the Middle East, but I've been spending quite a bit of time in the States lately. Listen, do you feel well enough to get up? Since you're not leaving right away, maybe we can continue this conversation at a proper table, or at least standing up. The first time I introduce myself to a gorgeous woman, she's usually not flat on her back.'

'Yes, I'm OK, I think. Were you standing beside me when I lost it?'

'Sort of, I was coming down the stairs. When I got to the landing, I noticed you weaving a bit and trying to find the railing. I caught you just as you were going down. My bag of film has been serving as your pillow while you were coming to.'

So that's what it was, she realised now.

'Yes, I can get up now I think. Oh, what a mess.' She looked down at her white cotton dress, which was now filthy. The back of the dress was wet and sticky. She had landed in an area where someone had recently spilled a Coke. Her left stocking had a run in it. 'They're going to have their work cut out for them to get me ready for tonight.'

'Do you have a big event to go to tonight?' he asked thoughtfully, holding her elbow and escorting her to the top of the stairs.

'Well, it's not an event in the social sense of the word. It's work. You see, I'm going to fill in for Stewart, the anchorman, just in case he's too shook up to make it tonight. He does the six o'clock news. Everyone else is either on vacation or too far away to make it back in time. They usually don't let the Special Segment reporter go on live, but I've done some live work before, and I've got a producer with a lot of faith in me.'

They were outside the station now. Her head began to clear.

'I never thought I'd be happy to be outside in this heat. But I am. And I've been quite slow in thanking you, Mr —' She realised she didn't know his name.

'Nicholas, Nicholas Tate. And you're very welcome, Miss —'

'Jennifer Martin.' She felt funny extending her hand to shake his. Nicholas had had his arm around her waist the entire time since she stood up. She also realised that it had been a very comfortable, pleasant feeling.

'Jennifer Martin,' he repeated in his oh-so-charming voice. 'Sounds terribly all-American. You aren't a native New Yorker, are you?'

'No, not at all. Like most people in this city, I'm an import, a transplant from the heartland of America, the Midwest.'

'I should have guessed that, tall, blonde hair, blue eyes: a perfect example of the best that America has to offer.'

'People usually think I'm the stereotypical California girl.'

'No, California girls have a sharp edge to their looks, from just one too many summers on the beach. They always dress very aggressively. I don't know, it's difficult to describe, but they always appear a little hard to me. You, on the other hand, seem to have been raised on the freshest dairy products available, lots of hot oatmeal with brown sugar and cream in the mornings in wintertime, and I'd bet that you don't even own a garment made of leather.'

'Well, you're right about the oatmeal, it's one of my favourite treats, but you're dead wrong about the leather. No clothing, but I do have this marvellous collection of little whips and stuff.' She laughed at her own outrageous comment. She was usually the one gathering all the information instead of volunteering all these personal titbits. What had possessed her to say something like that? Especially to a perfect stranger!

He wasn't shocked, in fact he seemed to be amused by it. 'Delightful,' he said, 'with any luck perhaps I'll be invited to view your collection one day.'

'And you, Mr Nicholas Tate, you are now in possession of two of the most intimate details of my life, and I know virtually nothing about you.' She began to look really closely at him, to see each of his features, and now that he was standing up she realised that he was in fact a very handsome man. Her trained reporter's eyes took in the entire package with lightning speed. He stood about six foot two, maybe three, she estimated, and was dressed casually but appropriately for an unbearable New York summer day. Khaki pleated trousers and a cream-coloured linen shirt with long sleeves that had been rolled up to reveal tanned, muscular forearms. He was wearing beige cotton socks with Ralph Lauren's latest crocodile loafers with tassels. She noticed that his belt with its sterling silver tip matched the shoes. The only jewellery he had on was an antique Rolex sports watch with a green grosgrain band. She reminded herself that lots of married men did not wear wedding rings. Why was she even thinking about those things? Most unlike her. Here it was, seven something in the morning, and she was wondering about this stranger's marital status and mentioning whips. Maybe it was the heat; she should really get back to work. Now!

'I can't off the top of my head think of two intimacies to match yours, but I am sure of one thing – we should both get back to work before they clean up the station and I have no photos and you haven't found your anchorman.'

Once again, she thought, your stupid, silly sarcasm has frightened this guy to death. Jennifer conveniently used her role as a reporter to keep people at a distance, never allowing anyone to know more about her than she did about them. But for some reason this man seemed so easy to talk with; she found herself wanting to tell him even more about herself.

And now her momentary return to her reporter mode had turned him off completely.

'You're absolutely right.' Business tone. 'I can't thank you enough for helping me this morning. I'm sorry; I've probably made you miss some important shots.'

They turned and started to walk back toward the entrance to the station.

'I doubt it. I'm sure they haven't been able to do much with the train yet. The guy who did this must have been very anxious to destroy someone or something that was on it. He seemed very thorough.'

'So it was a bomb, not some mechanical problem?'

'Oh, absolutely. You can see by the damage. I think there were several explosives involved.'

Back inside the terminal, Jennifer spotted her camera crew. They were set up at the entrance to the train platform trying to get some footage.

She got her press card out of her bag to show the police and had already started down the stairs when she realised she hadn't said goodbye to Nicholas. He was crouched down in back of her on the stairs, loading his camera. She turned back immediately.

'I see my crew over there. I'm going down to be with them. Thanks again for everything.' She figured she should be quick, since she was certain he was more than ready to be finished with her.

'Be careful, Jennifer. And good luck tonight.' He looked up from his film, camera in lap, and gave her a beautiful smile. Perfect gleaming white teeth, too!

You fool, she thought as she turned to go down the stairs. Tragedy is all around you, and tonight could be the most important of your life.

'Jennifer, be careful. We've got wires all over the place. Watch your step.' Kevin, the head cameraman had spotted her trying to make her way to them.

'Thanks.' She waved her way through the set up, grateful for the current flat shoe craze. 'I'm OK. Where's Stewart?'

'No sign of him, and we're pretty worried,' he said,

reaching out to give her a hand over the wires. 'We can't find him, and he's not on any of the paramedics' ambulance lists. Do you think he could've walked out of here and taken a taxi to the hospital?'

'I don't know. He only talked to Sid this morning, as far as I know, but Sid said he sounded pretty bad. Maybe Sid's talked to him again by now.'

'Hope so. This is awful, huh? It's the worst mess I can remember in a long time. The guy who did this really wanted to hurt some people. The sides of the train are all blown to hell.'

'Do you know anything at all yet? Any police reports issued?'

'No, it's still too early. We got a couple of eye witnesses on tape before the police got here en masse and started questioning everyone. People who were on the train and survived it just want to get out of here. Can't say that I blame them.'

'Well, I don't think it's going to be possible to speak to anyone now. Sidney simply wants me to get an overview of the situation,' Jennifer answered. 'Now I just want to get to the studio and see if we can find out what happened to Stewart.'

'That's probably the wisest thing to do. I'll keep everyone here for a while just in case something breaks. And, oh, by the way, Jennifer, Sid mentioned that you'll be substituting for Stewart tonight. Good luck. You know we'll do everything we can to make you look great.'

'Thanks, Kevin, you're the best.'

'But, before you go, tell me one thing. How'd you get so dirty and messy-looking so early in the morning? I've never seen you look like this,' he asked.

'Promise you'll never tell?'

'OK, I promise.'

'Well, this rough 'n' tough reporter took one look at the disaster and fainted dead away.'

'I'll never mention it. I didn't feel too good when we first got down here either. I'm just sorry I wasn't there to catch

41

you when you fell. I hope there was some great-looking guy nearby.'

'As a matter of fact, there was,' she replied. She picked up her bag and waved goodbye. Yes, there certainly had been someone, she thought. Someone pretty terrific!

7

'*DEAD?* There must be some mistake. It just can't be.' Jennifer clutched the doorframe of Sid's office. She had rushed back from the station to give him an update on the situation and to start preparing and editing the day's news.

'I'm afraid there's no mistake, Jenn. I was just at the hospital to make the identification. It was Stewart. He doesn't have any family in the area, except for the sister he was visiting last night. She's on her way down. The rest of them, his parents and a brother, are all in some small town outside of Pittsburgh. They've been notified and are going to start making the funeral arrangements today. I spoke with his father and told him we'd be available to help in any way we could, although I don't know what that would be. Oh God, Jenn, I feel so responsible. If I'd realised how badly he was hurt, I might have been able to get help to him sooner, maybe he could have been saved. They found him collapsed in the phone booth. I was probably the last person he spoke with.'

'Sidney, don't be so hard on yourself. It sounds as if he was very badly hurt – even *he* didn't realise how badly. I'm sure there wasn't anything more anyone could have done.' She tried to comfort him as she had done so many times in the past two years.

'He was such a terrific kid. He had become almost like a son to me, especially after Rita's death.' Tears clouded Sid's eyes. 'He really loved this crazy business and he was doing so well. It's damn tough to believe he's gone. Well, Jenn, I'm down a good friend and a top anchorman. I'm really going to count on you more than ever now.'

'Don't worry,' she assured him. She moved to his side and gave him a warm, comfortable hug. 'We'll do just fine. But I must say you've given me a tough one first night out.'

'You'll be great. I'll be right there at the monitor with you every minute. I think everyone's ready for you. Let me know this afternoon how you're doing. We should begin review and final edit by four-thirty or so. But right now,' he sighed, 'a long walk is the best thing for me.'

'Does anyone know yet?'

'Yes, I told everyone when I came back from the hospital. I'm sure the word has spread to those coming in. I'll write the obit for him for tonight's programme. We can do it at the end. On your way out, can you ask Cindy to get an appropriate photo and have the art department prepare it?'

'Sure . . . go take your walk.'

She hugged him once more and went out in search of Cindy, Sidney's secretary. She found her in the coffee room with one of the editors, teary-eyed and upset. Jennifer's request for the photo brought on more tears from both of them, and Jennifer felt her own strength begin to fade.

'I know, Cindy, it's a tragedy. Stewart's death is going to be hard on all of us, especially Sid. He's really going to need you more than ever now, so please try and pull it together for him, OK?' Her voice was shaky.

'Yes, sure, Jennifer, I'll try, but –' she couldn't continue as the tears started again.

'I know.'

Throughout the day, the newsroom was as frantic and tense as Jennifer had ever seen it. Telephones ringing constantly. Telexes working so hard that they couldn't keep up with the output of paper. By three, police reports indicated twenty-two people dead, seventy-eight wounded, and of those several remained in critical condition. The most frustrating element was the continuing search for those still missing, buried in the debris. That number was only speculation at this point.

44

The dead included the chief operating officers of three of Wall Street's most prominent investment houses, a top financial analyst at one of the city's largest banks, and a partner at Davis, Polk & Wardwell, the law firm representing several clients attempting to recover funds they had lost as a result of Richard Collier's actions.

The skeleton of Richard Collier's revenge plan had been pieced together by late afternoon. Because he was by now halfway to Brazil, he had not shown up for his deposition scheduled that morning for ten a.m. When contacted at their home, his wife was surprised to learn that he was not in Washington at a meeting.

Ross Chamberlain, a fellow passenger who had observed a well-dressed man moving from car to car for a reason that was just now becoming clear, had telephoned the New York City Police Department shortly before arriving in his office. All morning, his conscience had been bothering him, and he felt that perhaps he had witnessed something important. Something that might help to solve this senseless crime. His description of the man confirmed Richard Collier's presence on the train.

All this information led police to issue a warrant for Richard Harding Collier, aged forty-one, resident of Connecticut. He was now charged with murder.

Sidney had left his office almost immediately after seeing Jennifer. He entered Central Park at 81st Street and wandered across to the Delacorte Theatre. He sat in one of the stone seats and stared into the empty space. He cried. He cried for Stewart and the senseless loss of such a talented young life. He cried for his own losses, first his wife and now a young man that he had believed in and had come to love. The heat of the morning became increasingly unbearable. No wonder, his watch indicated that he had been outside for nearly two hours. The only answer to him seemed to be to return to work, to get on with it. Work had been his saviour once before; it was again time to block his grief and drive headlong into it.

A first draft of the evening news was on his desk when he returned. The details that had surfaced in the last few hours were remarkable. The depth of one man's hatred and fear were hard to understand. The lives he had touched with this crime were many, and the ramifications on Wall Street were mind-boggling.

'Mr Lachman, I know you asked not to be disturbed, but it's a woman named Alicia Clemson on line two. She says it's very important, about the train bombing. Can you take her?' Cindy's Brooklyn-bred voice rang out from the intercom.

His hand shook as he picked up the receiver.

'My God, Alicia, please don't tell me David was on that train?'

'No, no, thank goodness. He took the six-fifty today. No, he's fine, I just spoke with him. But he's certainly involved. The firm's been trying to get Rich Collier for a long time. In fact he's the reason I'm calling. I think maybe some of your people might want to talk with David. Perhaps he could be of some help.'

'That's a great idea, Alicia, I appreciate your thinking of me, and I'm so relieved that he's OK. Personally, they can't catch the son of a bitch soon enough for me. My anchorman was killed as a result of this madman. Do you ever remember seeing Stewart Howrath – he was on at six?'

'Sure, I do – I even remember you talking about him the last time we had dinner. Apart from business you were quite fond of him, weren't you? Sort of a mentor to him. He wasn't very old, was he?'

'No, only thirty-eight. At any age, too young to die this way.' His voice cracked.

'Oh, Sid, I'm so sorry.'

'Me, too, Alicia, I'm glad you called. Thanks for the information. I'll be in touch with David and we'll get together soon. Let's talk next week after this settles a bit.'

'Take good care, Sid. David will be at his office all day. You have the number, don't you?'

'Yes, thanks again.'

What a small sometimes sick world we've created, he

thought. He buzzed Cindy to have her get David Clemson on the phone and then gather the evening crew for a final edit.

'OK, I think we're ready. The clock says we've got to be anyway. If anything breaks during the programme, is everyone clear on signals? Jennifer?'

'Yes, I understand.' They had met for over an hour. Make-up had worked on her during the meeting and she looked fantastic. Their magic had been able to camouflage the signs of stress from the horrors she had seen today.

'Five minutes, Jennifer, how're ya doing?' Kevin called out.

'Fine, I think. You'll let me know about six-thirty-two.'

'Are you kidding? Six-thirty-one. OK, everyone, places. Let's go, now.'

She was on the air. Concise, professional, straightforward reporting. Jennifer was in total control from the minute she went on to the last second. Her timing was perfect, and the programme flowed from story to story, news to sports, sports to weather without a hitch. She delivered a brief obituary on Stewart Honwrath without losing control of her emotions, although her eyes were shining with unspilled tears.

As the cameras shut off for their last commercial, she took a deep breath, and left the desk immediately. Inside, even she was amazed at how smoothly it had gone.

'Thank you, everyone,' she yelled out.

Congratulations followed. She looked at Sidney, and saw that beneath the sadness in his eyes, she had pleased him also.

'Do you want to see the tape now?' asked Kevin.

'No, not tonight. I can wait till tomorrow. It's been a big day.' For so many reasons, she thought.

'C'mon, star,' Sidney said. 'I'm offering a ride uptown and a drink, dinner if you want.'

'I'm not interested in dinner, but two out of three will be great. A drink never sounded so good.'

Jennifer left her bag with the cosmetics and accessories in her office – it seemed like she would need them again tomorrow if the backup people were still out.

The limo took them uptown to the Carlyle. The Bemelmans

bar was unusually crowded, and talk centred on today's tragedy.

Sidney ordered a double scotch and Jennifer asked for a Campari and soda. Raising his glass, Sid toasted her, 'I hope you know how pleased I am with you tonight. I'm only sorry that Stewart's death clouds my enthusiasm.'

'Please, let's just drink to him,' she asked.

They sat for several minutes in silence. The couple at the next table, a handsome, well-dressed man and an attractive woman were talking quietly. But their accent was clearly English. Jennifer turned to look at them. Had she expected to see Nicholas Tate? It was the first time she had thought of him since this morning. It seemed like decades ago.

'I can go a long time without another day like today.' Sid's thought broke the silence.

'Me, too, I'm going straight home to a hot bath and two aspirin. I'm beginning to feel the bruises forming from my fall this morning.'

'What happened to you?'

'Oh, I took one look at the scene today and passed out. I think I might have hit my elbow on the way down. But there was a charming prince, or at least an Englishman, there when I woke up.'

'That's the least you deserve on a day like this.' He silently wished he had been the prince. 'I hope you're not hurt.'

'Not at all, just a little sore. The bath will cure all.'

'Let's get you out of here and home, then. You've got to go on tomorrow night and maybe for many nights after that.'

Jennifer's mind raced with the implications of Sidney's statement. Could this possibly be the opportunity to come one step closer to realising her dream?

'Sidney, what do you plan to tell Jim and Steve when they get back? I can't continue after they return, can I?' Jennifer tried to sound as casual as possible, but failed miserably.

'I don't know yet,' he answered honestly. 'If tonight wasn't just beginner's luck and you continue like that, there'll be no reason to change. You're stronger than both of them together.'

'Thanks, Sidney. Thanks for your support. I really can't believe this is all happening. Let's hope the viewers feel the same way.' Allowing her happiness to take over, she reached across the small table and kissed Sidney on the cheek.

She had the car drop her at the small deli/grocery on the corner. Flowers, yoghurt, bananas, freshly squeezed orange juice and Häagen Dazs ice cream. If only her mother could see this assortment. Thank heavens she wasn't nearby; she was one person that Jennifer didn't have the strength for right now.

The phone was ringing inside the apartment while she fumbled in her handbag trying to find her keys. What a fool, she thought. She was reminded of those people who never had their money ready for the taxi driver when they reached their destination. Who did they think was going to pay the fare? And who did she think was inside the apartment to open the door for her? Five, six rings, and no keys. They were nowhere to be found.

Just as she turned the key in the lock, the phone stopped. 'If it's that important, they'll call back,' her mother's voice from her childhood echoed in her ears.

Two seconds after she had submerged herself in the luxury of Calèche bath bubbles, the telephone rang. Ah ha, she smiled. She had determined after countless wet footprints on her hardwood floors that nine out of ten of the telephone calls she received came while she was either in the shower, the bath, or putting on make-up. She had solved the problem by having a phone installed in the bathroom. A hands-free phone that she could talk on while bathing or applying blusher. On the third ring, she lifted her long leg out of the water and pressed the 'on' button with her perfectly pedicured big toe.

'Hello.' The only problem with the speaker phone was that it sounded as if you were speaking from a cave.

'Did anyone tell you that you were brilliant tonight? No one could convince me that you haven't been doing it since birth.'

Nicholas Tate's voice resounded throughout her bathroom

as she scrambled out of the tub to pick up the receiver. Water was everywhere.

'They didn't say brilliant, but good enough to do it again tomorrow night, same time, same channel.'

'Well, that's good enough. I'm just making a follow-up call; I do that for all my fainting women. Did you hurt yourself today?'

'Not really, but after the programme I started to feel some bruises on my arm. I'm soaking them in a bubble-filled tub right now.'

'A delicious image, I must say. You know, I promised my second-born to the studio for your phone number. They're very protective of you.'

Second-born, she thought, he *must* be married.

'That's good to hear. The island of Manhattan is chock-full of loons.'

'Well, this one slipped through. I made up a very convincing story about being an old friend of your family. Told the secretary I would only be in town for a short time. It's not a lie altogether, and it seemed to have worked!'

They both laughed. Why did it seem they had known each other longer than a mere twelve hours?

'I'm leaving for London Thursday, but I'd hate to go without having dinner with you. Are you free on Wednesday?'

'Yes, I'd like that,' she replied, maybe a little too quickly.

'Wonderful, please pick the restaurant. It's much better for the local to choose.'

The local? It sounded as if he went from city to city, date to date. Strike two.

'That didn't sound quite right,' he continued immediately. 'Seems as if I do this in every port.' Could he read her mind? Did he have one of those phones where you could actually see the person you were speaking to? Don't get carried away, she thought. Nevertheless, she grabbed a towel and wrapped it around her dripping body.

'All I really meant was, I'd like you to choose the restaurant. Once in London, however, that would change.'

'Let me think about it. Can we talk Wednesday morning? I'll have some ideas by then.'

'Of course, but I think we should probably speak tomorrow also, just to make sure you're working on it and for an update on the bruises. I'm a full-service chap.'

'Good, I think I'd like that.'

'Terrific, I'm at the Pierre, room 809, if you want to reach me. Good night, pretty lady.'

'Night, Nick.' She hung up the receiver gently, refilled the tub with hot water and added more bubbles. Was it Wednesday yet? she wondered.

8

On Tuesday, the activity level in the newsroom was markedly reduced from the day before. The usual chatter and gossip were missing, the mood was sombre. In their shared silence everyone was mourning the loss of a friend and colleague.

Additional details about those who had been injured or killed continued to pour in. There were not many further developments concerning Richard Collier. One of the Channel 7 reporters had driven to Greenwich and had somehow caught Collier's wife, Sandy, and their two children leaving the house. She had not said anything, except that her attorneys had advised her not to talk to reporters, and she would appreciate it if everyone would leave her family alone. There were looks of extreme confusion and grief on each of their faces. The staff watched the tapes of this scene during the final edit in the afternoon.

'Surely we're not going to use that, Sid,' said Jennifer when the tape had finished.

'Why not?' He seemed amazed.

'Because it is a sensationalistic piece that isn't giving the viewer any information that they don't already have. How can we intrude on that poor family's privacy?'

'Jenn, don't be ridiculous. This is an exclusive tape –'

'That's exactly right,' she interrupted. 'It's not as if if we don't show it all of the other stations will have it.'

'Exactly the point,' he insisted with finality. 'We'll use the footage, and you'll announce the story.'

So the executive overrules, she thought.

The phone was ringing as she entered her office. She reached across the paper-strewn desk to answer it.

'Jennifer Martin.' One hundred per cent business.

'Is it true that female anchorpeople only eat raw meat for dinner?'

'Not funny,' she said, and meant it. There was such a fine line between femininity and the attitude it took to get the work done in an effective, professional manner.

'OK, sorry, sorry, small joke.'

'Very small,' she answered tersely.

This was Nicholas's second call of the day. The first, earlier this afternoon, had been to inquire as to how the bruises were doing and how she felt. That had been sweet of him, she thought, and she appreciated it.

'Well, I was only calling now to see if it was time for dinner yet, and if you've decided where we should go.'

She laughed. 'It's only Tuesday afternoon.'

'I know,' he said, 'but I've got an idea. Maybe we should do a practice run and eat together tonight. If you don't have any plans.'

'Actually, I do,' she lied. Her big plans were to stay late in the studio and finish up the Special Segment stories she had been working on.

'I suppose that's to be expected,' he said. She could hear the disappointment in his voice, and she was pleased. She also knew she wanted to see him tonight.

'My plans will be finished about ten. If you're interested in a late dinner, you're on.'

'That's perfect for me. Where shall I pick you up? Please not off the ground again,' he joked.

'At the studio, it's on 57th Street and Tenth Avenue. I'm on the fourth floor. Just come up and ask for me,' she said.

'Good. Do well on your newscast tonight. I'll see you later.'

Even with all the work she had to do, the afternoon passed extremely slowly. Finally, it was airtime.

Jennifer was superb. They had a mix-up with the audio

53

portion of one report, but since she had studied the scripts so well, she was able to ad lib without any problems. She was sure that one of the fundamental keys to her success would be that she always, *always* knew her material. They watched the tape afterwards, and even against her strict standards Jennifer had to admit to herself that she had done pretty well. However, there were still certain areas that definitely needed improvement. She asked for a duplicate tape to send to her father. He had always been her best critic. She'd see what he thought.

'Good work, kids,' commented Sidney as he left the room. 'See everyone tomorrow.'

Jennifer and the crew went back to work on the Special Segment materials. They finished editing the Marvin Traub piece. It would go out tomorrow. They also put the finishing touches on a story she had done on new restaurants that had opened during the summer and another one on what to do on the hottest days of the year if you're stuck in the city. That's good, she thought, one for tomorrow and, after that, two more stories in the can. They would cover her regular position while she was filling in until one of the backup anchors returned. She assumed Sidney had contacted them and advised both Jim and Steve to return to New York as soon as possible.

But she was dead wrong about that.

Sidney had decided not to call either Jim, Roger or Steve back early from their trips – Jim and Steve on vacation and Roger on assignment. Jim and Steve both had plans to return in ten days. That afternoon Sidney had asked Cindy to pull all the ratings sheets from the period when either backup had been on the air during any illness or when Stewart had taken a holiday. He studied this information and created his own chart to track the show's rating for the next ten days. He hoped his premonition was correct. Inexperienced as she was, he was betting that Jennifer was strong enough to carry the show and even to improve their audience share.

'Jennifer, possibly the most knock-out-looking guy ever to roam these halls has just shown up and asked for you. Not only is he terrific to look at, but what an accent! Direct from across the pond.'

Jennifer looked up to see Andrea Whitlock, one of the late-night production assistants standing in the doorway. She had just announced Nicholas's arrival to everyone in the conference room. No chance for secrets around here, Jennifer thought.

'Hot date for Jennifer tonight, huh guys?' Teasing jeers all around.

'Thanks, fellows, I don't really need your help on this one,' she responded.

'Listen, if you're not ready for him right now, I'd be glad to entertain him for a while,' Andrea continued.

'No, thank you, let's give the guy a chance. He's just here to take me to dinner,' Jennifer said. 'Please tell him I'm on my way. I'll be out there in five minutes.'

She gathered up her things quickly and said goodnight.

'Don't stay out too late.' 'Be a good girl.' 'Don't be late tomorrow or you're in big trouble . . .' And on, and on. It all reminded her a little of college and some of the close male friends she had made there since she never had a brother. In fact, in a city as difficult to work in as New York, she really loved the camaraderie they all shared at the station.

She gave them one final will-you-please-get-off-it smile and left the room.

Andrea had apparently decided not to try to pursue a conversation with Nicholas. She had shown him Jennifer's office and left him to his own devices. He was studying the bulletin board, which held an assortment of items ranging from the most important, like a production schedule, to the very inane and humorous – a *New Yorker* cartoon that she had thought was hilarious, and a New York Islanders goalie mask they had given her after she covered one of the post-game parties. There were many pictures of Jennifer and her sisters playing tennis, water-skiing on the lake last summer, and one picture of the entire family that her mother had insisted on using as a Christmas card last year. Nicholas's back was to her. Cute, she thought. She took one look at him

55

and wished she had gone to her apartment to shower and change before meeting him. He looked so fresh and rested in his summer-weight beige gabardine slacks and blue blazer. She could see the cuffs of a perfectly starched white shirt just showing beneath the sleeves of his jacket.

Shit, she said under her breath, he looks terrific and casual and you look like a refugee from a secretarial convention! Well, not that bad maybe, her peach linen unconstructed dress from Ralph Lauren was from the current season, but it was long and loosely cut, and didn't show off her legs at all. Well, the comfortable, sensible, crocodile flats didn't help much either. But at five foot seven she didn't look dumpy. Too late now. Wednesday night would be a different story. She'd wear something a little more suggestive. Like what? She hadn't needed an outfit like that lately. She would worry about finding some time for shopping tomorrow. Well, at least her hair and make-up had been done just a few hours ago.

'You can find out a lot about a person by studying the collection of stuff that makes up their bulletin boards,' she said.

He was involved in a serious examination of the board and was startled to hear that she was in the room.

'Yes,' he said turning around. The white shirt was open at the neck, his eyes sparkled, and Jennifer thought he looked extremely handsome. Even more attractive than she remembered.

'You must be especially proud of this accolade.' He was pointing to a blue rosette ribbon with gold printing. It looked like the rosettes awarded at horse shows or swimming competitions. This one was a little different. Imprinted on the centre of the rosette it said:

To: Jennifer Martin
Awarded this eighteenth day of June 1986
First Prize – Channel 7 Blow Job Competition

'You Americans are becoming much more blatant about the methods you're using to get ahead!'

'Yes, that's right. The realities about women in business can be frightening, but if your filthy mind hadn't drawn its own conclusions about my prowess, you would appreciate the true meaning of that award.'

'OK, beautiful, I withdraw my hastily drawn conclusions. Please tell me the significance of your rosette.'

'Every year Channel 7 sponsors a party in June for some of the city's handicapped kids. We all get together and create the events. Each staff person is assigned a group of fifteen or twenty kids and we compete against each other for prizes. My group was extremely skilled in the balloon blowing-up contest. Hence the innocent ribbon which you have so shamelessly defiled.'

'Indeed, that's very admirable, Ms Martin. But I must admit I prefer my own erotic theory.'

'As you wish, Mr Tate.'

'Some of the straight stuff is pretty interesting too. Are these all Martin siblings?' He had removed a photo taken about three years ago, on a rare occasion when all her sisters had been at home at the same time. A friend of their father's had taken the picture as they were docking their boat. They had been out on the lake all day, water-skiing and swimming. They were tired, sunburned, and just a little drunk from the beers they had had after they finished skiing. But it had been a wonderful day, a day that had reminded Jennifer of when they were all growing up together. They had laughed and joked and told each other things that they never talked about on the telephone. She smiled as she took the photo from Nicholas's hand.

'Yes, these are all the Martin girls, "Ken and Marion's bevy of blondes" everyone used to call us. Except for Christie, that is. Somehow she ended up with that raven-coloured hair. It makes sense, though. She's the least like any of the rest of us in almost every way. That's obviously Christie on the left.'

Christie was sitting on the side of the boat, leaning backwards. Her long, tanned legs were spread into a V and extended into the air at a forty-degree angle. She had a mug of beer in one hand, and was waving to the audience dockside with the other. Her long, dark hair was piled on top of her head and tied with a brightly coloured scarf. She was wearing a very tiny neon orange bathing suit, which revealed a perfectly toned body.

'Christie is the youngest and by far the wildest looking,' Jennifer continued. 'It must come from being the last child – a relaxation of discipline on the parents' part or something. She's a lot of fun, very bright, and she's doing very well. Don't let her looks deceive you. She's one smart cookie.'

'Where does she live?' he asked.

'She lives in L.A., near Westwood, and works at UCLA. She's one of the top cancer researchers in the medical school there. She got her degree from UCLA, but never wanted to go into private practice. She has always wanted to commit herself to research, says it's the most rewarding. I've always thought that her rowdiness and her outrageous manner of dressing were her ways of escaping the seriousness and what I'm sure is the frustration of her work. She's been promising to come back to New York and visit, but in the two years I've been here I've been out to the coast four or five times and she's never been here. She works constantly, she's very dedicated.'

'How old is she?'

'She turned twenty-six in May. She's the baby by two years.'

'And this lady with child?' Nicholas asked, pointing to Susan.

'That's Susan. She's Pat's twin. Normally they look very much alike, but in the ninth month I think even your face becomes totally different. Three days after this picture was taken, she delivered a little boy. He just had his third birthday a couple of weeks ago. She's married to a terrific guy, an attorney, and they live about five miles from my parents. She's probably the most like my mother, which makes her the most distant from me. We're close, but she leads such a predictable life that we really don't have all that much in common. This is Pat,' she said, pointing to a great-looking girl with very short blonde hair, enormous blue eyes, and a perfect smile. 'Pat is the fashion plate in the family. She's really my favourite, if it's OK to admit that you have a favourite. She's also married. Her husband is an architect, and they live near my parents also, but not quite as close as Susan. Her husband's family is German, so they spend a lot of time in Munich. I saw her last weekend, and she's just about to give birth to twins. She's enormous and very uncomfortable. She can hardly wait. And finally, that's me,' she laughed. It was a great picture of her. She had returned only a week before from a vacation in Mexico and she was very tanned. Her black bikini bottom, cut very high on the thigh to accentuate her long legs, and the bandeau top which barely covered her ample bust was very conservative in comparison to Christie's, but it revealed more than enough of her glorious body.

'Some family,' he commented. 'Your father must have had many sleepless nights wondering about you girls. No brothers?'

'No, he kept praying, but after Christie arrived, I think he gave up. I'm the closest one to a son I think. We've got a wonderful relationship.' She put the picture back in its prominent place on the board.

'That's a synopsis of the Martin clan, except for Ken and Marion, which is a whole different story. I'll save that. And you know even more about me, and I'm still completely ignorant about you.'

'We can correct that situation over dinner. It seems we're always talking standing up. What do you think about going somewhere to eat now? I don't know about you, but I'm starving.'

'Now that you mention it, I am too. Let's go.'

It was almost eleven, so they opted to go downtown, where the restaurants stayed open later and there was more activity. They went to Lola, on West 22nd Street. It was a fairly new, hot restaurant that served eclectic Caribbean-style food to a young, trendy group. Without reservations, they had to wait for half-an-hour. Sitting at the bar enjoying their drinks,

Jennifer was anxious to learn everything about Nicholas Tate. She had already revealed more to him about herself and her family than she had to anyone in years.

'OK, your turn,' she said. 'Apart from knowing that you give terrific aid to ladies in need and that you are now the heartthrob of all of Channel 7, I don't know much about you.'

'I don't have any family pictures to show you,' he said. 'I only have one sister. I'm basically the product of two people I never really got to know. My parents were busy travelling and moving around the world, so I think I must have been plenty for them.'

'Why were you moving so much?'

'My father, Lord Tate, was a senior diplomat with the British Foreign Office for many years. He would be sent out on postings ranging from six months to two years. We always wished the postings had been reversed – every place we stayed for six months we loved, and the two-year stints, to places like Tokyo, seemed interminable.'

'What was your favourite place?'

'Africa, hands down. We lived in Nairobi for a little over two years, an extended stay that my father begged for. The schools were quite good, so my education wasn't being interrupted, and we all loved it there. I knew that when we returned to England I'd have to get into boarding school and stay there, if my plans for university were to be fulfilled, so I was delighted for the extra months there. I think Africa is where my interest in photography really began. The terrain, the faces of the people, the costumes, and of course the animals – it was all like one big treasure chest for me. I was insatiable. All of the other children went off riding or hunting or playing polo, and I'd be perched on the top of a Land Rover with all kinds of equipment dangling from my neck, waiting to get the next great shot.'

'I envy you,' Jennifer said. 'I always wished that we had travelled more, seen more places. But when you're raised in Wayzata, the big trip is to Minneapolis!'

'There are pluses and minuses to every way of life. For

example, I don't think my son would adjust well at all to moving about constantly. He's very much a homebody.'

A son, she thought. Jennifer's eyes must have divulged her thoughts. Was there a wife, too? Despite knowing her such a short time, Nicholas was very sensitive to her reactions.

'Jennifer,' he said gently, 'your eyes are truly a window to your thoughts. You must always wear dark glasses when gambling.' She laughed. 'My son, Christopher, is ten years old. He lives with me in London. When I'm not there, which is frequently, too frequently, I'm afraid, he stays with my sister in the countryside south of London. His mother, from whom I am divorced, unfortunately has a very serious drug problem. She's been in and out of a clinic for a couple of years. Now she's checked herself in full time. She's been living there for three months. It's the British version of the Betty Ford Clinic, I suppose. Hopefully, some day she'll come to terms with it. She is, or was, a wonderful woman and a superb mother until cocaine became more important and consuming than all of us put together.'

'I'm sorry,' Jennifer said, really meaning it and imagining how hard it must be for him to be raising a child and travelling constantly.

'It's been a challenge for all of us. I must say, it forced me to reevaluate my lifestyle, and I almost gave up my work, but I don't think that's the answer either.'

'Welcome, Jennifer, it's so good to have you here again.'

Here was Lola, the restaurant's raison d'être. She was a sensational-looking black girl who had come to New York from Jamaica just a few years ago and now owned one of the most successful and trendiest eating spots. She and Jennifer had met last year when they both were invited to appear on a local TV chat show as members of a panel. The panel theme was 'Women with Style', and in addition to Lola and Jennifer the guests had included a woman who worked on Wall Street, an artist in the Soho community, a very successful shoe designer, and a pilot with American Airlines. They were on the show for three days, and each day they were questioned by members of the audience or people calling in:

61

they discussed clothing and fashion for work, for the evening, and weekend and casual wear. Jennifer had enjoyed herself, and she was happy about the acquaintances she had made. Lola had been the most outgoing, the most amusing person in the group. They became friends and saw each other a few times after that, mostly at the restaurant. She was seeing her now for the first time in several months.

'Hi, Lola,' she replied, reaching out to take her hand and kiss her on the cheek. 'I'd like you to meet Nicholas Tate, Lola Bell.'

'Very nice to meet you. I hope we're taking good care of you,' she said. Lola's accent had that beautiful, charming, mellifluous sound that was always associated with the islands. In its own way, it was as peaceful and soothing as Nicholas's.

Lola was dressed very chicly in a short black linen backless dress. She had it belted tightly with a bright pink sash. On her feet were the highest, strappiest sandals of the season. Enormous silver earrings dangled from her ears. She looked, as always, glorious and sexy. Looking at her, Jennifer felt more conservative than ever in her business attire. Tomorrow night, she would remedy that, she promised herself.

'A pleasure to meet you,' he responded. 'I think you're taking excellent care. It's a fun restaurant. I wish there were something like it in London. The city could use it.'

'Maybe that'll be the next one, although keeping this one going is plenty. So, Jennifer, you're looking good on the evening news. You're the new anchor, I hope?'

'Thanks, Lola. We'll see; it's all very much up in the air right now, after Stewart's horrible death.'

Just then one of the waiters came over to their table looking for Lola.

'Excuse me, please, Lola, we need you at table thirty-one. There is a problem and the guy is starting to go a little wild.'

'I'll be right there. See, everyone thinks this is such a glamorous job. Dress up every night and greet the people. No such luck. A crazy in every group. I'll see you later. Have a wonderful evening. Good to meet you, Nicholas. Jennifer, please call . . . and stay on the air!'

She dashed off across the room to try and rectify the situation at table thirty-one.

'Lovely lady,' Nicholas commented as he watched her begin to speak with the irate customer. 'She's right, though, what a tough business to choose. Especially in New York, where the restaurant casualty list is filled with great concepts that never caught on or were popular only for a short time. So, why were you so evasive about your job?'

'Well, it's the truth. The two backup anchors are out, one's on vacation, the other's on assignment. I'm really just filling in until they return, although I'd love for it to be otherwise. The producer is my biggest fan, which is why I even got the chance to substitute at all, but he can't risk the ratings by taking someone in my position and making them the anchor.'

'I don't see any risk at all. You handled it as if you'd been doing it for years. Leaving you there is probably exactly the right thing to do.'

'You're very sweet. Nothing would make me happier right now. The difference between doing the Special Segments and the anchor is vast, to say the least.'

'I have a feeling that it's going to be permanent.'

'From your mouth to the viewers' ears!' she said, raising her hand with crossed fingers.

Their dinners arrived, and they were excellent. The fresh red snapper was grilled to perfection, and the wine that Lola had sent over to them with her compliments was superb.

'Good choice of restaurant,' Nicholas commented. 'I hope you can choose something equally terrific tomorrow night.'

'I'll do my best. You do seem relatively easy to please.'

'As long as you keep coming up with the best!'

They talked and talked. Nicholas was only in New York for two more days. He was leaving on Thursday for London, going back to spend the weekend with Christopher. Then he was off to India for two weeks to cover the World Conference on Hunger.

They talked at length about his work. He loved what he

did. He enjoyed the travel, the excitement, and the ability to communicate world events, or just daily occurrences, through photography. He spent some of his spare time teaching in London at the Royal Photographic Society of Great Britain and he had done some work and had had several shows at the International Center of Photography in New York. A series of his on children was in the permanent collection of the Museum of Modern Art.

Jennifer felt that he was one of the few men she had met who was as passionate about his career as she was about hers. Even more pleasing, he seemed genuinely interested in her and what she was trying to achieve. In addition to work, Nicholas was very devoted to his son; he spent as much time as possible with him, often taking him on assignments when it was feasible. Last year they had been to Tokyo and Venice. He spoke about Victoria, his ex-wife, with great sympathy. Her drug problem had grown during the past year to such proportions that he could no longer count on her to take care of Christopher. She had become irresponsible and unable to cope with daily pressures. Their divorce had become final two years ago and the courts had granted Nicholas only temporary custody of their son. He lived with the fear that Victoria could try to take the child away from him before she was cured.

Jennifer was startled when their waitress came to the table to tell them that the kitchen was closing and if they wanted anything else they needed to order it now.

'My gosh, how did it get to be one o'clock already?' She was genuinely surprised.

'You know the old saying . . .' he said. They ordered espressos and a dessert to share.

'Since I didn't pick you up, I'm not sure where I have to take you home,' Nicholas said as they walked toward Sixth Avenue to get a cab. 'But I'll bet that you're an uptown gal – some chic address on the Upper East Side.'

Jennifer laughed, striking a snobby pose. 'Absolutely right. I'm *so* glad I project the sophisticated image that an out-of-towner has of an uptown-dweller. Actually,' she explained, 'it's the most convenient area for anyone to live. I'd much prefer to be downtown in the Village or even Soho, but it is harder to get back and forth from there. Maybe someday. But for now it's 77th and Madison.'

They rode uptown in silence. Nicholas reached across and took Jennifer's hand in his. She felt her breath quicken as she returned his gentle squeeze. She looked over to smile at him. Cupping her face with his other hand, he leaned over and kissed her, a soft, caring kiss. She returned the kiss, at first tentatively and then more aggressively as they travelled north on Madison Avenue. By the time they reached 77th Street their arms were wrapped around each other and they were oblivious to the amount of time the taxi had been at a standstill.

'Trust me, a couch or even a bed is much more comfortable than the back of my cab,' said the driver, whose identification photo posted just to the right of his meter indicated that his name was Jack O'Shaunessey. Jennifer and Nicholas opened their eyes, looked at each other, and immediately broke into embarrassed laughter. Nicholas paid Mr O'Shaunessey, tipped him generously, and thanked him. They were still giggling like schoolchildren when they reached the lobby of Jennifer's building. Alberto, the night doorman/elevator operator, was as usual comfortably camped out in a chair listening to his classical music and reading a science fiction novel. He was surprised and pleased to see Jennifer with this handsome man, their arms wrapped tightly around each other.

'Good evening, Ms Martin . . . sir,' he nodded toward Nicholas as he unlocked the front door and led them to the elevator.

'Hi, Alberto. Nice night, seems to be cooling off a little.'

'At least the weather is,' he replied with a smile as the elevator stopped at the eighth floor. 'Good evening,' he offered as they stepped out. He was glad to see her looking so happy. Usually she was alone and coming home from working late or having a business dinner. They often talked for a minute as he took her upstairs.

Jennifer unlocked the requisite Medeco deadbolt and second lock, and held the door for Nicholas to follow her inside the apartment, which was in a wonderful building referred to as 'pre-war' in the world of Manhattan real estate. This differentiated it from all the newer, often shakily built buildings constructed after World War II and usually meant the apartments had good-sized rooms, ample kitchens, and sometimes very acceptable bathrooms. Jennifer's apartment had all of these. It had two bedrooms, two bathrooms, and faced south and east. The large living room had a fireplace and French windows that opened on to the terrace, a fairly large one by New York standards. The apartment was in superb condition. It had been painted recently, windows scraped and re-paned, and the herringbone parquet floors were sanded and polished. It was, by all accounts, a lovely, well-located Manhattan apartment. The only problem was, since Jennifer had purchased and moved in nearly two years ago, she had not taken the time to furnish or to decorate it in any way. Except for a king-size bed in her bedroom, two twin beds in the guest room, and a single chaise longue on the terrace, the apartment was virtually empty. When she had left Kansas City and the apartment that she and Jeffrey had furnished together, she had made the decision to leave everything, even some pieces she had felt very strongly about. All of that was an attempt not to disrupt his life any more than she already was by stepping out of it completely. The only thing she took was a large canvas by the painter Clyfford Still. She had purchased it ten years before at auction at Sotheby's. It was the only real piece of art she had ever owned, and she never tired of its bright orange and red stripes, nor of its continuing appreciation in value over the past years. As she switched on the lights and looked at the empty space, she was torn between shock and embarrassment at the fact that this was where she lived. It was as if she was seeing her existence for the first time. For a fleeting moment she thought that for once maybe her mother was right. She would, she decided, arrange to get some furniture ordered soon.

'Your apartment?' Nicholas questioned, wondering if she had unlocked the right door, or if she had been burgled during their evening out, and cleared out of everything including curtains and carpets.

'Yes, my apartment,' she replied.

'You didn't mention that you were such a devout follower of minimalism,' he said as he wandered into the living room, trying to decide whether to sit on the floor or perch himself on the window sill. He chose the latter.

She surveyed him from the entry foyer, her handbag and attaché case still in her hand.

'Well, I admit that I don't like clutter, but maybe I've carried it a bit too far. You don't realise, however, the expense of creating this look, sparse yet functional. And it's murder to keep clean.'

'OK. I'll stop with the jokes. You must really be very busy if you haven't found the time to even buy a couch. But I do admire your taste in art. If I could only have one painting I might wish for a Still also.'

He knew his stuff, she thought.

'Yes, you're right. I should call someone and get some furniture ordered. It really looks silly now that someone else is in here. But I can offer you a drink on the terrace.'

They decided on hot tea, which Jennifer prepared in her meagrely equipped kitchen. He must think I am truly one-dimensional, she thought as she took out cups and saucers, not even sugar or milk to offer him. She found that if it wasn't in the apartment she wouldn't eat it. Hence, no sugar, no biscuits, only an occasional tub of ice cream.

Her refrigerator served as a storage bin for a range of colours of nail varnish filling the space usually reserved for eggs. The top shelf held Elizabeth Arden and Lancôme astringents that she liked having cool during the hot weather. She shut the door quickly when she heard him approach the kitchen. Seeing a refrigerator turned into a cosmetic case might be too much for one evening.

They shared the single chaise longue and sipped their tea quietly. Soon they were back in each other's arms, at first

67

kissing softly, subtle exploratory kisses that led to more passionate, eager embraces. Jennifer was excited by his touch, by his hands around her shoulders, on her neck. But she couldn't help thinking how familiar, how right, it all seemed. She felt strangely comfortable, as if they had known each other for a long time.

Nicholas suddenly pulled back, leaving Jennifer immediately wanting him to touch her again.

'I'm sorry, but your ploy won't work. I can see it now, a *New York Post* headline, "Brit Falls for No Furniture Ruse" – the *Daily News*, "Londoner Seduced by Empty Apartment Scam".'

'You're very presumptuous, Mr Tate. What you see here is just the result of an overworked, underorganised lady – clearly not an effort to keep you for the night. If it had been raining, I'd never have invited you in.'

They both laughed and fell back into each other's arms.

'I really must go, Jennifer. It's after two, and we've both got to be up early in the a.m.'

'A school night, we used to say.'

'Well, it's still true. Only one gets paid for attending classes now. I have really enjoyed myself. It may sound silly, but I can't wait to see you tomorrow night.'

'Me too,' she smiled. 'It was a wonderful evening.'

As they walked back through the empty apartment, Nicholas stopped to look at her painting.

'I hope you've owned it long enough to enjoy it, as well as the outrageous increase in value that it's had,' he said.

'Yes, it was a wise investment.' Wonderful, she thought, another subject he is interested in and can talk about. None of the rest of the men she had dated in New York had half the range of interests that Nicholas Tate seemed to have. But then again he wasn't a New Yorker, and also she'd never given anyone else the opportunity to comment on her painting. Nicholas was the first man she'd invited upstairs since she'd lived there. Except for Sidney, who had spent several nights in the guest bedroom during his wife's ordeal.

'Good night, pretty lady.' He took her face in his hands,

looked at her with his delicious blue eyes, and kissed her good night. 'Be spectacular tomorrow on the news, and I'll see you afterwards. Is nine o'clock OK?'

'Yes, and I'll make the reservations.'

'I trust you implicitly.'

The elevator door opened, and he waved goodbye. She could hear Alberto beginning a conversation with him as they descended.

Jennifer locked the door, turned out the lights and was in the bed, she figured, before Nicholas had hailed a taxi to take him downtown to the Pierre.

She snuggled under the covers, a smile on her face. For some reason, she was not bothered at all tonight by the sound of the air conditioner.

9

JENNIFER had the soon-to-be-proven-correct feeling that it was later than she would like it to be. A strained glance through a half-opened eye at her Cartier red enamel bedside clock indicated that it was eight-ten, forty minutes past her normal rising time. Well, she would just have to move a little faster than usual. But for right now she granted herself another ten minutes of luxury. She pulled the covers up snugly around her neck. Her thoughts immediately turned to last night and the very impressive, very charming Nicholas Tate. She had had such a good time; so comfortable, so easy, and yet so stimulating. Jennifer was anxious for tonight to come. A quick clock check indicated that she had two more minutes to dream, to remember his touch, his caresses.

Up, showered, dressed, and out into the street in search of a taxi in less than an hour. Not bad. She had a long day and, most possibly, a long night ahead of her. She smiled at the thought.

The newsroom was buzzing as more details of the Grand Central bombing came in. The owner of the plane that carried Richard Collier from Teterboro Airport just across the border in New Jersey to a destination still unknown had been identified and police were searching for him.

Funerals for the dead continued.

Jennifer passed Andrea in the hallway en route to Sidney's office.

'Lookin' tired, Martin. I bet that little British number is some fun,' she teased.

70

'He's not the worst thing that's happened to me lately,' Jennifer replied.

They began a review of the first stories, and Jennifer was delighted when they broke for lunch at twelve-thirty. They would regroup in two hours. She had just enough time for a quick shopping spree.

The Calvin Klein boutique at Bergdorf Goodman was fairly crowded. Jennifer always found very special things here, because Calvin made them exclusively for the store. Most of the customers were just looking, and her regular saleswoman, Marina, was at Jennifer's side in a minute.

'It's been for*ever*,' she greeted her. 'What have you been wearing?'

'Mostly what you've seen me in on the air. I've really been a hermit for the past few months. But now, you've got to come through for me. I need something very special, but it's for tonight, so I hope you've got something in stock.'

'Dress or pants?'

'Dress, I think, short, maybe black, or I'll consider a colour.'

'OK, sit down or have a look at the stock on the floor, and I'll see what we've got in the back.'

Jennifer looked through the merchandise on display but didn't find anything she loved.

Marina returned five minutes later with several possibilities. At once, Jennifer spotted a bright red, really a lipstick-red silk dress. It was sleeveless, with a round neck, very simply cut, with just one button on the side at the shoulder. It was very pretty.

'I like that. With a belt it could be terrific.'

'I knew you'd like it. With your colouring it should be sensational. We've sold several of them, but it takes a body like yours to do it justice. Let me get you a belt – in the meantime you can start trying it on.'

She put her in one of the oversized dressing rooms.

As she started undressing, Jennifer was struck by the reality of what she was doing. She was buying a new, fairly expensive outfit, in order to look very beautiful when she had dinner tonight with one Nicholas Tate, a man she had just met. That much was easy. She also faced the reality that she hoped the evening would end in bed, making love. As much as she wanted to trust him, to believe everything he had said, there were still many unanswered questions, questions that in the old days no one would have even thought of asking. In Jennifer's past, it had always been very simple, boy and girl met, boy and girl liked each other – the 'right chemistry' was the catch-phrase – they dated, and eventually went to bed. But, as everyone knew, all of that had changed dramatically. It was no longer safe to trust one's instincts about a person, certainly not about someone known for only a few days. Jennifer had done numerous stories on the AIDS issue, she had visited patients, reported on the facilities caring for those infected, interviewed both victims, lovers, and survivors. She had even gone so far as to take the test herself at one of the clinics she had visited. But she had never discussed the issue with a prospective partner. How did other well-informed, sexually active women handle this problem? She wished she'd thought about doing a story on that a few weeks ago, but there was obviously no time for it now. She was certain that Nicholas must have other lovers, how many she couldn't guess. He was divorced, very attractive, and travelled all over the world, why shouldn't he? They would just have to discuss it, she decided. When and where were another matter. Right now she needed to get this outfit and get back to the studio.

'Here are your belt choices.' Marina held up a black patent three-inch-wide belt, and an equally wide red belt covered in the same fabric as the dress.

'Definitely the self-belt, don't you think? The black one will only cut the lines of the dress.'

'I agree,' Marina said and handed it to her. 'It is a *hot* dress.'

Jennifer stepped out of the dressing room into the boutique. Looking at herself in the three-way mirror, she felt the admiring glances of the other women in the boutique. A distinguished-looking gentleman who was seated in a corner waiting for his wife or mistress also gave his approval.

'Lovely,' he commented. 'Lucky fellow to be taking you out.'

Maybe she should ask him how he was handling the AIDS dilemma, she thought whimsically, but quickly decided against it when she saw a woman who was obviously his wife emerge from the dressing room.

'Now what about shoes?' Marina asked as she adjusted the belt so it fitted properly on the dress. 'I saw a great pair of Maud Frizon pumps. They're red leather with black inserts – you know, her basic style with high heels – they'd be perfect. What size are you? I'll run up and get them while you're dressing.'

'Six-and-a-half A in her shoes,' Jennifer said. 'That would be terrific. Then I'll be finished.'

The shoes were a perfect colour and a great fit. She charged the clothes, extracted a promise that everything would be delivered to her apartment by six, thanked Marina for her help, and left. As always, the cab situation was hopeless, so she ended up walking across town. She arrived in her office hot, sweaty, and moderately cranky.

One brilliantly formed, single rosebud was in a Baccarat vase on her desk. Whoever had brought it in had placed it in the middle of a great pile of papers. The rose was almost the exact colour of the dress she had just bought. An envelope indicated that the flower was from the florist at Maxim's on Madison Avenue, just around the corner from the Pierre Hotel. She tore it open and was delighted to see, in real boarding-school handwriting, a note. It read, 'I think you are quite terrific. Is it time for dinner yet? Nick.' Nice. Sweet. Thoughtful. All those things. The qualities she thought he possessed. She tucked the note in her bag and left for the final editing session.

The afternoon passed extremely slowly, and her twenty-two minutes on the air seemed like twenty-two hours. She couldn't wait to get out of the studio.

Sidney was surprised to see her dashing toward the elevator after the broadcast.

'You've decided that anchors should keep bankers' hours?'

73

'Oh, not exactly, Sid,' she said, a little embarrassed. 'I've just made some plans for tonight and I need to get home first and change.'

'I'm just kidding,' he relented. 'It is seven-thirty. I think that's enough for one day. You're having quite a week. The tapes look good; so do the ratings.'

'You haven't told me when Jim and Roger are due back. I need to start lining up some Special Segment shoots, I've only got two more left after tonight. Quite honestly, I thought one of them would be back by now.'

'Let's talk about it next week, Jenn. You'll be just fine. Don't worry about it now. Have a great time tonight.'

The rose on her desk and the especially bright smile on her face all day had not escaped his attention. He selfishly wondered whom she was seeing tonight. On the other hand, he was happy for her. She deserved someone very special in her life. She was beautiful, warm, caring and intelligent. His good wishes didn't stop him from feeling extremely jealous.

The packages, all neatly wrapped in Bergdorf boxes, were waiting for her when she arrived at the apartment. Thank God for Bergdorf's, she thought! After all the other big New York stores had lost their personality, as Saks Fifth Avenue had on its road to becoming the J.C. Penney of speciality stores and like Henri Bendel, which now sold inexpensive cotton sweaters on the main floor, Bergdorf's had managed to retain its position as a fashion leader, all the while never forgetting their dedication to customer service. Whatever the reason, she loved Bergdorf's even more for having delivered her beautiful new dress and shoes on time.

Air conditioners on full speed and a warm, luxurious bath were all she wanted right now. She laughed to herself as she walked through the empty living room. She added an extra capful of Calèche foaming bath oil to the water and submerged herself in the tub.

The dress was even prettier than she remembered, now that she had a chance to take a really good look. The shoes, as only Maud Frizon could cut them, accentuated her well-shaped calves and made her legs appear even longer than they were.

When Nicholas arrived, he was visibly pleased with her transformation from conservative, serious newscaster to femme fatale. He remembered the picture of Jennifer in a bathing suit, but tonight she really looked sensational.

'You didn't tell me you also had an incredible figure,' he commented. 'I was content with your beautiful face and outstanding genius as a reporter. Content with a vision of an amorphous blob from the neck down. Now this –' He turned her around in his arms. 'The whole package. Cancel dinner and call for Chinese.'

She was laughing uncontrollably. She could also tell that he was genuinely delighted with the way she looked.

It was apparent that several other men were equally impressed when they entered the restaurant. Chanterelle was a very small, intimate, well-rated restaurant in Soho with just ten tables. Only thirty people could be seated at one time. It was difficult to be unaware when new arrivals entered, let alone when a knockout blonde in a bright red minidress and a handsome bearded Englishman made their appearance.

Once again, her choice of restaurant seemed to please Nicholas. The food, nouvelle but not too pretentious, was superb. Specialities such as tuna carpaccio with sea urchin, lobster ravioli with coriander, and the featherweight chocolate soufflé they shared were exquisite.

It seemed they had so much to talk about, so much to share, that they often had to take turns.

'No, go ahead, please, you go first.'

'No, you, I'll be happy to keep eating.' Then they would both end up with mouths full of food, and neither talked.

They left the restaurant fairly early, and once outside, Jennifer was delighted that Nicholas had a car and driver waiting. The car headed uptown on Sixth Avenue. They hadn't done more than three blocks when they were in each other's arms, kissing frantically.

'Could I interest you in stopping at the Pierre? I've a wonderful suite, complete with a couch and the proverbial nightcap.'

'Are we there yet?' She smiled.

His suite overlooked Central Park, beautiful even at night in all its summer glory. She was looking out the window, loving the city and all its lights. He stood behind her, his hands around her waist. Gently he bent down to kiss the back of her neck.

'Jennifer Martin, we've been in this situation before,' he said. 'Nothing has felt so familiar, so comfortable for a very long time.'

'You're right. I've been thinking about that all day.'

'Let me take you to bed now. I want hours and hours to make love to you.'

She nodded in agreement as he unfastened the single silk-covered button that held up her dress. Jennifer's breasts were so firm that she rarely wore a bra, and almost never under evening clothes. Tonight she had on a short slip, just a little longer than a camisole. It was black, and trimmed with a delicate French lace. She wore nothing under it. Nicholas's breathing was audible to her as her dress fell to the floor.

'Ah, Miss Martin, you are truly exquisite.'

It was a compliment that didn't require an answer. She pulled his head to her breasts. He led her to his bed and stood above her as he undressed. Naked at last, they lay in each other's arms, exploring one another's bodies in a way reserved for first-time lovers. Their fingers never stopped touching, stroking, caressing. Nicholas held Jennifer's wrists with one hand, as he ran the fingertips of his other hand over her nipples, down across the flatness of her stomach. His fingers opened her, and she arched the small of her back upwards to him, forcing them deeper inside. She came quickly with a passion and fury foreign to her. She opened her eyes to find him smiling gently at her. A soft purr of contentment was the only noise she could make. Nicholas reached across and opened the drawer in the bedside table. He took out a small package which Jennifer immediately recognised as a condom. Does he always keep these in stock, she wondered? And why were they already in the drawer? Had he put them there when he arrived for the other women before her?

He sensed her anxiety and answered her questions at once.

'Jenn,' he said, for the first time calling her by the shortened form of her name, 'I know we didn't talk about this, somehow we both managed to avoid it, but regardless of how you are feeling about me, I'm sure you have many unanswered questions. I assure you there is no reason for fear. But now is no time to ask you to take my word for it. So, I bought these for you, for us, to use, hoping you would be more comfortable. I just got them today, wishing that what is happening now might happen. I must admit, it's really a new experience for me – a forty-year-old man buying condoms. It brought back many memories, of a long, long time ago.' He laughed at his thoughts. 'I hope this was the right way to handle it.' His eyes were begging her for a response.

She reached out and took him in her arms. 'Thank you, sweet man. Yes, it's a completely new situation for me, too. I must admit, I thought about this today, what I would be able to say, or do, and I really didn't have an answer. Thank you for making it so easy.'

He looked so relieved. They began to kiss again, and soon experienced the new way to make love in the eighties. Jennifer respected him even more for the responsible way he had handled this sensitive problem. She would be delighted, however, when she could rest assured that there was no reason to fear that either of them was infected, and they could return to a freer, less complicated type of love-making.

They rested for a short time, but soon found their hunger for each other had returned. Nicholas took her again several times in the night, sometimes by merely stroking her with his fingers. Their bodies were always entwined in some way.

She awoke from a sound sleep with that startling feeling – where was she and what time was it? Light was pouring in through the windows in the living room of the suite. She reached over, but the bed was empty.

Then she heard his voice from the other room.

'Yes, I understand that, but I would like confirmation on the afternoon flight. It's flight number four, I think.'

Silence, while whoever he was speaking to responded.

'Yes, however, I have just missed the nine-thirty departure. I'm still in Manhattan. What time is the next Concorde flight?'

Again silence.

Oh, great, Jennifer thought. How late was it? It couldn't be after nine-thirty already.

'Fine, I'm confirmed on the one-forty-five Concorde then,' the conversation continued. 'Thank you for your help.'

He hung up and walked lightly back into the bedroom.

Jennifer smiled at him from beneath the covers. Ever the gentleman, he was wearing a polo green-and-white striped cotton dressing gown and slippers. He looked extremely handsome and, she felt, quite happy.

'Good morning, angel. You look fairly content. Maybe we should both retire right now and live here, in this very bed, forever.'

'They may be retiring me from my job as we speak. How late is it?'

He switched on the bedside light. Eight-forty-five.

'Still early enough for me to wake you in a manner to which you could become accustomed,' he said as he slid his hands under the covers and grabbed her around the waist.

'Not on your life, Nicholas Tate. Take your hands off me immediately.' They wrestled each other for a minute before kissing seriously.

'I'm not kidding,' she pushed him away.

'All right, but I suggest you be very decent to me. Who else is going to go get clothes for you so you can leave here dressed properly?' Oh God, he was right. She hadn't spent the night out for so long, especially a 'school night', that she had forgotten the hard realities of the mornings. Now she was at the Pierre Hotel, one of New York's finest, with a black slip, no underwear, high heeled shoes, and a red minidress.

'Anything, my love. Anything.'

While they waited for room service to arrive, Nicholas showered and dressed.

'OK, I'm ready to serve you. The list please.'

Nicholas had offered to go up to her apartment and get everything she would need to dress for the day, saving her the embarrassment of getting into a taxi at the hotel. She had accepted at once.

'You're a fine-looking messenger.' She loved the classic tailored way he dressed. This morning he had put on a blue-and-white striped shirt and navy pleated pants. His tie was a dark blue silk background with just the tiniest pink dots. The monogram, on the left front of the shirt in dark blue thread, read NAT.

'What's the A for?' she asked, suddenly reminded of how little she knew about this man she had just spent the night with.

'Alexander, after my mother's grandfather.'

'Nice, I like a messenger boy with a sophisticated name. Now here's the list. I think you'll be able to find most everything. I'm pretty organised.'

'If I don't get lost in the maze of furniture, I'm sure I'll be fine.'

'Don't be a wise ass. And Nicholas, please hurry. They usually expect to see me long before now.'

'At your service, m'lady, and I'll hurry.' He kissed her forehead and left her midway through her coffee, fresh pineapple, and *The New York Times*.

She telephoned the studio to tell them she'd be late and also her doorman to tell him to let Nicholas up to the apartment. Just as she was stepping into the shower, there was a knock at the door. Wearing the pyjama top Nicholas had given her, she opened it tentatively.

'Good morning, ma'am,' said the uniformed bellman as he entered carrying a large basket wrapped with bright-coloured paper and tied with a ribbon. 'Mr Tate said you would require these at once.' He set the basket down on a table in the living room and left.

She pulled the wrapping off to reveal a large white basket filled with life's essentials: a toothbrush; the *Wall Street Journal*; a small travelling hair dryer; Calèche soap, eau de toilette, and body lotion; and a large bouquet of double pink peonies. The card read, 'These should keep you busy until I get back.'

What a thoughtful, wonderful man. She could get used to this very easily!

Nicholas returned with everything on her list. She dressed quickly, and they left the room together, Jennifer clutching her fragrant peonies under her arm.

'I'll drop you at the studio, if you'd like; I've got a meeting downtown.'

'Is it with the publisher?' she asked.

'Yes, I'm hopeful that I can finally convince them to commit to the project. It's been over a year already. After I missed the flight this morning, I called him on the off chance he might be able to see me. Maybe an informal pitch will get them moving.'

Nicholas had mentioned a project he very much wanted to work on – a book showing the other sides of the war in the Middle East, photos of the people, the land, and the villages that the public never saw – photos that depicted the real devastation that the war was causing. He felt it was important to document that side of the crisis, not just the battle fronts. Hunter & Weiss Publishers had shown an interest in the book, and he was anticipating their final decision soon.

'I hope so, too. It's a very important idea.'

The cab was going west on 57th Street, moving faster than she wanted it to.

'Jenn,' he took her hand in his, 'I've had a wonderful two days. I love being with you.'

She smiled but didn't speak.

'I'll call you from London. I really don't know when I'll be back, but we'll talk and make plans as best we can.'

He hugged her tightly when they arrived in front of the building.

80

'Thanks for a wonderful time.' She knew if she tried to say any more, tears would overcome her.

'Goodbye, pretty lady.'

She grabbed her flowers and entered the building without looking back. She didn't want him to remember her with tears running down her cheeks.

10

EVEN though it was well past ten, Jennifer allowed herself five minutes' more privacy in the ladies' room. She washed her face and reapplied the small amount of make-up she wore during the day. Andrea came in just as she was gathering up her flowers and the laundry bag with the Pierre logo imprinted all over it that contained her dress and shoes from the night before, plus all the Calèche products Nicholas had sent up. She took one look at Jennifer, with her face not completely recovered from crying, and decided that a simple good morning, without any extraneous comments, was in order.

Cindy informed Jennifer that Sidney was still out at a breakfast meeting, but he was expected shortly. Thank heavens for small favours, she thought.

There must have been ten or fifteen minutes during the day that she did not think of him, but as she climbed into bed that night, exhausted, she couldn't recollect when they had occurred.

She ended up working most of the weekend on new material for her Special Segments because she was convinced that after everyone returned, which she was certain had to be during the coming week, she would be forced really to scramble to get stories ready on time once she returned to her regular position. She did take time to call her favourite New York decorators, Zajac & Callahan, and advise them that she was finally ready to do the apartment, which had sat empty for so long. Edward Zajac and Richard Callahan represented the best of elegant classic design in all their work and their client list included some of the most tasteful people in New York. Good, she thought, Eddie and Richard should know exactly what to do.

But there was an overriding distraction that clouded everything she did. Nicholas had been gone for three days now, and she hadn't heard from him. Of course, she asked herself, did you really expect to? And the answer was always; yes, absolutely. There was no answering machine or service to pick up the phone in the apartment, but he definitely had the studio number. With each hour on Sunday afternoon, her disappointment grew.

Sidney had wanted her to attend a movie screening that evening, and she forced herself to go along. It was a lightweight summer romance, along the lines of *Romancing the Stone*. Each time the heroine was kissed, she felt Nicholas's lips on hers, each time they made love she relived Wednesday evening in her mind, detail by detail. By the end of the picture, she was lonelier than ever.

Finally, after she had been home for several hours that night, the phone rang. She hesitated to pick it up, certain that it was her mother wanting a report on another dateless weekend from her eldest daughter, but something made her answer it.

'Hello, lady anchor.' It was him.

'Hi,' she said, a little brusquely.

'I've been trying to call you since I got home. It was too late on Friday night when we finally got to the country and on Saturday there was the most incredible rainstorm in years. All the power in the entire village where my sister lives was knocked out. I got through once, the phone was ringing, but it went out again almost immediately. Christopher and Lisa and I had a nice weekend, but I've been missing you terribly.'

'Me too,' she admitted, her voice much softer in tone after hearing his voluntary explanation.

'But, have I got a proposition for you.'

She laughed. 'Yes, I'm ready.'

'Can you come to London next weekend? I'd fly back to

New York, but Christopher has a rugby match on Sunday and I'm afraid I have to go and support. Particularly since I'm off for two weeks after that. It would be the only thing planned for the weekend, however. The rest of the time we could be together, doing whatever makes you happy. I've a car, and we could go to the country or stay in town, whatever your pleasure.'

'What makes me happy doesn't necessarily require a car, although we could try it,' she said.

His laughter was clear even through the transatlantic connection. 'Well, what do you think?'

'It sounds wonderful, I think I can work extra hard during the week so I won't need to go in over the weekend. But I may still have to do the Friday night edition.'

'If that's the case, perhaps you should take the night flight, it leaves around nine, and then you can take the Concorde back on Monday morning. The one that leaves here at ten-thirty a.m. gets into New York in time for the first story of the day on Monday.'

'Oh, Nicholas, I can't wait.'

'Good, I'll have the tickets delivered to the apartment, let's say, by Wednesday of next week. I'll also arrange for you to be met at the airport. In the meantime, behave yourself and give good news! Good night.'

London for the weekend! How wonderful! But she knew the week would take forever to pass.

She was right. It was only Wednesday, and the week was dragging. She had packed and repacked twice in an effort to take just the right clothes. On Monday she had left the office early to go shopping, buying new things for the trip – two casual yet fitted linen dresses, a chic black Vicky Tiel fancy dress in case they went to the theatre, and two new nightgowns, a long silky Christian Dior with a matching robe, and a short peach-and-ivory patterned nightshirt. She had not been so excited about a purchase in years.

Riding the escalator down from the third floor of Saks, Jennifer heard a familiar voice calling her name.

Glancing over to the up escalator, she saw her good friend

Wendy Grimaldi. Wendy and her husband, Tony, had founded one of the premier cooking schools in New York. Their speciality was Italian cuisine, and they offered a variety of classes for all levels, from the New Yorker who weekended in the country and found himself with a workable kitchen on his hands to the most serious gourmet. Some of the city's finest chefs held a diploma from the school. Quarterly they took an eager group to Italy for instruction on location. Jennifer had been so fascinated by their business that she had made them the subject of one of her first Special Segments. Charmed by their dynamic personalities and the most outrageous tortellini she had ever tasted, a strong friendship developed. Besides her sisters, whom she was able to see less and less frequently, Wendy had become one of her closest friends. Still, with the hours Jennifer kept, she never had as much time to spend with her as she would have liked.

Wendy scrambled down the up escalator.

'Boy, when you hit the big time, you really leave your friends in the dust,' she teased her.

'You're right, you're so right,' Jennifer said ashamedly. She hadn't called since before the Grand Central catastrophe. 'I'm a rotten friend, but I do think about you often. How is everyone?'

'Tony and the kids are in Italy, and I'm having the time of my life. I haven't been alone like this since Elizabeth was born,' she said, referring to her twelve-year-old daughter. 'Now I remember the good points about being single!'

'Sounds like a nice break. Where are you off to now?'

'Actually, I'm finished for tonight. I was on my way home.'

'I'm done, too. Should we have something to eat?'

Wendy surveyed all Jennifer's packages and suggested they drop them off at her apartment on 54th Street instead of carrying everything to the restaurant.

'A good plan,' Jennifer agreed.

When they reached the apartment, Wendy offered to 'whip up something light'.

'What a treat,' Jennifer replied enthusiastically. 'I've eaten out so much this last month, I've forgotten what a home-cooked meal is like. Especially one of yours.'

So they stayed in and enjoyed a bottle of Chianti, and what Wendy referred to as a 'designer pizza', but most of all, the company. They brought each other up to date on their respective lives, Jennifer sharing the dual excitement of her temporary assignment and, of course, Nicholas.

'So that's what all of those packages are about,' Wendy squealed.

'Yes, I probably went a little overboard buying new things for the trip,' Jennifer admitted.

'Don't be silly. I can't think of a more suitable reason to overspend. Let's see everything.'

Like two schoolgirls, they carried on past midnight, Jennifer modelling all her new clothes and talking incessantly about Nicholas.

They also discussed Jennifer's concerns and fears about meeting his son for the first time. Wendy's son Sean was almost exactly the same age as Christopher.

'Just don't try to pull any punches with him,' she cautioned. 'Be straightforward. Kids at ten today are so much smarter than you and I were at twenty. But you've got to remember that, no matter how mature he may be, he's been through a lot for a child his age. It's difficult to be separated from either parent, but especially the mother. Don't worry, Jenn, it may take a little time, but I'm sure you'll get along fine.'

When Jennifer finally returned to her own apartment she realised how good it had felt to share her feelings with another woman, especially someone as supportive and caring as Wendy.

As she arrived at the studio on Thursday morning, she was surprised to see the lights on in the office two doors down from hers. Steve Wykowski, one of the newscasters who had been on vacation when Stewart was killed, had apparently returned. Jennifer dropped her things on her desk and walked down the hall to welcome him back. She thought the first effort should be hers. At thirty-seven, Steve was a newscaster of moderate talent. Sid had inherited him when he moved over to Channel 7, and he had never been one of his favourites. Steve's more-than-slightly arrogant manner, both off and on the air, made co-workers and viewers uneasy with him. Jennifer had always been professionally friendly with him, believing that a person should always at least try and develop a working relationship, even if the other party wasn't responsive. They had, in fact, thanks to her efforts, achieved at least a civil attitude toward each other. Last year Steve had got himself into a bind; he couldn't make a deadline on two stories he had promised. He had come to Jennifer late one night and asked for her help.

'Say, Jennifer, do you think you could just put the finishing touches on these two pieces? I'm really late, and they're due tomorrow morning.'

'Sure,' she had agreed, figuring that it couldn't take long just for 'finishing touches'. But the truth was that the pieces were barely started. They required additional research and many more factual details before they could be perceived as valuable reporting. By the time she discovered their real condition and went to look for Steve, he had left. It was not her nature to break a promise, and she had agreed to help. But, even more important, she could not submit poorly done or incomplete work, regardless of whether or not her name was on it. So she had stayed, using the research library and trying to pull the pieces together as best she could. When she dropped them off on Steve's desk at four-thirty that morning, she left a note: 'You give new meaning to the phrase "finishing touches". I hope these are all right.'

Quite honestly, she had expected a gesture from Steve in gratitude for basically saving his bacon on the two assignments. A fur coat or a Mercedes would have done the trick – better yet, a thank-you note. But nothing like that happened. Steve used the materials exactly as she had written them, never once mentioning to anyone how grateful he was to her. Not even to Jennifer. After that incident Jennifer had remained civil but greatly distanced from Steve.

He was on the phone. From the look of his tan, he had had

great weather on the trip. He was not handsome at all, she decided as she stood in the doorway looking at him. His nose was too big for his face, his head was too small for his body, and he dressed rather poorly. She suspected that natural fibres never went near his body. A tan and almost two weeks of vacation usually made anyone look his best, but Steve appeared as self-consumed and unattractive as ever, his feet propped on his desk, phone to his ear. He seemed certain that the anchor slot, which he wanted so badly, was in the bag.

'Morning, Jennifer,' he waved. 'Come in, I'll be off in a minute.'

'That's right. A convertible. I'll be there at one on Friday to pick it up. Don't let me down, honey,' he said to the rental car agent. 'If I can't get to the Hamptons this weekend, I'm in big trouble.' Jennifer was sure that someone taking his car reservation wouldn't give a damn about his weekend, much less know anything about where or what the Hamptons were. She also thought it was terrific that after his vacation he was planning to leave early on Friday. Such dedication.

'Welcome back,' she offered. 'It looks like Alaska was warm and sunny.'

'Too sunny. The temperature reached a hundred degrees a couple of times, but it was fun. Beautiful country, but not many social activities out in the wilderness.'

What did he expect? The Palladium West?

'I understand you've been trying to hold down the fort while Roger and Jim and I were out.' Condescending bastard, she thought. Not one mention of Stewart, the tragedy of his death, or the deaths of all the others. No, none of that, just concern that he get back on the air at once and save the ratings.

'I've tried. Everyone has been very helpful. Very supportive. It's been a tough couple of weeks.'

'I'm sure. But we'll get it back on track now,' he assured her.

'Yes . . . well, I'll let you get through the mail. It really piles up. I'll update you later, whenever you're ready.' Just keep being pleasant, no matter how difficult it is, she told herself.

She turned and left the office before saying what she really felt.

Roger Hartson was just stepping off the elevator, his morning coffee in one hand and briefcase in the other. When he spotted Jennifer, he put both of them on the nearest desk and walked toward her with open arms.

'Good morning, gorgeous.' He hugged her and lifted her up off her feet in greeting.

'Welcome back. Boy, am I glad to see you.'

'Me too, but I've got to admit I love being out there on the road. You really feel so close to the action. Santa Fe was terrific. Great weather. Fun people. We'll kill everyone else with our stuff. But it's sure sad coming back here, knowing that Stewart won't be around. We were all shocked when we heard about it. Couldn't work well at all that day.'

'You're right. It's a different atmosphere. A lot of us still expect him to come in again some morning. But . . .'

'Yeah, I know. But it's not going to happen. I hear you've become an instant success. Everybody downstairs says you've been great.'

'We're trying. Last week was something else.'

'Well, I guess the mail is waiting. Will you be around for an update?'

'All day . . . you know where to find me.'

Cindy came around the corner at full speed. 'So that's where you two have been. I've been looking in your offices, how foolish of me. I should know by now that all important stuff is decided in the hallways. Anyway, now that I've got you, Mr. Lachman has called an all-staff meeting at ten-thirty in the conference room. Do not be late, and do not bring anything – those were his exact words,' she said. 'Oh, by the way, welcome back, Roger, I missed you,' Cindy yelled back to them.

'Sounds serious. We'll be there.'

The chairs around the conference table had been pushed back against the walls, and those who had arrived early and had taken a seat were now blocked by others standing two and three deep in front of them. Jennifer arrived just at ten-thirty and took a place leaning against the back wall. Roger and Steve were across the room, chatting with each other. Sidney entered about five minutes later, empty handed. So it wasn't a review of numbers or expenses. But it was the first time he had called everyone together since Stewart's death.

'A little quiet for your producer, please,' he opened. The room settled down at once. They all laughed and joked together during work, but they were all smart enough and professional enough to know when to straighten up. It fell so quiet they could hear the constant hum of the fluorescent ceiling lights.

'Thank you. Each of you in this room deserves a special thank you from me for your efforts during the last two weeks. We've all suffered a great loss, each of us to varying degrees. Certainly all of us have lost a professional, likeable co-worker, and, I would venture to say, most of us also lost a friend. Stewart's death would have been a tragedy had it occurred from natural causes, but the fact that it didn't, that it happened because of the selfishness, the craziness of one man, makes it even more difficult to accept.' His voice cracked. 'But you're all to be congratulated, you've pulled together, and we've been able to carry on and do our job, which is to report the news to the public in the best way we know how. I know it has been tough, and I thank you all.' The silence became more noticeable. No one moved. They sensed that he wasn't finished yet. They felt that there was another very different reason for them all to be gathered in the crowded, overheated room.

'A tragedy such as this,' he continued, 'a tragedy that takes the life of a key person, leaves a big hole in the operation. In my judgement, it is prudent to fill that spot immediately and to begin rebuilding a team as rapidly and efficiently as possible. This, of course, assumes that there are individuals ready, willing, and capable of filling that slot. I've always felt blessed in this job, because I was able to attract and develop competent people. After all, a producer is useless if his productions can't be carried out by his actors, or, in this instance, his reporters. But I've always felt we were on the road to becoming number one in the New York area.' This last remark brought cheers and clapping from everyone.

'Stewart's death makes that goal more difficult now. We're going to have to rebuild, regain the attention of our viewers by providing them with the best, most up-to-the-minute reports on anything and everything that concerns them. I'm confident that we have the people to meet this challenge. In the past two weeks, you'll all have observed, and many of you have been directly involved in producing, a top-flight broadcast with Jennifer Martin as anchor. I think you'd all agree that she has embraced the position with sincerity and a style of her own.' The room showed its agreement with more clapping. Several of the camera crew yelled out, 'Go Jennifer!'

'All right, let me finish. Jennifer is by no means a seasoned newscaster. Most of you know her only from her performance on tape, entirely different from a live show. But, I believe she has the potential to become one of the best. She is dedicated and committed.'

More cheers. At this point, everyone felt that Sidney was merely recognising her, and thanking her for filling in. Now that Steve and Roger had returned, things would switch back to them, and the roles they would play in the new structure.

No one was more surprised than Jennifer at what came next.

'Quiet down, please,' Sidney implored. 'It is for this reason that I've made a crucial decision for this station. Jennifer Martin will be the new anchor on the early evening edition –'

They didn't allow him to finish. The message had been delivered. They went wild – Andrea, standing next to Jennifer, grabbed her and kissed her. Everyone was clapping. Everyone except Steve Wykowski. Jennifer could see across the room to where he was sitting. Roger, seated next to him, was clapping loudly, smiling at her. Steve was looking straight at her, straight through her, she felt. His eyes did not mask what he was thinking. She smiled at him, and looked away.

Sidney was attempting to bring the room back to order.

'I gather from your response that I can count on all of you to give Jennifer your continued support.'

'You bet,' yelled Kevin, and the others echoed his sentiments with more applause.

It was evident to Sidney that he had made the right choice. But he couldn't help noticing the look on Steve's face. Unprofessional bastard, he thought, it just confirms what I've always believed.

'Please allow me just a few more announcements. Roger Hartson will be promoted to lead roving reporter. He will spend most of his time in the field, on the road. He is topnotch and is most effective in that position.' More cheers showing support for Roger. He was well liked by everyone. 'Steve Wykowski will continue as backup anchor.' The room gave a short, light applause. Just enough so that they did not appear rude, but not enough to make anyone think they really cared.

'That's all for now,' Sidney continued. 'Now I believe we've got a news programme to produce. Back to work, everyone, and thank you again.' He left the room through the door at the other end from where Jennifer was standing. Jennifer was immediately surrounded by everyone congratulating her.

'Way to go, Jenn.'

'Best of luck.'

'We're behind you all the way.'

'It's about time we got a woman in the top spot.' This from some of her female colleagues.

She was ecstatic, and she accepted their wishes graciously. As soon as she could, she broke away and went directly to Sidney's office.

'You sure know how to surprise a girl. I'll take you for shock value any day.'

'Jenn, I hope you'll forgive me for handling it that way. I really felt it was the best way, the easiest. And I'm certain it was the right decision, even more so after I saw the crew's reaction. Also, the ratings show it. You've gained more share of audience in the last ten days than we had when Stewart was here . . .'

'So?' he looked at her questioningly.

'Thank you. I couldn't be happier. You know it's what I want. Don't worry, I'll do you proud. I think Steve may have some serious problems with it, though. Just a couple of hours ago he was preparing his acceptance speech. If looks could kill –'

'I saw him. The best thing that guy could do right now is leave. I've spelled it out for him in letters ten feet high. I won't tolerate his attitude any longer. I don't subscribe to the idea that there has to be one bad apple in the barrel.'

'Well, I've got more important things to worry about than him now. What are your plans for the Special Segment position?'

'I met a woman in Chicago during the broadcasting convention last month. She desperately wants to move to New York. I thought I'd call her and see if she could fly in to meet with us this weekend.'

Sirens went off in Jennifer's head. She couldn't exactly interview this person from London.

'How do you feel about one night next week? If we did it early in the week, we're still covered for three weeks. I've got three more segments.' She prayed he would agree.

'Not planning to be around this weekend?' He was immediately aware of what she was asking. They knew each other so well; Jennifer sometimes forgot everything they had been through together.

'Well, actually I've been invited to go out of town.' She smiled. 'London.'

'London? Well, that doesn't sound cancellable. I'll have her come in on Monday night. We'll talk with her then.'

'It seems all I do lately is thank you. Thank you again, for everything.'

'Say hello to Nicholas for me. He may not remember me, we purchased a series of his work for the Museum of Modern

Art permanent collection a few years ago. I met him briefly then. He is extremely talented and quite nice.'

For the second time that morning, Jennifer's face held a look of shock.

'Incredible – how on earth do you know about him?'

'Word travels fast around here. Actually, I saw you two leave together the other night. From the smile on your face these last days, I merely assumed a romance was budding. I'm happy for you, truly, and I wish you a great weekend.'

'You're amazing. You don't miss a trick.'

'Not if I'm interested in something, or someone,' he added. 'Now out of here. You've got plenty of work to do between now and the time you get on the plane.'

'Right again,' she said as she left his office.

'That's it. Don't let anyone ever tell you that women still aren't sleeping their way to the top. That bitch just did it – fucking the producer is still the quickest way to the next rung on the ladder, in this case my rung, rightly deserved. And now I'm upstaged by some untalented blonde cunt.'

Jennifer stopped dead in her tracks. It was painfully clear who was the 'blonde cunt' to whom Steve was referring.

His back was to her. He was standing in his office pontificating to Roger. Roger immediately leapt to Jennifer's defence.

'I'm not sure I agree with you, Steve. I know you're disappointed about not getting the slot, but what you've just said is pretty powerful stuff. Jennifer is not exactly untalented, in fact she's pretty sharp, and about sleeping with Sidney, even if . . .'

She stormed into the room. 'Yes, even if I were, which I am not, it's none of your goddamn business. Absolutely none. Now I'd like an apology, Steve, in fact I'd like your assurance that you will keep your filthy mouth shut from this minute on. You'll either get over this and decide to work with me, decide that maybe I do have some talent, which is apparently what the most recent ratings show, and we'll go from there. Or I'll make your life more difficult than you can possibly imagine. I don't appreciate both a personal and a professional assault.'

The two men had never seen a display of temper from Jennifer. Steve was shaken.

'Jennifer, I didn't know you were outside.'

'Of course not, but thank God I was, so that now maybe I have a chance to stop your poisonous, malicious gossip from infiltrating the entire station.' She was not finished with him.

'I'm sorry. I guess my disappointment really got the best of me.'

'As far as I'm concerned there is no "best of you".' Roger showed his agreement by lowering his head and laughing to himself. 'Just keep your disgusting thoughts to yourself, or I'll rally every one of those kids, whose support I obviously have, and we'll make your life here less than wonderful. That's a promise.'

She left them both without waiting for a response.

The whole incident had upset her. She knew that Steve was not high-quality material as a person, but she didn't think he'd stoop quite that low. Lady Luck had smiled at her, but she had worked hard to develop a talent capable of handling this position, and she'd be damned if she would allow anyone to ruin it for her.

She had meant what she said. Any more problems, and she would see to it that Steve was off the show in short order.

11

JENNIFER tried to reach her parents almost immediately after she learned of her promotion, only to be told by Doris that they had gone to the theatre in Chicago with friends, and wouldn't return until Friday.

When she finally reached them, Ken Martin shared Jennifer's news with the level of enthusiasm she had come to expect.

'Oh, honey, it's wonderful. It's just one step away from a network slot. Do you realise how quickly it happened? I can't wait for the tapes, can you send them weekly?'

'I suppose, Dad, now that I'm the anchor, I'll get more secretarial help. I'll have someone make sure they get them to you.'

'And you're off to London for the weekend. It sounds like things are going very well in your world.'

'Yes, no complaints this week. How is everyone there?'

'Your mother is anxious to get on. I'll let her tell you.'

Her mother's voice came on the line.

'So what story are you going to London for?' she demanded immediately. No congratulations, no recognition, and she of course assumed that a trip to London could only be for business. Time to surprise her.

'It's not a story, Mother, it's a man.'

Jennifer was certain she heard the phone drop.

'Mom, are you still there? Yes, I know it's shocking, but it is the truth.'

'How on earth did you meet someone from London?'

96

Jennifer's mother's perception of the world was far-reaching.

'Well, they now have trans-Atlantic flights, and he was daring enough to take one. I met him in New York.'

'Your sarcasm is not appreciated. I am your mother and I expect straightforward answers.' Then ask halfway intelligent questions, thought Jennifer.

'OK, I'm sorry. I met him in New York, we spent some time together, and he invited me to spend the weekend in London with him and his son.'

'His son?' she asked incredulously.

'Yes, a small, male child, ten years old.'

'Is he married?'

'Not this weekend,' she giggled. There, she did it again, she couldn't help herself.

'No, Mother, he's not married.'

'Divorced?'

'Yes, for two years. The man's name is Nicholas Tate, and he's a photojournalist.'

'One of those people that travel around the world taking pictures?'

'Exactly,' Jennifer agreed. Why try to explain anything at this point? She just wanted to let them know she'd be out of town.

'Well, have fun, but I don't know why you can't find someone who's single, and in New York.'

'He is single, Mother. I can't help the fact that he doesn't live in New York. Anyway, it's just for a fun weekend. Now what's going on there?'

'Well, Pat's due any day now. We can't keep Jason out of the swimming pool, and the Jacobsons are getting a divorce.'

The Jacobsons were two of her parents' closest friends. The two couples played bridge together and belonged to the same club.

'I'm sorry to hear that. I'll try to call Pat tonight before I leave. I've got to leave for the airport in an hour, so if I can't reach her, please give her my love.'

'I will. Your father said something about a promotion. I hope it's what you want.'

'It is, Mother, thank you. I'll talk to you next week. Bye.'

The Jacobsons. She was sorry about that. Quite frankly she was surprised her parents were still together. She chalked it up to the fact that her father possessed many saintlike qualities.

She was able to get a lot of sleep on the plane. It was a throwback to the time when she travelled a great deal. She had to admit, however, that it was much easier to sleep in a first-class seat than in the cramped quarters in economy.

She was thankful Nicholas thought so too.

As she disembarked, at eight-forty London time, an imposing man approached her. He was dressed in a suit, neatly starched shirt, and tie. On his head was a blue hat, which he tipped as he spoke to her.

'Miss Jennifer Martin?'

'Yes . . .' She hesitated.

'Hello, good morning, rather. Welcome to London. I'm Basil Cummings, Mr Tate's chauffeur. He's asked me to meet you and drive you to the house. If you'll be kind enough to give me your luggage tags, I'll get your bags for you.'

'I didn't check anything. This is all I have.' She indicated the Vuitton duffel and garment bag.

'Excellent.' He liked her already. 'That will speed things up dramatically. It always takes them so long on these morning arrivals.'

The number plates on the enormous black Daimler read 'TATE I'. She wondered if there was a TATE II. So much to learn about this man. She realised yet again how little she did know.

It had been almost three years since her last trip to London. She and Jeffrey had flown there for a weekend shortly after she was offered the job in New York. They had stayed at the Connaught and had gone to the theatre and to some museums, but the trip had been marred by her knowledge that their relationship was soon going to change dramatically, possibly even end, when she finally moved to New York. Jennifer had surprised herself by not even thinking of Jeffrey recently. She realised that while she and Nicholas were making love, and even after when he held her in his arms, not once did her thoughts turn to Jeffrey. Usually when she became intimate with someone now, she would make comparisons to the previous lover. Not so in this case. Nicholas was someone very special, very different.

'How much longer?' she questioned the driver.

'With this traffic, I'd estimate another twenty minutes, Miss Martin.'

Enough time to recheck her make-up and hair. She had spent a long time in the bathroom on the plane, brushing her teeth, washing her face and generally trying to pull herself together after the long flight. She took a last look at herself in the small travel mirror, not totally pleased with her appearance, but it was not terrible considering she had gone directly from the studio to the plane.

Two minutes later Basil stopped the car in front of a large white Georgian house. The entrance was bordered by a black wrought-iron fence. The first floor had three large windows draped with what looked like tie-back curtains. The second and third floors, what must be the bedrooms, she assumed, were concealed behind brown shutters.

'Here we are, please step out and go directly in. I know Mr Tate is expecting you. I'll deal with your luggage.'

'Thank you.'

She smiled past him and walked toward the front door. A discreet brass plate indicated that indeed this was the Tate home, No. 18 Grosvenor Crescent.

Before she reached the bell, the door swung open and she faced a smiling woman, dressed in black and a white eyelet pinafore and starched cap to match. She pulled the heavy wooden door open to allow Jennifer to pass.

'Good morning, ma'am, and welcome. Mr Tate is expecting you. Just go up the stairs one flight, please. Basil will be bringing your things in shortly.'

She started up the stairs slowly, trying to get a glimpse of the main floor salon. It was decorated in a very traditional way — chintz upon chintz, lots of overstuffed furniture flanked by delicate wooden side tables. Only a small part of the room was visible, the rest was hidden behind a pocket door that had been pulled partially shut.

'Welcome, beautiful.' It was Nicholas at the top of the stairs standing in a doorway that appeared to lead into a library. He had on a different robe from the one she had seen in New York, this one an intricate paisley print in silk with a multitude of beautiful colours. The robe was tied at his waist with a belt in the same fabric, with tassels hanging from the ends. On his feet were burgundy glove-leather slippers.

'You look terribly English this morning.' She was now on the first-floor landing, only a few feet from him.

'How do you know what English men are supposed to look like in the morning?'

'From the movies, where I get most of my useful information.'

He stepped out of the doorway and took her in his arms.

'Oh, Jennifer, I am so glad to see you.' They kissed formally, then came the same light teasing kisses, just like in the taxi on the way to her apartment.

'I'm awfully glad to be here.'

They went through the doorway where he had been standing. He pulled the enormous mahogany doors shut. She had been correct, it was his library. To the full height of the fourteen-foot ceilings, the far wall was lined with books – art books, the classics, books on film, architecture, and, of course, photography. She spotted some current things also, the new Picasso biography and every adventurous man's favourite, the latest Robert Ludlum. A copy of *Les Liaisons Dangereuses*, in French, was on top of the pile of books and magazines stacked casually on the oversized desk. The side of the room facing the street had huge paned windows, partially hidden now by the drapes that Jennifer had seen when she was getting out of the car. On the opposite wall was an ornamental carved marble fireplace. The floor was covered with oriental rugs; they looked old and worn and very appropriate for the room.

Nicholas led her to an inviting red leather Chesterfield

couch. He held her and told her again how happy he was to see her. Had Basil found her easily enough at the airport, he asked. She nodded her head to indicate yes, not wanting to remove her lips from his for even a brief moment. His hands were soon inside her blouse, his fingers teasing her rock-hard nipples without mercy. She pulled open the sash of his robe, and as he stood up to allow the sleeves to fall from his shoulders, she saw that he was as hungry for her as she was for him. She pulled him down on to her, rubbing her bare breasts against his chest, nipple to nipple. He made her stand before him, as he sat on the couch, while he unfastened the elegant buckle on her Kieselstein-Cord belt, unbuttoned the metal buttons on her jeans, and slid them down, over her bottom to just above her well-defined calves. The blue silk panties she was wearing were stained with her wetness. He cupped his hands over the blonde hair, gently pushed the thin strip of material aside, and entered her with the full length of his second finger. He soon traded his fingers for his tongue. Jennifer's sighs were uncontrollable now, she tried to be as quiet as she could, but from time to time she realised her moans were loud enough to be heard outside the library doors. She desperately hoped that Christopher wasn't anywhere in the house. The desire was too great, and if she continued to allow his tongue to assault her, she would soon reach a point of no return. She pulled back, released her legs from the skin-tight jeans, and straddled Nicholas with her now wobbly legs. There was a brief moment of hesitation as she poised her open lips above his fully swollen cock. He had been so prepared the last time, the first time, that she was slightly confused.

'Trust me, love,' he pleaded with her. 'We'll talk about it later.'

Something, her deepest instincts, told her that it was all right, that everything was going to be OK, probably even more than just OK. She lowered herself on to his hugeness. He allowed her all of the movements. She controlled the speed at which he opened her. Finally, selfishly, knowing that he had not yet reached his orgasm, she thrust herself recklessly, repeatedly on to him, gripping his shoulders with all her strength. She rode him forcefully. The orgasm overtook her, and for a moment, as she stared glassy-eyed into his beautiful face, she was lost, floating, the centre of her being focused between her legs. Nicholas came just as she was finishing her wild movements, at the time when she had recovered enough to feel the heat of his burning life pour into her, a sensation she had missed terribly under the conditions of their last lovemaking.

She rested peacefully, her head on his shoulder, her legs still wrapped like a child on a carousel horse. When they finally did move, the weight of Nicholas's arm caught some of her dishevelled hair, and pinned it to the back of the couch.

'Ouch,' she squealed. 'Be very careful. You have just made love to the new official anchorwoman, anchorperson, whatever, of Channel 7.'

'Oh, Jenn, congratulations, darling. That's wonderful. When did it happen?'

'Just yesterday. So this could really be considered a celebration weekend.'

'I'm delighted for you. I'll have to think of something very special to do. How about this for starters?'

He kissed her again as he rearranged her body so that she was lying stretched out, completely naked on the red Chesterfield. He found the sash of his belt and, spreading her legs apart, ran the sash in between them and reached under her thigh to grab the other. He held both ends with his hand, pulling the paisley silk until it was taut between her lips, still swollen from his recent departure. The tassels became gentle whips that he used teasingly on the inside of her thighs. He continued to kiss her, but the realisation of what he was doing, how he was touching her, and manipulating her in a manner unlike any previous lover, sent her into new spasms of desire.

'Does my lover need my tongue on her?'

'Yes, yes, Nicholas, please now, take me again.'

'Yes, darling, will you come for me?'

'Yes, I promise.'

Not one to break promises, Jennifer came almost as soon as his tongue pushed aside the fabric of the sash, and answered her wish.

Again they drifted off for a time.

She woke him with her giggles.

'Will we stay in this room all weekend? I didn't have to bring so many clothes.'

'Love them and discard them. An old trick. I suppose you're hungry now too.'

'Well, you're not entirely wrong.'

The breakfast had been set by Anna, Nicholas's cook and housekeeper who had greeted Jennifer at the door, on the terrace in back of the library. Its glass top was usually closed, but on a glorious summer morning like this, she had pressed the buttons that automatically made the entire roof disappear into storage. She had set the table with beautifully starched linens, fresh flowers, and a bucket with ice and a bottle of Dom Pérignon as Mr Tate had requested. Now she was downstairs seriously considering whether she had misunderstood him. She had been waiting in the kitchen with eggs, bacon, sausages, toast – all the ingredients of a hearty English breakfast – for over two hours. No, she was sure he had said, 'Miss Martin and I will take breakfast on the terrace around ten. Please prepare everything.' It was now almost twenty to eleven, and there was no one in sight, not one buzz from the bell upstairs. Oh, well, she could wait. She turned her attention back to her morning tabloid, the paper she couldn't live a day without, the *Sun*. She had already read it twice this morning, but she was looking through it again. Besides the scandalous photos and sizzling headlines, there was always some additional titbit of gossip hidden in the small stories that she usually missed.

Eleven o'clock. Almost time for her to start preparing for lunch, and not a single egg had been fried. But she was excited at the thought that her proper boss, the epitome of good English manners and dress, was upstairs in his library or wherever fucking the pants off the beautiful American

103

who had arrived this morning. God knows, he deserves it, she thought. After that rich spoiled Victoria – a very unstable individual and poor excuse for a mother, who paraded herself around London as an up-and-coming fashion designer – had literally turned this lovely house into a drug dealer's haven; after all the pain she had inflicted on Mr Tate and that charming boy, Christopher, he deserved some fun. Someone who really cared for him. She decided that he really deserved to fall madly in love.

At noon Nicholas appeared in the kitchen.

'Can we change the meal on the terrace to lunch?' he inquired of Anna, in a manner more appropriate to a four-year-old asking for another biscuit than the master of the house.

'With pleasure,' Anna replied, noting a distinct rosy tone in Nicholas's skin. 'I've caviar, poached salmon, and a delightful green salad. Do you still want the champagne?'

'Fine.' He was only half listening and already headed back upstairs.

They lunched and then took a long walk through Knightsbridge and later went to Hyde Park.

While they talked, Nicholas thanked her for trusting him this morning. He announced that last week, when he was getting his inoculations for his trip to India, he had had the doctor run a blood test, one that would eliminate any concern that he could be a carrier of the AIDS virus. It was, thankfully, negative and he announced with great happiness that there would be no more need for 'those little slipcovers for my friend.' She shared his laughter, but inside was seriously grateful.

'Are you happy, my sweet?' he asked as they strolled together.

'Very, but I'd be much happier if we were back at your house now.'

'That can easily be arranged.' He was hailing a taxi as she spoke.

Jennifer couldn't recall a time when she had been so content, so satiated. But as soon as they finished making love, she wanted more. He was like a Chinese dinner, you always thought you'd never be hungry again, but just a few hours later . . . She couldn't seem to get enough of him.

They returned to the house on Grosvenor Crescent, and Nicholas offered a tour. She realised she had spent the entirety of her visit so far upstairs in the library.

'Sure, just in case I sleepwalk tonight I'll know where the kitchen is.'

He opened the downstairs room to reveal a room right out of *The World of Interiors*, an article entitled 'A Country House in Town'. It was larger and grander than she had imagined from the brief glimpse she had on her way upstairs. A large gilt-framed mirror on one wall made the room appear larger than it really was. But by any standards, even Wayzata's, the room was spacious. The furniture was all English period; two chintz-covered sofas flanked an elaborate eighteenth-century fireplace. Two round, cloth covered tables, one on either side of the larger couch, held a multitude of photographs, each in its own silver frame. She was immediately drawn to the table, her interest a combination of wanting to know more about this man and also her curiosity about what the woman, in whose living room she was standing, looked like. Nicholas skiing with a large sign indicating St Moritz behind him; Nicholas on a boat with a handsome young boy standing in front of him, Christopher she presumed; Nicholas in black tie, joking with several other men. Then she saw them, nestled in the third or fourth row of frames: pictures of a beautiful woman, jet-black hair, creamy-white skin that looked like it rarely, if ever, saw the sun, with penetrating almond-shaped green eyes. She was holding a baby. The baby, whose sex was undetermined, was dressed in an elaborate lace christening gown. The woman was seated, and the hem of the child's gown almost reached the floor. He was grinning up at his mother. There were many other photographs, taken at various places around the world, that portrayed the activities of a handsome, affluent family. Their expressions defied the unhappiness the future held for them. She moved across the room to the other table, wishing to see as much as she could without seeming overly curious.

All the pictures on the smaller table were of Christopher. Several of them had been taken very recently. They must have a limitless supply of silver frames! she thought. He was a terrific-looking young boy, having inherited his father's colouring and height, and his mother's haunting eyes. She was attracted to a shot of him dressed in his rugby kit. Two of his teammates surrounded him, their arms around each other. His head was cocked to one side as if to say, 'We look like winners, don't we?'

'Handsome young man,' she commented. 'I'd expect nothing less from a father like you.'

'Yes, he's pretty terrific. Lisa, my sister, will bring him into town tomorrow morning. Her house is in the country, in Exbury, about a two-hour drive from here. His match is at one. I must warn you, I have no idea how he'll react to you. You're the first woman he's seen in his home since his mother left. I hope he doesn't behave rudely.'

'I'll understand even if he does. It has to be rough on him.' Even as she said this, Jennifer realised the high level of anxiety she was experiencing in anticipation of meeting Christopher. She had very little exposure to children or young adults. Was a ten-year-old a young adult? She supposed so. Wendy had warned her how advanced kids were at that age. Jason was the only child she had spent much time with, and, at three, she still considered him an infant.

'Does he see his mother often?' Maybe if she had more details about the situation, she wouldn't be so apprehensive.

'Not often enough to have any kind of relationship, I'm afraid. Victoria's really not in any condition to relate to anyone right now. We went up to visit her a few weeks ago. It was definitely a mistake. She's extremely hostile, sometimes disoriented. She's in the worst phase of withdrawal, when the body's physical reactions are the most severe. Christopher's a very mature little boy, but Victoria's condition at the moment is difficult for anyone to understand. The only positive aspect of the whole mess is that I'm sure he won't be interested in trying drugs when the time comes, if it hasn't already.'

'Well, I hope my being here doesn't confuse or frighten him even more.'

'I don't think so. He'll be so involved with his big game he won't have any time to think about it.'

The tour continued through the kitchen, where Anna was preparing the contents of the picnic lunch to be taken to tomorrow's game.

Fried chicken, pasta salads, freshly baked bread, cheeses, seasonal fruits, and assorted cutlery, plates, and paper napkins were all lined up on the stainless steel work table that dominated the room. Two wicker baskets, their lids propped open, were waiting to receive the goodies. The smell of brownies baking was overwhelming.

'This looks like a very American spread, I must say,' Jennifer commented as she surveyed the beautifully prepared food.

The work space was the size of a Manhattan studio apartment. Except for an open hearth oven on one wall, there was not a trace left of the original room. Even the Victorian-style wall mouldings had been removed to accommodate the ultra-modern, ultra-sleek design. Everything was white, the walls, the German ceramic tiles that covered the floor, even the high-tech movable light fixtures that hung down from beams in the ceiling. The white reflected whatever light was available, and it made a room look not only larger but more inviting. It had worked beautifully in the kitchen that Nicholas and Suzanne had designed when they had moved into the house. Light reflected off the stainless steel double sinks and counter surfaces. The eight-burner Garland stove-top and grill were shined to military standards by Anna and the second housekeeper, Martha. A complete selection of glistening stainless steel Sitram cookware was arranged by size on the Metro wire shelving that covered an entire wall. Plates, glasses, and cutlery for everyday use were stacked up neatly on the opposite wall. More formal dinnerware, champagne and wine glasses, and silver were kept in a floor-to-ceiling custom-made cabinet. Jennifer realised that they must have entertained extensively when things were good. This arrangement could easily provide food for a hundred people with no strain on the staff. She wondered if Nicholas missed that part of his previous life.

Jennifer continued to admire the glorious kitchen.

'What a terrific setup! Is there anything missing here? It seems that everything a real cook would want is at your fingertips.'

'Just about,' Anna agreed. 'But when Mr Tate gets going in here, all of my organisation is shot down within seconds.'

Jennifer turned to him. 'You never mentioned your cooking skills. What do you specialise in?'

'He specialises in mess,' Anna commented before Nicholas had a chance to answer.

'Very funny, Anna. She's merely jealous because the crust on her steak and kidney pie doesn't hold a candle to mine. Despite numerous tries on her part, my pie is consistently better.'

Steak and kidney pie, one of my least favourite culinary treats, Jennifer thought.

'Jennifer Martin, your eyes betray you yet again. Don't be afraid, English cooking is not my forte. I'm best at fish and orgasmic pastas.'

At the mention of pasta, all traces of disgust left her eyes.

'Aha, that excites you. Now I know the real reason why we get along. Forget what they say about chemistry, roses, et cetera, just give the girl a bowl of pasta and she's yours forever. Pasta on my mind . . .' He began to hum an old Neil Diamond tune with his new lyrics as he grabbed Jennifer and, with her in his arms, started to dance around the kitchen.

Anna looked up and then back to her chicken quickly, shaking her head. Secretly, however, she was so happy to see Nicholas smiling and joking again. It had been so hard on him, ever since that awful Victoria had destroyed their marriage.

'OK, wise guy,' Jennifer said as he twirled her faster and faster around the enormous room, 'what's for dinner?'

'Oh no, I'm taking you out on the town. I've made reservations at Langan's, and then we go to Annabel's afterwards. *Quelle danseuse, ma chérie,*' he announced, supporting the upper back and bending her gently backward into a final dip to announce the end of his song.

'*Je veux rester ici ce soir.*' He was surprised at her perfect French accent, far better than he had ever heard from the mouth of an American.

'*Vraiment?*'

'*Vraiment,* truly, yes, I want to stay here tonight. I think it would be fun to stay here and watch you destroy this magnificent kitchen with your reckless cooking.'

At this, Anna gave Jennifer a final shake of her head, plus a wink, and left the room. Jennifer noticed she had replaced the proper black shoes with pink high-top Reeboks for her kitchen work. She decided then that she really liked Anna very much.

Nicholas moved close to her and wrapped his arms around her waist. He nibbled on her neck and moved his hands up underneath her linen skirt.

'Are you sure you want to stay home tonight? I would tie you to the centre table with my apron strings and bring you to climax by stroking you all over your body with al dente fettuccine.'

'Just think what we could do with the pesto sauce,' she added. 'Yes, if you're up to it I really want you to cook for me tonight, but I suggest you fix a large portion for yourself and eat every bite.'

'Oh yes, and why is that?'

'Because you're going to need all the strength you can get for what I'm going to do to you tonight.' She wriggled out of his arms. 'Now we better get moving.'

'Anna, we're off to Harrods for shopping – groceries, not clothes,' he yelled as they left the kitchen, arms wrapped around each other's trim waists.

'Dear Lord, give me strength,' Anna reentered the kitchen and raised her head upwards.

'The whole family needs strength to survive your visit.' He

pinched Jennifer on her firm, delicious behind as he trailed behind her, out of the house and off to the great Harrods Food Halls.

The Food Halls were as glorious as Jennifer remembered them. On her last visit here with Jeffrey, they had walked the aisles, drooling over the enormous variety of cheeses and sausages, counted over three hundred different kinds of jams and marmalades, examined the butcher shop, the exotic fresh fish, and the extraordinary selections of teas and coffees. It was such a pleasure for the eyes and the nose. The skill with which each item was displayed, and the delicious smells! She remembered wishing that they had a kitchen to prepare some of these things in, but they were at the Connaught with no facilities, so they settled on some butter biscuits from the bakery, which they devoured before leaving the store. But today it was all different, and her wish was being granted as she watched Nicholas scurrying around, throwing package after package into his trolley. He knew the aisles intimately and was very thorough. They only had to retrace their steps once when he discovered he had forgotten some badly needed ingredient.

'Jenn, run back to the third aisle from the left, about four yards down on the right, and grab a jar of Crosse & Blackwell capers, will you, love?'

She was not the least bit surprised to find them exactly where he said they would be.

They returned to the house an hour later.

'Now, upstairs to the library or bedroom, wherever you wish, for a nap or a read, but please try to leave me alone for a couple of hours so I can create something edible for you.'

'Gladly,' she said, climbing the stairs, but truth was that she didn't feel like being away from him for even two minutes; two hours seemed like forever.

He found her almost three hours later, sleeping in his bed, a copy of *Tatler* magazine resting on her chest where it had dropped when she had fallen asleep while reading. She had removed her skirt and blouse and put on the silky Dior robe. Her long legs were crossed under her. Nicholas opened her robe and uncrossed her legs slowly. She moaned and turned over, trapping his head exactly where he desired it. He licked her slowly with his tongue, spreading her warm hairs gently. Instead of awakening completely, she groaned again and reached down to guide his head more securely between her thighs. She was happy to have him take her like this, secure enough in their lovemaking already to know that pleasing her was almost as good for him as pleasing himself. Slowly she met his tongue, and then suddenly her thrusts became stronger. She needed not only his tongue but his fingers inside her to take her fully. He responded quickly, just in time for her not to lose her rhythm. Her breathing quickened. He heard her giggle once before she finally released herself completely to him. He held on to her until she was finished and she reached for him to take her in his arms.

'Dinner is served, my love.'

She smiled up at him. 'And you've already had your appetiser!'

The table on the terrace had been set for their dinner, but this time Anna had chosen the palest blue linen tablecloth with coordinating napkins. 'I thought the colour would look lovely with your blonde hair,' she told Jennifer the following morning. She had selected the last of the brilliantly coloured summer flowers, peonies and daisies and irises, and had arranged them in two vases and placed them on each side of the table, instead of making just one centrepiece that would have blocked their view of each other. Not good for a romantic dinner! Anna really had an eye for lovers' details. The pink Reeboks had clued Jennifer in that despite her English countenance, at heart she was great fun. The Baccarat wine goblets and Christofle silver glistened in the candlelight.

Nicholas hadn't been joking about his culinary talents. She would find out later that Anna hadn't been kidding either about the mess he left.

In the few short hours while Jennifer slept, he had created a true gourmet meal. They started with a cold asparagus soup, chilled perfectly and topped with fresh ground pepper. The pasta, unlike anything she had eaten before, was a fettuccine with seafood. The fettucine had been tinted deep black with the ink from the squid. It was superb.

A simple but perfectly grilled swordfish with parsley and lemon butter followed. All this was accompanied by ample quantities of cold white Californian Riesling. Dessert was a heart-shaped Italian mascarpone with fresh blueberry sauce. At any other time, at any other place it would have been corny, but not now, not here. Jennifer was touched by his sweetness and his efforts. That night they made love with a new sense of closeness, another dimension in their rapidly growing attachment to each other.

'Good morning, gorgeous.' He startled her. She had slept so soundly that she wasn't sure how late it was.

'Hi, chef.'

They lay quietly in each other's arms.

'I've spent worse weekends, but I don't remember when,' she joked.

'Me, too. But the beauty of this morning is that I don't have to take a taxi anywhere seeking ladies' underwear and stockings. I assume you brought some,' he said.

They had just a couple of hours before Lisa arrived with Christopher for the game. They chose to spend it making love again.

'I hope that will keep you quiet for a few hours till I can get to you again,' he stroked her calmly, quieting her down after the last wild orgasm.

She hit him square in the face with one of the many down pillows from the bed as she went into the bathroom.

'Speak for yourself, you sex-crazed maniac.'

Lisa Tate Phillips was a female version of her older brother. At thirty-six, she looked twenty-five, a result of spending many hours each week horseback riding with a large hat covering her waist-length fair hair and every inch of exposed skin well-moisturised.

'Not that there's much sun in Exbury, but whatever does come through can wreak havoc,' she said flatly. Jennifer agreed and quickly dropped the subject when she glanced at her own sun-freckled flesh.

Lisa was a writer, twice published, once with some critical acclaim. Both her novels were about families in conflict. There were always two families in each story, one from a previous century, and one from today. Their problems and crises were similar, one just an updated version of the other, but the solutions were very different. They were moderately literary works and enjoyed fair success. Her second book would be available in the States some time in the autumn. She was quiet and caring, and she and Jennifer got along at once.

Lisa and her husband, Jonathan Phillips, lived in Exbury, a hundred miles to the southwest of London on the Solent, just opposite the Isle of Wight. They lived there basically, as Jonathan would later explain, so that 'we can ride as often as we like, avoid the nonsense of London, and always be nearby when the rhododendrons first blossom.' The riding he was referring to was their stable of thirty plus thoroughbreds, the nonsense of London was the pressures and tribulations of his society banking family, and the rhododendrons were the 250 acres of gardens nearby, where one member of the Rothschild family had spared not one penny to create one of England's most visited and most glorious gardens.

Lisa and Jonathan didn't have any children. They preferred to live a very carefree life, coming and going as they pleased, which meant travelling to exotic places on a moment's notice or joining one of their friends in Paris or Rome or Istanbul.

Lisa mentioned in passing that they had not totally ruled out the possibility of having children, but for now they were blissfully happy with the life they led, and having Christopher for several days at a time when Nicholas was away shooting seemed to fulfil their desire to have young people around. Christopher was more of a pal to Lisa than a son. Because he was so mature for his age, they had developed a strong friendship, based on similar interests such as riding and tennis. They spent hours together on the trails surrounding

113

the Phillips estate in Exbury, often leaving just after a hearty breakfast with a backpack stuffed with sandwiches and drinks and not returning until almost dark. Lisa had always felt that her close relationship with Christopher, which had really developed over the last two years, was a direct result of the fact that she had never tried to replace his mother. She merely liked being with him – he was an attractive, smart boy whose company she enjoyed. Because of her attitude they had developed an open, free relationship. He often told her how he felt about his mother, how he wished she would get well and come home to live with him and Nicholas. He wanted them to be a family again.

Jennifer's first meeting with Christopher was not as pleasant as she had hoped it would be. When he and Lisa and Jonathan arrived at the house, he gave her a perfunctory 'hi' and dashed off to the kitchen to examine Anna's preparations for the day. He joined them half an hour later when they were all having tea in the living room.

Jennifer offered him a gift box, brightly wrapped in green paper with the Bloomingdale's 'B' logo on it. He accepted it politely.

'Rugby's a much better game than American football, you know,' was his response as he held up a multicoloured football jersey with the number 22 emblazoned on the front and back.

Jennifer was surprised at his remark. 'Yes, I'm sure you're right. I'm really looking forward to your game today. I don't know a whole lot about it. But I thought you might like having something very American, like a football jersey.'

'Why'd you bring me this? Do you think it will make me like you better?'

She heard Lisa's gasp of surprise, and she could feel Nicholas getting ready to reprimand the boy. Quickly she turned and looked at him. Once again he was able to read her all-telling eyes correctly. Jennifer wanted to handle this by herself. She remembered Wendy's advice – just be straight with him and you'll be fine. Nick could discipline his son later, privately.

114

'No, Christopher, I actually brought it to you because I was always taught that it showed good manners to bring a gift to someone in whose home you were going to be a guest. I chose that particular gift because I sincerely thought you'd like it. As for liking me better, or at all, that's something you'll have to decide for yourself. That's one thing a person can't buy.'

He looked directly at her, with his mother's piercing eyes. She knew she had got her message across to him.

'We better get going, Dad, or we'll be late,' he said to his father. 'I'll just take this up to my room. I'll be right back.' He grabbed the wrapping paper, tissue, box, and shirt with both hands and ran from the room.

The hardest part of the meeting between Jennifer and Christopher was over. They both had a clear understanding of each other and had crossed the first bridge. She knew it wasn't going to be easy to win the child's friendship. But she was committed to continue trying, and she felt secure that she had Nicholas's support in her every effort.

The game was hard fought and Christopher's team emerged victorious with a score of 18 to 9. Christopher played prop forward. He was very athletically skilled for a ten-year-old, and he had a good sense of team spirit. Next year, he later told Jennifer, he wanted to be the team captain.

Anna's picnic was a big hit. They ate almost everything in the baskets, polished off all the hearty English beer, and then switched to white wine with their dessert of fruit and cheese. The boys devoured the brownies and biscuits as if they would never eat again. They laughed and drank into the evening while Christopher and his friends began another impromptu game. Jennifer loved being with all of them. She sat with her legs crossed, leaning against Nicholas, holding his hand, while Jonathan regaled them with very funny stories of Lisa trying to master the skill of mountain climbing during their recent trip to Tibet. They had loved it and planned to return in the spring for another ascent. Jonathan had that extra-ordinary English humour that fascinated Jennifer and, in fact, most Americans. He was witty, and at the same time sarcastic. But he was very interested in many things and seemed to enjoy life immensely. The fact that he was independently wealthy and had nothing else to do but travel and play and enjoy life made him even more appealing.

Everyone piled back into Jonathan's cherry-red Jaguar about eleven, with a much lighter load because of the empty baskets, and headed back to the house on Grosvenor Crescent. They dropped Nicholas and Jennifer at the front door, refusing an offer to come in for a quick drink.

'Princess Lisa and Count Christopher are riding at dawn. They need their rest,' Jonathan announced.

Lisa giggled and said she hoped very much to see Jennifer when they stopped in New York next month on their way to San Francisco.

On the drive back to Exbury, Lisa mentioned to Jonathan that she couldn't remember the last time she had seen Nicholas so relaxed and seeming to enjoy himself so much. He agreed and said he thought Jennifer was terrific. Even Christopher cautiously voiced his approval.

Monday morning came too quickly, and Jennifer awakened from a light sleep feeling tired and wishing that the weekend were just beginning instead of already over. The two days seemed more like two minutes. They had both slept fitfully, not wanting to stop touching each other's naked bodies, not wanting to waste one precious minute of their last night together. When they finally drifted off to sleep after countless kisses, the dim lightness of a mist-shrouded London sky announced the beginning of a new day.

Even though they were both aware of it, they hadn't discussed the fact that Nicholas was off to India the following week for two weeks. With his travel schedule and Jennifer's new position, it was going to be difficult to see each other as often as they would like. However, they also both knew they couldn't stand to be apart.

'It seems like I just got out of this car, and now it's time to

116

go back again,' Jennifer said as Basil loaded her luggage into the trunk of the TATE I.

Nick held her close to him, keeping her warm against the cool, wet morning air. 'I know, my love, but let's not talk about it now. I'll call you tonight to see if we can make some plans soon. If the deal with Hunter & Weiss goes through, I'll have to be in New York within the next couple of weeks.'

She made a mental note to remember to see if she could find somebody who knew somebody at Hunter & Weiss. She'd be willing to pull any strings she could find if it meant seeing him again soon.

She looked up at the bleak sky, ready to teem with rain. 'Any chance of the plane being delayed for two or three days?'

'At best, for an hour or so. They always seem to get the Concorde off relatively close to schedule. It's the least you deserve at that price. I'm sorry I can't go with you to the airport, love, but if I don't get my papers for India this morning, I'm out of luck.'

'It's OK, I understand,' she answered. Maybe it was easier this way.

He hugged her again, and then gently pushed her away.

'In, go, no . . .' She covered his mouth with her lips. Basil turned away from the door he was holding open and pretended to be studying the British pavement.

'Ciao, my sweet.'

'I miss you already,' she called out to him as he waved from the front door and Basil slowly turned the Daimler away from the kerb. As they turned the corner she saw him disappear behind the imposing black Georgian panelled door.

The Concorde was on time to the minute, and as the speed indicator in the front of the cabin, which was visible to all the passengers, dropped from Mach II to Mach I to advise them that the aircraft was making its descent into New York, Jennifer realised that for the past forty-eight hours she hadn't

117

once thought about Channel 7 or, for that matter, anything associated with the studio. It was at that exact moment that she also realised she was madly and perhaps hopelessly in love with Nicholas Tate.

12

*T*HE New York weather was as humid as before, Jennifer's apartment was as empty of furniture as ever, and the studio was exactly as it had been when she had left it two days ago. But somehow, everything seemed just a little different. Was this what being in love with someone three thousand miles and five hours' time difference away meant?

She could think of nothing else, from morning until the time she finally fell asleep from exhaustion after lying awake, tossing and turning, missing Nicholas's sweet voice and loving caresses.

From the number of phone calls, he apparently felt the same way. Even with the time difference, they managed to talk twice a day, once early in the morning (she could almost depend on his early calls instead of her alarm clock) when he would tell her how the early part of his day had been, and then later on after Jennifer's broadcast, when he would call her in the studio to see how she had done.

Almost without fail, Andrea would pick up the phone in the taping room and yell out, 'It's the trans-Atlantic hunk on the line,' which signalled Jennifer to stop whatever she was doing and run to her office seeking some privacy.

Sometimes he would call her at home later if he had been out – to tell her about a new restaurant or play he had been to. She never asked whom he had gone with, thinking it might sound too nosy since she didn't know any of his friends, and she also figured if it was a date she really didn't want to know.

She was working extra-long hours because they needed a few more Special Segment reports to fill the time slots until the replacement arrived and was familiar enough to go out on her own. The woman from Chicago, Janet Rileson, had been terrific, and they had offered her the job that very night. She was cute and believable with a perky personality. Most important, she was a competent reporter who would fit the slot perfectly. She accepted readily, but even though she was moving as fast as she could she wouldn't be in New York for another three weeks. Jennifer rationalised that although it meant carrying two assignments for a while, it would keep her busy while Nicholas was in India. Besides, she would do anything to help Sidney over this rough period when he was down on staff members. It was the least she could do for him after the golden opportunity he had offered her.

Nicholas left for India the following week. He would be gone for almost two weeks, less, he had said, if he could get all the shots he wanted before then. He wasn't particularly fond of the country, having had enough of it when his father was posted there when Nicholas was eleven. He also didn't like leaving Christopher with his sister for such a long period of time. Even though he knew it wasn't a burden, he didn't want to impose more than was absolutely necessary.

They had talked up to the minute of his departure for Bombay, and he said he would call as soon after he arrived as possible. But he warned her that some of the meetings, especially the ones he wanted to cover, were being held in some fairly remote, primitive villages. So he didn't have any idea how elaborate the phone systems would be, if they existed at all.

Apparently they didn't, because it had been five days since he had left London, and Jennifer hadn't heard from him. She'd rush straight back to her office if she'd been at a meeting or out of the building, ignoring everyone in the newsroom to see if there was a pink message slip with his name on it. Then she'd frantically dial the new answering service she'd hired to pick up her calls at the apartment. Each time she heard the click and then the eerie, computer-

120

generated voice – 'There are no messages for you at this time' – she would slam down the receiver in frustration. Once she even called the main office to ask them to check and make sure the line was working. When they called back later that day she was almost disappointed to hear that nothing was out of order.

'Are you absolutely sure? You checked all the lines?' she asked the repairman.

'Yes, ma'am,' he answered in a voice that had been trained to sound courteous even when dealing with the most exasperating customer. 'Let me ask you, please, ma'am, did someone say they had tried to call you and couldn't get through or that the answering service didn't pick up? What made you think your line was out of service?'

'No, no,' Jennifer answered, 'no one said they called. I just haven't been receiving any messages, and usually I have some.'

So that's it, he thought. Right away he had her number. The repairman had named this group 'the wishers'. These were women who were wishing that someone would call them. Most of them had either just lost a boyfriend or just left one and couldn't believe that he wasn't calling, begging to be let back in to the women's lives. Some others had just met someone new and couldn't believe he wasn't calling every ten minutes. If it didn't happen, they were convinced that something was wrong with the lines. Almost one hundred per cent of the numbers of these 'false check' requests were registered to single women. Yes, he'd seen so many of them during his seventeen years on the job that he'd developed a pat answer for them, which he now used with Jennifer. 'Well, you can be assured now that the line is open, and I'm sure you'll start receiving calls today.' That always seemed to make them feel a little better. It was the best he could do.

Every hour at night she'd refigure the time difference and try to imagine what Nicholas would be doing. There were several times when she had decided that he could be trying to call her. But nothing happened.

Finally, as she was halfway through the broadcast on Friday night, she heard Kevin's voice through her monitor, 'I've got Nicholas on the line from India, he says he'll hold until you're off the air.'

Her eyes lit up as she nodded to Kevin. Her smile told him to keep Nicholas on the line at all costs. She tried to suppress the glow she felt in her cheeks as she reported on a devastating fire in Staten Island that had destroyed several homes, and on the parade activities for the weekend. She heard herself turn the last segment of the show over to the meteorologist. It was the last report, but she had to stay on the show, in her place, to say good night to her ever-growing audience. The weather report seemed to last for ever, and they still had one more break before the five-day forecast, which included the weekend weather that everyone else was so anxious to hear about. Would it ever be over?

'It's currently seventy-eight degrees and cloudy, barometric pressure . . . I'll be back in just a minute to give you the five-day forecast. But first . . .' At last, the final break. She looked pleadingly at Kevin, and he immediately indicated that Nicholas was still holding.

The credits started to roll and Jennifer ripped off her microphone and ran out. She slammed the door to her office and grabbed the phone from the other side of the desk.

'Nicholas, is that you, sweet?'

'Hello, Miss Jennifer Martin, please.' She heard the scratchy voice of the international operator. Every few seconds there was a sharp crack and then a clicking noise, which indicated that the connection wasn't very strong.

'Yes, this is Jennifer Martin.'

'Go ahead, sir.'

'Jenn, love, are you all right? You have no idea how I miss you.'

Just hearing his voice soothed her – she felt all the tension and worry of the last few days dissolve. Her shoulders relaxed and she reached back to massage her neck with her free hand.

'Yes, it's me, darling. I was so worried. You must really be in the country.'

'You've no idea. You have to queue up early in the morning, in this small village, to put in your request for an international call. Only two or three go through each week, and then the connections are lousy. This one sounds pretty strong, but it could go any time. It cost me three packs of cigarettes plus a Swatch watch to the mayor of the town to get moved up on the list.'

'A Swatch watch? What were you doing with that?'

'I took two dozen of them along and I've only six left. They are the hottest bribe items in the country. The Indians love them. I found out a long time ago, when we lived here, that little "gifts" go a long way. It really helped this time; I probably would never have got through to you without them.'

'Whatever it took, I'm sure glad you had it. How is the trip?'

The line started to click and buzz more frequently, and the connection became weaker. She could hardly hear him over the crackling.

'Jenn, the line is going. I'll call you as soon as I get back to Bombay. I miss you.'

'Me too,' she yelled just as the call was disconnected.

Even though they had been able to talk for only a few minutes, she felt so much better. She was anxious to tell him of all her discoveries about the Richard Collier case, but it would just have to wait. He'd be back in London in ten days. She thanked Kevin for keeping him on the line.

She switched her mind to the business of reporting. She had made Sidney promise to stay late that night. She needed to share some information she had uncovered – information that would give them an exclusive, powerful story. A story none of them would ever forget.

13

'No wonder I haven't seen you around much this week,' Sidney said. 'You've really been on a dig.'

'No kidding,' Jennifer agreed. 'But it was well worth the effort. It's good stuff, isn't it?'

'Damn right it is. I'm really proud of you. You've got so much here that none of the other stations will have.'

'I think that's true. Thanks to David – he pointed me in precisely the right direction. He's so close to the case, and he was extremely hesitant to talk. The most he would do was nod if I guessed right about something. So I don't think anyone else was able to get nearly as much material as we have. At any rate, I didn't see anyone I knew while I was doing my research. So I'd agree that it's pretty much ours.'

Jennifer had spent all of her afternoons and three late nights doing her own investigation of the Richard Collier story. Following Sidney's suggestion, she had tried to convince his friend David Clemson to talk with her.

She had gone down to Wall Street with high hopes. 'Can't you give me anything else?' she had pleaded. 'Any other sources, anyone I might be able to talk to? Right now I don't have any more information than what's already been in the papers.'

He had hesitated to divulge anything to her that could possibly influence their case. He sat in the green leather club chair in his distinguished partner's office and offered his apologies.

'Jennifer, I'd love to tell you everything I know, but you are as aware as I am how imprudent that would be.'

'A thread,' Jennifer insisted. 'Just a lead, and you have my word that no one will ever be able to trace the source.'

'OK, I have one idea for you, and I'm not even certain it will help that much, but it's a possibility.'

Jennifer sat expectantly on the edge of the camelback sofa. She could feel her heart quicken and her eyes grow wide with anticipation.

'Francisco Rivera is in town.'

At the mention of the name, Jennifer's entire face lit up. She had done enough homework to know that Francisco Rivera was the father of Richard Collier's first wife, Isabel. He was one of the most powerful men in Brazil, and it was through his connections that Richard had been able to make such inroads into the South American market. Apparently some of those connections still existed, which was why Collier had planned his escape to Brazil via private plane after the bombs had been planted aboard the train.

'Do you think he'll talk to me?' Her voice was full of hope.

'I don't know, Jennifer. First you'll have to find him. I have no idea where he stays when he's here, I only heard he was in town. Now, please, I don't mean to be rude, Sidney's a good friend, and I'd do anything for him, but I'm afraid that's as far as I'm willing to go.'

'You've been terrific, thank you,' Jennifer said, as she left his office, her mind racing a thousand miles a minute with plans for her next move.

Half an hour after leaving Wall Street, she had two of the station's reporters on the phone trying to locate Francisco Rivera. At the end of the first day, they had nothing. Forty-three of New York's top hotels had been called; none showed that he was either registered or expected.

'Keep going,' was her only comment on the reported lack of progress.

Later that evening, one of the reporters she had on the story entered her office looking optimistic. 'It's a long shot, but the Essex House has a Frank Rivers registered.'

Jennifer dropped what she was doing.

'That's him. It's *got* to be him,' she declared. After several unsuccessful attempts to reach Mr Rivers, she decided the only way to find out for sure was to see him. So, as inconspicuously as possible, she parked herself in the hotel's lobby.

Just as a combination of sleepiness and the late hour convinced her that the elusive Mr Rivers, her only possible lead, was out for the night, the revolving doors began to move, and into the hotel walked one of the most handsome men she had ever seen. Dressed impeccably in a blue blazer and light slacks, looking like an ad for a cruise-ship line, was Francisco Rivera. She had an idea of what he looked like from the news clippings she had uncovered. But the grainy newspaper reproductions did not do this tanned Latin god justice. At sixty-three, Francisco Rivera looked at least fifteen years younger. It was evident from the way his clothes fitted that he kept himself in top shape. Several of the photos showed him astride one of his prize polo ponies or aboard his enormous yacht. Jennifer was captivated by this extraordinary-looking individual, but she managed to gather her bearings and approach him as he walked toward the elevator.

'Excuse me, Mr Rivera,' she said.

He turned around sharply and smiled at Jennifer.

'Yes?' he asked questioningly. 'Forgive me, do I know you?' His manner of speaking was as charming as his looks.

'No, no you don't, but I would appreciate it if I could speak with you for a moment.'

'Well, as you can see, I am quite busy, and it is also quite late, even by New York standards.' For the first time Jennifer noticed a young woman standing near Rivera. She appeared to be in her mid twenties but Jennifer figured that underneath the make-up she was no more than eighteen, twenty at the most. They were obviously spending the night together, and the woman seemed anxious to go upstairs.

'Yes, I see,' Jennifer said slowly, hesitating about whether to push him or to try to make a date for the next day. She

126

decided that delaying a man on his way to bed with a young girl would be a big mistake.

'My name is Jennifer Martin, and I'd like to talk to you about Richard Collier – some time tomorrow if possible.'

The man's face tightened at the mention of his ex-son-in-law's name. His sable brown eyes grew narrow, and his look was piercing.

'What interest do you have in Mr Collier?'

Jennifer knew that she had struck a chord. Rivera appeared repulsed by the mere mention of the name. Her time was up. She would have to state her cause and pray that he would cooperate.

'Well, I'm a reporter covering the case. Actually, I'm the replacement for a man who was killed in the train bombing. I'm trying to get a more complete story, and I'm very hopeful you'll be willing to help me.'

Rivera seemed to be touched by her honesty, if more than a little reluctant.

'Tomorrow,' he finally said abruptly, torn between his willingness to help Jennifer and his desire for the young woman who now clung to his arm. 'Can you meet with me tomorrow?'

'Yes, yes, of course, what time would be convenient?'

Glancing briefly at the girl, he said, 'Breakfast, eight o'clock in the dining room here.' With that, the elevator opened to take Jennifer's only viable lead to his suite.

She stared at the metal door as it slid closed. It took every bit of her self-control to keep from jumping up and down in the lobby. Hoorah, she cried inside, she had at least got to first base!

The night couldn't pass quickly enough. Jennifer was astounded at the clock's insistence that only a few minutes, at most fifteen, had passed since the last time she had checked. Time never went this slowly when she was with Nicholas, she reflected.

At seven-thirty the next morning she was anxiously awaiting Francisco Rivera in the already-crowded dining-room. At eight-twenty, she was concerned. At eight-thirty, after several cups of tea, she was convinced that he wasn't coming. As she was deciding whether to call upstairs or just for the bill, he appeared in the doorway. Looking rested and as elegant as he had the night before, he saw her immediately and crossed the room to join her.

'My apologies, Miss Martin. South Americans, I'm afraid, are notorious for their lack of punctuality.'

Jennifer was so relieved to see him she was barely listening. She would have been more than willing to sit there until dinner was served if she could just speak to him. He was her only hope for a story she wanted desperately.

As it turned out, they spent over two hours together, Jennifer's pencil working nonstop attempting to record all the facts while she was trying to separate them from Francisco Rivera's raging contempt for his ex-son-in-law.

Back in her office she had amassed enough material, plus a few additional leads, to pull the story together.

What they were looking at now was the result of her investigation.

On paper, Richard Collier could easily be portrayed as an American success story. With just a little help from his not-impoverished family and two marriages, one of them to Isabel Rivera, he had climbed the ladder of corporate success very quickly, skipping uninteresting or tedious rungs along the way.

Collier had been a dean's list student at Princeton and had gone to the Wharton School of Finance, where he graduated with honours. His career in banking had begun at one of the city's oldest, most revered, most profitable financial institutions. He had remained there for the last fifteen years. His early success in managing large portfolios for several prominent, wealthy individuals in Latin America had helped to pave his way and virtually guarantee his future success with the firm.

He had embraced his assignment to Brazil almost a decade ago with a passion that produced such phenomenal results for the firm that no one ever thought to question his tactics.

It was at about this same time, Jennifer had been able to determine, that he had begun to lead a dual life – one as an energetic, effective officer of a prestigious investment bank, and the other as a deceitful, calculating criminal. The criminal and the deal-making minds appeared to work in tandem to create an environment that looked great from the outside. For a long while everyone – the banks, the clients, and probably even Richard Collier – was exceedingly happy.

His timing had been perfect. The new Brazilian government had been very anxious to pursue an aggressive foreign investment programme. Their external debt began to grow wildly, tripling from one year to the next. Richard Collier became their man. His propensity for deal-making, plus his social connections and familiarity with the South American mentality, allowed him to become the most powerful banker in the country. He earned the respect and trust of several key clients, among them his father-in-law.

Once the trust had been established, Collier was rarely if ever questioned about what he was doing with the clients' funds or exactly where they stood financially at any time. It had been simple for him to begin diverting funds, in small amounts at first, graduating to larger sums siphoned off more frequently as time went on.

These unauthorised withdrawals of clients' money, deposited to the Collier account or to phony companies he controlled, went unnoticed for years.

Richard Collier, of course, had continued to report a growing but still believable income to the US Internal Revenue Service. At the same time his lifestyle had been improving dramatically. He had begun to buy art and antiques at auction. Through Rivera, Jennifer had been able to contact his dealer and review all Collier's purchases. He had stockpiled these acquisitions and stored them in a warehouse somewhere in Queens. When they were finally discovered, and valued at over six million dollars, his second wife, Sandy, had had no idea he had owned any of them.

Things had only begun to sour two years earlier, long after Richard and Sandy had moved permanently from Brazil back to Greenwich.

One of his wealthiest clients had discovered some serious discrepancies in the accounts that Richard Collier had managed for so many years. The client reported the problems to Collier's replacement in Brasilia, who, after some investigation of his own, was baffled as well. Finally the accusations and sums became so astounding that the senior officers of the bank decided that they had to start asking Richard Collier some serious questions.

Collier avoided the questioning for as long as possible, but finally, late the previous year, he could postpone it no longer. He was unable to respond to their questions to anyone's satisfaction, and it soon became painfully clear that the extent of the problem was far greater than anyone had previously imagined. He admitted to knowledge of several million dollars' worth of 'mismanaged' funds, which he promised to return. But, as the investigation continued, the firm could not be content with his simply paying back the money. They suspended Richard for several months and continued searching the records with a vengeance. After three months, they were unable to uncover anything more. Richard Collier returned to work, and to seeming normality, until just a few months before.

One of the senior executives of the firm had been tipped off that there might be more to the case than the bank had originally suspected. It was then discovered that there were other clients whose funds had met the same fate as those of that first wealthy Brazilian. Once the count reached seven large portfolios, the bank knew it could no longer remain silent but had to take the scandal public.

That was when Richard Collier had decided he could not face the music. He could not wait around to stand trial in New York, to be sentenced to federal prison, to pay the fines and the interest for his theft. It was about this time that his anger and resentment toward Wall Street, and the men who ran it, grew to such frightening proportions that for years to come he would remain a mystery to his family and everyone who knew him.

He arranged his escape from Teterboro to Brazil on the plane of one of his clients' partners, a man who had served as his cover on many questionable deals they had pulled off during his years there. The man, a cousin of one of the government officials, had little reason to suspect that he too was being investigated by the bank. This oversight led to the discovery that he had provided the explosives and helped in Richard Collier's escape. It was easy for the Brazilian government to track Richard Collier down at the resort home of José Rehado, just fifty kilometres outside Brasilia.

Now he was being extradited to the US to stand trial for murder, in addition to all of the tax evasion and bank fraud charges.

Jennifer was fascinated by the story, and she was pleased with the amount of information she and her team had been able to uncover.

Now that she had Sidney's blessing, she put the finishing touches on a long, comprehensive report that she knew would be edited dramatically. But she wanted to be as thorough as the information would allow. She wanted all the facts of this complex, sick human being to be brought to light so that, in turn, he could be brought to justice. She wanted to do everything she could to ensure that Richard Collier received a life sentence.

It was the least she felt she could do for Stewart's memory.

14

*J*ENNIFER became an aunt for the second and third time within minutes early in the morning of August 30th. Right after they wheeled Pat back from the delivery room, she grabbed her bedside phone. She was exhausted, but she couldn't wait to share the news with her. When the phone rang at four-thirty in the morning, Jennifer was convinced it was Nicholas calling.

'Jenn, wake up, it's me, Pat,' she heard before she even had a chance to say hello.

She temporarily forgot her sister's pregnancy.

'Is everything OK? Are Mom and Dad all right?'

'Yes of course, silly, it's me I'm calling about. I've just delivered two little girls, Lauren and Jessica – identical – a little over six pounds each.'

Suddenly Jennifer snapped to her senses. 'Fantastic, oh, congratulations, Pat – are they all complete – no problems or anything?' She hesitated, thinking that maybe 'complete' was an odd way to describe a newborn.

'Yes, they're complete – all toes, fingers, even quite a bit of blonde hair,' Pat sighed. 'I'm the one that's feeling ravaged. I've been in labour too long, eighteen hours, really an hour or two is all you need to get the flavour of the experience. I'm sure glad it's over.'

'I'll bet you are. Who's there with you?'

'The proud father just left, more exhausted than me, I think, a few minutes ago. Mother and Dad were here last night, they left about midnight, figuring I had a way to go.

132

Susan should be here as soon as she gets Jason off to day camp. I'd really just like to get some sleep now, but I wanted to call you first.' She sounded worn out.

'I'm so glad you did. I'm proud of you. This will give you something to keep busy with for a while.'

'You're not kidding. Thank heavens we were able to get the twin expert, or "multiples specialist" as they call themselves – she's ready and waiting. Dr Jacobs said we can go home the day after tomorrow.'

'It's really the best news. Send pictures right away.'

'Not right away, as pretty as I think they are I still think all newborns look like little raisins – I'm going to give them a few days before a photo session. I haven't even asked how you are. All OK? How's the English treat?'

'He's good – in India. It makes London seem like only next door. I miss him more than I should.'

'Exactly what does that mean? More than you should?' Pat demanded, sounding less tired and very interested in her sister's comments.

'It means I have lots of work to do here – to really maximise the opportunities I've got now that I'm the anchor. The next step should be the network job. It's a crucial time, one that requires my paying attention and really working hard, with no time for a long-distance romance.'

'Sounds like it's too late to worry about that. Sounds to me like you really like this guy.'

'Of course I like him,' Jennifer jumped to his defence at once. 'He's wonderful, handsome, sweet, terrific and a sensational lover. Oh, Pat, he's really special. He makes Jeff fade into a blurry memory.'

'Well, that's good, but it doesn't sound like all he does. Listen, I've got a great idea. When's he coming back from India?'

'He goes to London next week.'

'Good. Then why don't you two plan a visit to see your new nieces? We should be on some sort of schedule by next month. I hope so, or I'll be out of my mind. Anyway, come and stay with us – don't stay at Mom and Dad's, they'll separate you at night – come and stay here, we've got plenty of room. The kids are a perfect excuse for not staying with them. We'll tell Mom you really wanted to be close to the kids, you know, to get a firsthand idea of how it is. That'll make her crazy. Will you do it? Come, and bring Nicholas.'

'Well, maybe I'll mention it to him when he gets back. I'll see – it seems a little aggressive, doesn't it? He might think I'm making suggestions a little too quickly, don't you think?'

'Believe me, Jenn, you don't have to worry. I don't think anyone could misread a trip to see your two new nieces. Not with the way you carry on about your career. If you really wanted to settle down, you probably would have decorated your apartment by now.'

'Very funny. It's odd you should mention it. I'm working on that very project next week.'

'I hope it's done when I arrive for some rest and shopping in a couple of months; just as soon as I get this body back in shape, I'm coming to spend a weekend with you – just us!'

'You'll be surprised. It will be a mini-palace.'

'OK, OK, I believe you. Jenn, I'm getting tired, I need some sleep before they bring the babies in.'

'Thanks for calling. Give my love to everyone. I'll try to come soon – before they need braces.'

'Don't joke – we want you, and hopefully Nicholas too, soon. Bye.'

'I'll try! Now rest, and a big kiss. I love you very much.'

She was anxious to see Pat's children – Pat was the one sister she missed being with more than anyone, so she planned for a weekend in Wayzata the following month. It was a long shot, but maybe Nicholas could go with her if he was going to be in New York again that soon. She'd love him to meet Pat and her husband, and possibly Christie would come east if they made an event of it, like the twins' christening or something. She knew that he and Ken would get along just fine, they'd have lots to talk about. She would have to decide if she was willing to subject him to her mother's sometimes not-so-subtle harassment.

*   *   *

Zajac & Callahan started work on the apartment right after their first meeting. The floor plans had been drawn up, sketches made, and Jennifer had agreed to everything almost at once. She took the suggested plans home with her one night, and sat cross-legged in the middle of the empty living room, and studied them. The layout, detailed down to the last scatter cushion, had transformed the room into an inviting, luxurious space that maximised use of both the fireplace and the terrace. The seating plan allowed for several separate yet overlapping conversational areas, and since she didn't have a formal dining room, they had cleverly used screens partially to divide the living and eating spaces. One of the major expenses, which she felt was crucial to the look of the room, was the mahogany bookcases that would cover the entire wall surrounding the fireplace. She had agreed to those at once, and the cabinet-maker had already begun to select the rich, red wood. The decorators had also been very careful to highlight her Still painting, without making it seem that the room had been designed around it.

On a separate sheet was a list of all the items she would need to purchase to complete the room, in order of importance. In other words, she could live without the two slipper chairs if her budget did not allow for them right now, but the major sofa and two identically-sized Oriental rugs were vital to get the room started. As she reviewed the list – a Coromandel screen, the Regency-style dining chairs, the pedestal tables – she had a brainstorm: most of these pieces were English in origin, and what more convenient place to buy them than right at the source? If she could manage to take just one weekday off, she could take the Concorde both ways, and have plenty of time for shopping. When she had mentioned it to Richard, he had tried to dissuade her, telling her that the selection in New York was really superior to that in London. He also said that because of the weak dollar she would be paying at least as much, probably even more, over there than here. And that didn't even take into consideration shipping, customs and any damage that might occur during transit. But she was insistent, and he realised she was determined to buy overseas. At last he agreed, and created a list of the dealers she should see, and where they were located. Now she looked forward to Nicholas's return even more. But it was still several days away.

That week, she increased from three to four the number of times Anthony, her exercise trainer, came to the apartment – just to keep herself busy. As she surveyed the mats and equipment on her living-room floor, she wondered where they would work out once the furniture arrived.

Sidney had sensed her anxiety and had offered to take her to dinner or a movie several nights during the week. She had declined most times but had accepted his offer to go to the opening of a new Broadway musical. It was directed by a protégé of Andrew Lloyd Webber, and the show had been last year's rage in London. There was a black-tie opening gala and a dinner at Tavern on the Green following the performance. It sounded like fun, and Jennifer was not unaware of the need to become more visible outside the studio if she was to realise her dream. By appearing at social events, looking spectacular, and chatting with some of New York's movers and shakers, she would only increase her chance of a network slot later on.

She was just closing the side zip and adjusting the crinoline of her new Carolyne Roehm dress – made of bright pink silk with black satin trim, with a bustier and short skirt, it was one of the prettiest, most feminine dresses from Carolyne's hot new collection – when the phone rang. Certain that it was Sidney calling from the car en route to pick her up, she allowed it to ring one more time while she made a final check of her shoulders and back, both of which she had dusted with powder containing crushed pearls that would make her skin shine under the lights.

She was very surprised, and thoroughly delighted, to hear the long-distance crackle in the phone. It was Nicholas calling from Bombay to say he'd finished his work and was leaving for London in two days, almost a full day ahead of schedule. He asked how she was, and she told him she was just dressing for the theatre. There was a long silence, at the end of which he told her to have a good time and said he only wished it was him that she was going with. He promised to call the minute he got home, said he missed her and would see her soon. She hoped so – each time they spoke she realised how much she missed him, how quickly they had grown so close.

Nicholas's call put Jennifer in an entirely new mood. She was relaxed and happy to know that he was thinking about her, and she could go out tonight and concentrate on her career.

More people than ever would recognise her this time because just last week her picture had appeared in the business section of *The New York Times*, announcing her appointment as the new anchorperson for the Channel 7 evening news. It was unusual for them to devote so much space to an announcement like that. Most often, a biography like the one they ran, including her educational background, previous work experience, and achievements, was reserved for major management changes at 'Fortune 500' companies. Even rarer, they ran a picture under the headline, 'Jennifer Martin Appointed to Fill Anchor Spot.' It had been taken only last year, a flattering head shot with her hair slightly blown back, a warm smile revealing her perfect teeth. You could barely see the collar and opening of a soft silk shirt. Her only jewellery was a pair of Paloma Picasso gold love knot earrings and a simple gold necklace, a gift from her grandmother upon her graduation from college. She'd thought she looked very professional and very capable. She had clipped it out immediately and sent it off to her father, who she was certain was passing it around the golf club locker room with great pride. With his oldest daughter in *The New York Times* and his middle one just having delivered twins, Ken Martin had a lot of good news to tell his cronies. Of course, her mother would have much preferred that her picture appear in the social section under wedding announcements rather than on page two of the business section.

Even though he claimed to have no knowledge, she was certain that Sidney had had a hand in getting the story placed.

At six-forty-five sharp, Sidney's driver announced their arrival downstairs. Jennifer twirled out of the building rather theatrically in her glamorous new dress; long, shapely legs highlighted by the fullness of her skirt and high heels. She hoped that the next time she was wearing this outfit, she would be out with Nicholas. Her mind wandered for a minute to all the wonderfully erotic things he could do to her in this dress.

Sidney voiced his approval of her new creation, and when they arrived in front of the theatre, so did several photographers. Amidst the traffic jam of limos lining West 48th Street, she could see that the opening had attracted some of New York's most powerful faces. They were people who contributed generously to support the Broadway scene, and some of them were even genuinely interested in what was being produced.

The musical was entertaining and she guessed it would open to good, but not spectacular reviews. She enjoyed having the chance to see it, and she was always thrilled at being part of the glittering, black-tie audience for a first-night production.

The bevy of limos travelled northward on Sixth Avenue and through Central Park to Tavern on the Green after the closing act.

The restaurant, lit by thousands of tiny white lights in the trees surrounding it, shone like a precious jewel in the middle of the park. She had done a piece once that showed it was the single most popular restaurant in New York for celebrating 'special occasions' – such as birthdays, anniversaries, weddings. The ambience, service, and food were consistently excellent, and rarely were any of the customers disappointed. Tonight was no exception. As they entered the Crystal Room, a fantasy space glittering with light from enormous Hungarian cut-glass chandeliers, many of the women's dresses, beaded or paillette, added to the reflections in the already sparkling room.

The dinner tables for eight were beautifully set with

individual lavender roses in silver trumpet vases at each place. From the three wine glasses at each setting, she concluded that it was going to be a long meal. But her concern was eliminated when she and Sidney took their assigned seats at the number two table. Her dinner partner to the left was the show's producer, and on her right she had a very interesting, successful businessman, who was also chairman of the Arts Council of New York. Not a bad draw.

After dinner, the toasts began. Several key players responsible for the show's success took their turns thanking and congratulating.

When she turned her head to listen to the male lead give his short speech, she was startled to see, directly across the room, a very familiar profile. She looked quickly to see if she recognised anyone else at the table. Yes, it all made sense now. Seated not twenty feet away from her was Dr Jeffrey Sullivan, her Jeffrey, whom she hadn't seen since the night she moved out of their apartment in Kansas City. Seated next to him was a very attractive, very conservative woman. Her long hair was pulled back on each side and secured with combs. She was wearing a very simple, yet not-too-sophisticated, black sheath dress. Jennifer couldn't see the length of the dress or her shoes because she was seated, but she did notice a substantial diamond-and-sapphire ring on the third finger of her left hand. Jeffrey's right hand was resting on her thigh, and she was smiling sweetly at him, oblivious to the others at the table. Jennifer recognised Matthew Culbert, a classmate of Jeffrey's from medical school, and, his wife sitting on the other side of the table. He now practised in Kansas City, too. They were sitting with two other couples – one of whom she thought she recognised as old friends of Jeffrey's. She wondered if he had seen her earlier. She was difficult to miss in the pink dress, but on the other hand she had been surrounded by people all evening.

Surely she would have heard if he had got married. But maybe not, she thought, people were always funny about calling up and giving that kind of news, afraid of what the reaction might be.

Well, there was only one way to find out. Now that the speeches were over, she excused herself and walked directly to his table. Why did she feel so hesitant as she neared the table? Could she still be attracted to him after all this time? His back was to her, and she took a deep breath before she spoke.

He must have sensed her presence behind him, for she did not have a chance to speak before he turned and looked up at her, not a little surprised. But from his expression she was certain he had seen her earlier that night. Was he purposely trying to avoid her? He stood up and took her hand. 'Jennifer, it's been a long time.'

Yes, that was absolutely true.

'Hi, Jeffrey, welcome to New York. I thought it was you, and I recognised Matthew, so I wanted to say hello before the evening was over.'

Just then Matthew recognised her and got up to kiss her.

'Well, a class reunion. It's been quite a while since we've all been in New York together. Jennifer, you look terrific. How's the news?'

'Oh, it occurs daily and gets reported.' She didn't mean to sound so flip, but her emotions were a little confused.

'I read about your promotion in the *Times*. Congratulations.' He was only trying to be polite. But if he had seen the *Times* article, they had been in town for at least three days.

All heads at the table were now beginning to turn toward Jennifer, including that of the woman on Jeffrey's right. She looked up at him questioningly.

'Karen, I'd like you to meet an old friend of mine, Jennifer Martin. Jennifer, this is my wife, Karen.'

Karen smiled politely and Jennifer made some attempt to return the courtesy.

She turned back to Jeffrey and her face offered a mixture of surprise and happiness. She *was* happy for him. What hurt her was the fact that he had not told her or even any of her sisters, who could pass the news on. Maybe this was the way he wanted her to find out; she couldn't tell, and maybe she'd never know.

He responded to her questions with short, succinct answers. They had been married just three months ago, had taken a short vacation – he hadn't called it a honeymoon – and now they were on their way to visit Karen's parents, who lived in Copenhagen.

She decided there was really nothing more to say, and she excused herself to go and find Sidney. Later, as they sat in the bar at the Carlyle having a cognac, she described her feelings to him. She was surprised that they ranged from jealousy to anger, and finally to an odd sense of contentment that that chapter of her life was closed. She also realised that she was no longer in love with Jeffrey and that she was indeed pleased that he had found someone important enough to him to marry. No, with that chapter of her past laid to rest, her thoughts turned to the man she did love, half a world away.

15

*T*HE Richard Collier extradition story broke with a bang. Channel 7's ratings for the week skyrocketed, and Sidney's team was once again credited with delivering the most complete news coverage in the New York area. It was great exposure for Jennifer, and now they would have a chance to see if she could, on the strength of her broadcast, keep those new viewers they had attracted with their exclusive report.

Of course, everyone was thrilled, and Sidney called the entire staff together for a celebratory meeting.

'It's the largest single increase in one week in the history of the station,' he announced proudly. 'You're the best team in the world!'

The champagne was consumed within minutes, and several members of the support group went over to Jennifer to offer their congratulations.

'Couldn't have done it without you guys,' she insisted. But she knew the story had been good, solid reporting; she had pulled out all the stops to get it, and she was proud of the results. The viewers had responded, and in the final analysis that's what it was all about.

Rushing out of the office later that night she paid little attention when Sidney mentioned he felt her report was worthy of an award.

Later that week, Nicholas returned from Bombay sounding triumphant about his trip and full of other good news. They were back to their once-a-day, sometimes twice-a-day calls, and Jennifer's spirits were buoyant. England seemed so close after the vast time difference and enormous technological shortcomings of India. She still worried about becoming more and more involved with someone whose life was firmly entrenched so far away, but she couldn't help feeling a growing attachment, becoming stronger day by day. He was so caring, so interested and interesting, that she began to count on him for advice on many things, including her career – a subject about which she had previously never sought any lover's opinion.

It was obvious that the same closeness, the same trust, was developing in Nicholas also. He discussed his day-to-day activities with her, solicited her thoughts on new assignments and whether or not he should take them, occasionally asked about her family, even though he'd never had the chance to meet any of them and had only seen pictures on Jennifer's bulletin board and on her desk in the apartment.

That's why she wasn't too surprised when, as she mentioned Pat's twins one night and how she was so looking forward to seeing them, he suggested that they go to visit them together.

'Really, would you like to do that?' She tried not to sound too pleased, although secretly she was delighted at the thought of having him meet her family. She was certain they'd have a great time.

'Yes, love, it would be fun. I've not been around newborns for, well, it's ten years, since Christopher was born, and I was travelling quite a bit then, so I missed some of the all-night duty. Besides, I'm anxious to meet the rest or the Martin clan and see what the heartland of America is really all about.'

'Well, it wouldn't be a true picture, but you'd get the idea. When do you think we could go?'

'Hunter & Weiss has promised an answer on the book commission some time within the next two weeks. I'll give them a ring tomorrow and see if I can't move them along. If it's on, I'll come and close the deal in person, shouldn't take more than a day, and then we could go for the weekend. How's that sound?'

'Perfect. I hope it's soon. I miss you a lot.'
'Me too, love. I promise it will be soon.'

Three days later a DHL express courier package was waiting for her at the apartment when she got home. Nicholas had enclosed a group of pictures from his India trip, most of them in the convention setup and a few showing the primitive village and the post office from which he had tried, mostly without much success, to telephone her. There were two pictures of him, both of them taken outside a village hut. He was wearing khaki shorts and a bush jacket loaded with equipment. He had a full three or four days' stubby growth in those areas around his beard which were usually clean-shaven, and he looked tired and hot, but every inch the photojournalist at work. Attached to one of the pictures was a short note – 'Deal is ready for signature. Would you consider introducing this man to your family next weekend?'

She was ecstatic – it meant he would be here with her again in only a few days!

The following day she asked Andrea to get a copy of the tape of the Richard Collier exposé converted on to a European-compatible cycle. She sent it to him Federal Express with a card telling him she thought he might be interested in the report and that she missed him terribly and could hardly wait for him to arrive.

'You look awfully sexy in the newscast, my love. It's a good thing I'll be there soon,' he said that night on the phone.

She laughed. 'Don't flatter yourself. I've kept extremely busy while you've been in far-off lands.'

'Keeping busy and being extraordinarily satisfied are two entirely different things.'

'I couldn't agree more.' She felt herself becoming excited at the mere thought of his touch. 'But on second thoughts, when will you be here?'

'I've been able to move it up. I'll meet Hunter on Wednesday, finalise everything, and then we can leave Friday night. So I'll see you the day after tomorrow. I get in at four.'

'Come straight to the apartment. I'll be there within minutes once I'm off the air.'

'Can't wait.'

Knowing they would be together soon made saying goodbye this time a lot easier.

The plane from London was two hours late arriving at Kennedy, so the apartment was empty, not only of furnishings but of company, when Jennifer rushed through the door on the night of his expected arrival. After confirming the delay with British Airways, she had time to shower and change before he arrived. She put on her most flattering jeans and an oversized cotton shirt. She looked casual, fresh, and very anxious to see him.

The minute he walked in the door, it was apparent that their hunger for each other had only increased during the time they had been apart. Just as they had in London, they at first made love with a wild desperation, without words, quickly. They lay exhausted in each other's arms, the tension that had built up over the few weeks they had been apart drained from their bodies.

'Are you hungry?' she felt it necessary to ask, her Midwestern upbringing regarding proper manners as a hostess shining through.

'Not for anything I don't have right here,' he said, burying his head between her breasts and rocking her gently.

They made love again, this time with no concern for time, no pressure to release any pent-up emotions, for now they were together completely, even if only for a short while. Jennifer felt herself letting go, step by step, allowing herself to enjoy the passion of Nicholas's lovemaking, for she knew that when he pleased her, his pleasure, when he finally allowed it to come, was even greater. The first time she gave up total control of her body and let the power of her orgasm take her to a new sexual height, it frightened her so much that immediately afterward tears began to flow. She lay weeping in Nicholas's arms, looking up at him with unbridled happiness in her eyes.

. Despite all of their well-meaning attempts to avoid it, she was late getting to work the next morning.

When he arrived at the studio to pick her up for lunch, the expression on his face told her that the book commission was a done deal.

'You got the go-ahead, didn't you?' she asked, already certain of the answer.

'I must look like the cat that ate the canary.' He smiled even wider.

'Oh, sweet, congratulations. Did they agree to everything you wanted?'

'Well, almost, there were a few concessions on budget, but we've got enough to work with. We'll give them a good product.'

She gave him a strong hug. 'Oh, Nick, I couldn't be happier. When do you go?'

'I'll leave for Beirut the day after New Year. I thought we could make our plans, to go to Europe or wherever you would like to celebrate the New Year, and then I'll leave from there. The rest of the crew can go from London or wherever they are, and we'll all meet in Lebanon.'

So he planned to spend New Year's with her. She was glad he was thinking that way. Double happiness!

'Let's go celebrate. Where would you like to have lunch?'

She didn't hesitate for an instant. 'At the apartment.'

He looked at her and tried to create his best 'shocked' expression.

She wrapped her arm around his waist and escorted him to the elevator.

'Don't look so incredulous, Mr Tate.'

Even though they were under some time pressure – Jennifer had to be back for a three o'clock edit meeting – their lovemaking did not suffer. She was constantly amazed at her growing desire for him. That desire and excitement were evident when at last he touched her, and his hand became soaked with her wetness. She begged him to make her come the first time by merely stroking her with his fingers while

146

holding her in his arms, softly massaging her nipples with his other hand, and covering her mouth with his to stifle her whimpers. When she could no longer stand the teasing or his fingers around her swollen lips, she thrust herself up to him. In his desire to please, that became an instinctive signal for him to insert his fingers forcefully and let her ride them to a climax. Not for a second did he stop stroking her, his tongue and lips a constant source of pleasure for her.

They weren't planning to eat until after the theatre that night, so they grabbed a quick sandwich on their way back to the studio.

Jennifer laughed, perhaps a little too quickly, when later that afternoon the make-up man who had been assigned to her for the past month commented on how terrific her skin looked. He brushed the side of her well-defined cheekbones with Clinique powder blusher.

'Did you switch treatment products recently? Your pores seem to have disappeared.' He continued examining her skin as if on a treasure hunt. 'The whole texture has changed, improved. Tell me what the miracle cream is.'

She was tempted to speak the truth, but she didn't know him well enough and she still had three stories to familiarise herself with before airtime.

'It's nothing, really, David,' she insisted half-heartedly. 'Since I've been on the air every night, I've just paid more attention to what I've been eating.' Not a total lie. 'As much as I love it, I've cut out red meat entirely.' Jennifer had had her favourite prime rib at Christ Cella's just last week. So much for food fallacies. But it was true that inner happiness and contentment showed right through to the outside.

She felt, and it was confirmed by several others as they watched the tape later, that she was especially good on that night's broadcast. Nicholas had come to the studio to watch her, and as they smiled at each other through the partition that separated the set from the crew, sharing their intimate secrets of just a few hours ago, her job had never seemed easier, or more enjoyable.

*　　*　　*

Once again, because of the congested skies on a Friday night, their plane was delayed getting into Minneapolis. They didn't seem to mind, or even notice, as they sat comfortably in their first-class seats holding hands and having vodka tonics. Their only complaint was that the divider section between the seats was stationary, and couldn't be pushed back. They decided that was the one advantage of flying economy class.

Trustworthy, ever-loyal John was there to greet them as they stepped out from the gate. She found it incredible that her mother had not driven out with him to meet them. After all, this was the moment she had been praying for – Jennifer coming home with a man in lieu of a briefcase. It was so totally out of character that for a minute she panicked, before John put her concern at ease.

'No, no, Miss Jennifer, your parents are fine, excited to see you. Your mother wanted to stay at home and make sure all the preparations for tonight's dinner are taken care of. Doris isn't as sharp as she used to be when you girls were growing up, you know. I haven't been much help today, I've been out to the airport once already, to pick up Miss Christie. She sure is fine, mighty happy living in California. So far away.'

She couldn't wait to see Christie. It had been almost a year, and Jennifer had insisted last week that she take a weekend and come home. Telling her that Nicholas would be there made her agree. So all the Martin girls would be there for tonight's dinner – Ken would be in his element. She only hoped Nicholas was prepared for all of this.

'Miss Pat suggested I drop you two off at her house first so you can leave the luggage and change, I suppose. She's already at your parents' with the twins. Mighty cute, they are, and not just a little noisy. When the two of 'em get going, close your ears!'

Jennifer agreed immediately about stopping at Pat's. It was only ten minutes out of the way, and they could change. Plus, by having all their things there, it would alleviate any uncomfortable moments when they left her parents that night after dinner. It was amazing how coming home made her feel like such a child again, instead of a career woman with her own life.

Showered and changed, they made the short ride to Ken and Marion's. As always, John advised them of their arrival with his standard 'Here we are' when he turned the navy Lincoln Town Car through the white columns flanking the driveway. Jennifer detected a little more emphasis, a touch more pride in his voice as he said it this time, wanting very much to make a good first impression on Nicholas.

Her father's garden was as glorious as ever, but it had a totally different look from the way she remembered it the last time she had been home, just a little over two months ago. Instead of the bright pinks and purples of July, there was now a profusion of yellow and red, the colours of late summer.

The entire house was buzzing with activity, the hub of which was the kitchen where the twins were being fed by the nanny. Abigail, the twin specialist imported from Scotland two weeks prior to their birth, had them well under control. Dressed in matching light pink T-shirts and diaper pants, they were pressed together side by side. She alternated the two bottles from one hungry mouth to the next, her timing so finely tuned that any cries of hunger were deftly avoided. By the time Jessica realised she no longer had a nipple in her mouth, Lauren had had a drink and Abigail was ready for her again.

Jason sat quietly by Abigail's side, mesmerised by the two small beings, so beautiful with their tiny, perfectly formed hands and alert blue eyes. Wispy strands of golden hair covered the top and sides of their heads. The sameness of their faces was startling. The only discernible difference was in their size – Lauren was just a slight bit heavier than her sister. Jennifer practically had to pry Jason away to get him to say hello to her. She gave him the gift they had brought for him, a new floating toy, a combination raft and chair for him to play with in the pool. He thanked them politely, put it on the kitchen table, and immediately turned his attention back

149

to his cousins, fascinated by these wondrous new arrivals.

Dinner at the Martins' that night was as warm and loving an event as Jennifer could remember. Everyone knew that Marion had made a very special effort to make it a success, and they showed their appreciation with a few toasts and many compliments about the food.

As Jennifer looked around the table and saw her entire family gathered together, she became a little sad that they did not make the attempt to do this more often. She had never seen Ken and Marion look so happy, so delighted to have those most important to them all at home again for an entire weekend.

Ken carved the expertly cooked roast at one end of the table while Marion passed vegetables, potatoes, and salad – all the makings of a hearty Midwestern meal. Jason was seated on a child's chair, with one of his parents on either side in case he should decide to make an unruly move. Dressed in a blue blazer and proper white shirt, with a tiny madras bow tie, he looked to be the perfect little gentleman. Pat and her husband sat across the table looking just a little tired from the enormous changes that had recently occurred in their lives. Even with her arduous work schedule, Christie managed to look tanned and taut. She seemed to be fascinated with Nicholas, and they talked photography during the entire meal. Jennifer saw him turn to speak with her mother several times, and she only hoped Marion was not being her usual aggressive self.

After dinner, when they were all in the library having coffee and dessert, Abigail brought the twins in for Pat to feed. Watching them suck hungrily on her milk-laden breasts gave Jennifer the slightest maternal longings. She looked at Nicholas – he appeared relaxed and comfortable talking with Ken and Susan's husband. For a brief moment, she wondered if he would like to have another child . . . their child. Great wailing cries from Lauren interrupted her thoughts.

That night, in Pat's guest bedroom on the second floor, their lovemaking took on a new dimension. She felt closer, and more intimate with him than ever. As he tenderly stroked her breasts, taking them slowly in his mouth, she closed her eyes and fantasised about the miracle of a newborn child.

Pat awakened Nicholas at five the next morning so he could dress and be ready when Ken came to pick him up at six. The men had all agreed last night that the best plan for them on Saturday would be an all-day outing on the Martins' Chris Craft. They would already be miles out on Lake Minnetonka by the time Jennifer got up.

The three eldest Martin girls spent a lazy day poolside at their family club. Jennifer and Susan gathered up enough energy for a late-day singles tennis match, which was immediately followed by tall, cool gin and tonics in the clubhouse. They saw lots of old school friends and friends of their parents, and Jennifer enjoyed her mini-celebrity status, a result of her father's continual boasting about her career.

Christie had decided to spend the day with her mother; they went shopping for autumn clothes and last-minute presents for the twins' christening on Sunday.

Susan and Jennifer went out to the slip just as Ken was captaining the bulky Chris Craft into the harbour. Everyone looked sunburned and tired from a long day on the water, but the fishing had been very successful.

'Your Nicholas is a star angler,' her father yelled to her from the boat. 'He really showed up the locals.'

She was delighted that he was fitting in so well with everyone in her family. Everyone seemed to like him. Even her mother had offered a small hint of approval, a big step for her.

Nicholas had indeed been the big winner that day. He had managed to catch more, and larger fish than any of the others, and his catch enabled them to have a genuine fish fry at home that night.

They ate outside by the pool and barbecued the day's booty on the big grill. Dressed in bathing suits and shorts, the evening was a marked contrast to the formality of dinner the night before. Nicholas admitted that the wall-eyed pike and crappies had a different taste from what he was used to, but he did like them. He was especially fond of the tiny sunfish, deep-fried and eaten whole, complete with tail and eyes. Doris had prepared several dozen ears of Minnesota corn, and to everyone's surprise it disappeared almost at once.

They slept early and soundly that night, everyone exhausted from their day in the sun.

The christening was scheduled for nine in the morning, so they could breakfast together afterwards at the club and get Jennifer, Nicholas, and Christie out to the airport that afternoon for their flights home.

The small church on the lake was crowded with their friends, and white flowers – tulips, wisteria, daisies, and garlands of honeysuckle – covered the altar. Marion had saved the exquisite hand-embroidered dresses that Pat and Susan had worn for their christening almost thirty years ago, never dreaming there would be another occasion when both of the dresses would be required.

Pat held Lauren, and Peter held Jessica, while Abigail stood quietly and attentively to the side. Jessica slept soundly, undisturbed by her sister's screaming.

Jennifer held Nicholas's hand throughout the ceremony, thinking of the silver-framed photos of Victoria and Christopher on the table at Grosvenor Crescent.

The minister performed his duties quickly and efficiently. He was much older and a little less patient than he had been in the fifties, when he had performed these same rites for Jennifer Carolyn Martin.

On the flight home, Nicholas went on and on about what a good time he'd had. He gave her his impression of everyone in the family, and in most cases she thought his observations were right on target. From his report, her mother had been on her best behaviour.

He left from New York that night for London. He would stay there for a couple of weeks then go out on assignment over the Thanksgiving holiday. When Jennifer had found that out, she had immediately volunteered to go home to Minnesota then, hoping to spend Christmas with Christopher and him.

When she returned to the apartment from Kennedy that night, it seemed even emptier and quieter than ever.

16

*J*ENNIFER was surprised that the next few weeks passed so quickly. They were extremely busy at the studio, trying desperately to hold on to the increased market share they had captured as a result of the Collier story. Janet Rileson, her replacement on the Special Segment job, had finally settled down in New York and had taken over Jennifer's old duties full-time. Jennifer still had to spend a lot of time with her, but, all and all, both she and Sidney were pleased with Janet's grasp of the situation. The first two segments had been well received by the viewers.

The trans-Atlantic phone calls continued, and Jennifer was as happy with the relationship as she had been from the beginning. The distance did bother her, of course, and she fully realised the road to solving that problem could be rocky, but for now she was superbly happy.

She continued to accept offers from Sidney, and, during the course of a week, they usually attended at least two business-related events. She was becoming more and more recognisable from her nightly appearances, and she found she enjoyed the idea of always being able to get a table at the Russian Tea Room or Café des Artistes and tickets to major movie screenings. It made life in New York a lot more enjoyable.

Nicholas left for Deauville the first week in November to cover the Paris to Deauville vintage car race. In addition to that, he was going to attend the annual trotter sale, to try and find one for Lisa for her birthday. The trip was mostly social,

154

and he was really covering the event for a friend of his who was this year's chairman. Jennifer was a little disappointed that he had not asked her to go with him, even though it would have been difficult to take even one day from the newscast.

She was feeling exhausted when she went home late on Friday night. Zajac & Callahan had had the carpenters in all week working on the bookcases, and she was examining their almost-completed work when Alberto rang the doorbell. She had been home for almost an hour but was still dressed from work when she answered the door.

'Oh, I'm so glad you're still up, Miss Martin,' he said, relief showing in his face. 'I found this down in the mailroom and thought it might be important, with those overseas customs stamps and all,' he explained, handing her a Federal Express envelope.

'You're the best, Alberto. This could be my ticket to paradise!' She was more than surprised when she opened the envelope to find just that. Inside was a round-trip New York–Paris Concorde ticket, plus a short note in her favourite handwriting.

'This isn't the worst place to spend a weekend. Any plans? If not, I'll expect you at Orly Saturday night. A driver will meet you and bring you to Deauville. Look for your name on his card. It will read "Star". I love you.'

Her spirits soared, and she stayed up most of the night packing and repacking, trying to remember everything she had ever heard about the chic town on France's Normandy coast, known for its casinos and horses, just two hours from Paris.

As always, she overpacked, but her intuition had been right. In her new short dress from Chanel, she felt at least as well dressed as the other women in the casino, and her linen shorts and skirts were great for walking in the marina at Port Deauville. For the first time, Nicholas turned his camera on her and took several rolls of her at the pier. They spent Saturday night at director Claude Lelouch's Club 13, a charming, tasteful twenty-five-room hotel with a private cinema. On Sunday morning, they swam in the luxurious indoor-outdoor pool, and then spent the rest of the day in their room making love.

They drove back into Paris late Sunday afternoon so Jennifer would be able to make her return flight early the next morning. Their suite at the George V was so luxurious that they decided to have dinner in the room. They walked up the Faubourg St Honoré to Fauchon where they went wild, buying caviar and champagne, and bread just out of the ovens. They could not resist the glorious pastries, and chose three of the most irresistible to take with them. With two bags full, they walked the short distance back to the hotel. Nicholas requested china, crystal, and a champagne cooler from room service. Everything arrived almost at once, set up on a beautiful table with a vase of fresh roses. Nicholas put on his paisley silk robe, and Jennifer wore her Christian Dior silk pyjamas. They drank to each other and devoured the delicious, piquant black beads. But sitting across the table from one another was too great a distance, and they found themselves entwined in each other's arms in the enormous bed even before they had finished their beautiful meal. The pastries were long forgotten when they went back into the salon the next morning.

On the way to the airport, they finalised their plans for the holidays. Jennifer would spend Thanksgiving in Wayzata with her family while Nicholas finished up his last job – what he referred to as his 'last bit of civilised work' before his scheduled departure for the Middle East in January. They would meet in London on December 20th, shop for a couple of days, then go to Lisa and Jonathan's house in the country to celebrate Christmas. On the twenty-ninth or thirtieth they would travel to New York to spend New Year's Eve in the city. Nicholas would leave from there for Beirut on New Year's Day. Jennifer's birthday was December 29th, so they would have lots of activities during the two weeks.

But Jennifer could see that Nicholas was troubled. 'What's wrong, sweet? You're not comfortable with the plan. Tell me what's the matter.'

'It's Christopher. I just don't know what to do about him.'

Immediately she thought the problem was with Victoria, about whether or not she could see him and be with him over the holidays. Without hesitating for a minute, she volunteered to change plans if it would make it easier for him.

'No, love, it's not that at all. Christopher's delighted that you're coming over. He's already planning to lend you his favourite horse to ride when we're in the country. No, the problem is that Lisa and Jonathan are leaving for Tibet the day after Christmas and they'll be away for more than a month. I can't possibly take Christopher with me to the Middle East – it's far too hectic a schedule, and he'd just be in the way. I'm really nervous about leaving him with Anna, even for a week.'

'Can't say I blame you for that. I think the two of them would turn the house upside down.'

'You're right, plus it's just an enormous responsibility for her – one that I don't want to burden her with.'

They rode on in silence for a minute, until a bright smile crossed Jennifer's lips.

'I've got a brilliant idea. Listen to this, Mr Tate. He's never been to New York, right?'

'Right,' he answered.

'Well, we'll bring him back with us after Christmas. We can all have New Year's together in the city, and then when you leave he can stay on with me in the apartment. You're only away for six days, we can manage that. In fact, I think it will be great fun. We can go to the movies, the Bronx Zoo, the Museum of Natural History. What do you think?'

He was looking at her as if she'd just told him she wanted to change careers. As if she'd gone totally wacko. 'Jenn, are you kidding? And what would you do with him while you're working for twelve and fourteen hours at a time?'

'Aha,' she replied at once, 'I've already thought of that. I have a friend, a very good friend, Wendy, who has two kids, a boy about Christopher's age and a girl a little older; I'm sure she would be glad to take him during the day. Besides, there are only four days when I'm at the studio. I could be with him all weekend. So it's perfect. I think he would have a good time. Then when you're home I'll put him on the plane at Kennedy. What do you think he'll say?'

'He'll say it's the best idea yet. He's been badgering me for a trip to New York for years, ever since the Mets won the World series.'

'Then it's settled.'

He still looked troubled. He moved closer to her, put his arms around her neck, and pulled her face close to his. 'But, my love, what about our plans for a cosy, quiet New Year together, not to mention your birthday? You can't send Christopher out for several hours at a time, you know.'

'We'll chain him to the bed in the second bedroom, and turn on the TV loud enough to drown out my cries of ecstasy,' she joked. 'Don't worry; we'll be able to figure it out.' She reassured him with an extraordinarily sensual kiss.

'No breaks ever for us,' she complained as she read the departure board at Air France that indicated that both of their planes were scheduled to depart on time. 'We never get an extra second together.'

'Come on, love. This won't be so bad.' He held her tightly. 'You'll be back in London in a little more than three weeks. By the time you shop for all of my wonderful presents, pack your country and city clothes, and maybe deliver a news broadcast or two, we'll be together again.' His joking didn't stop her tears from coming this time.

He wiped her eyes with his monogrammed linen handkerchief, and held her face in his hands. His piercing eyes told her there was no one else in the world for him. He finally broke their embrace.

'I love you, Jennifer. Now go. I'll speak to you tonight.' And he turned her around and headed her toward the Concorde passenger entrance.

She looked back at the automatic doors and waved to him. She wanted so much to run back, to tell him how much she loved him, and to explain how painful it was each time she had to leave him, but she was sure she'd never be able to respond to him without falling apart completely. So she continued toward the aeroplane. The next three weeks would be an eternity.

17

'So just how long has Nicholas been separated from his wife?'

'He's not separated, Mother, he's divorced. There's a big difference. It's been final for two years, but they haven't lived together for almost three years. She's got a serious drug problem.'

'A drug addict?' She made it sound like only a street disease, certainly nothing that could exist in the homes of the middle and upper classes.

'Yes, I suppose you could call her that. Just like Mrs Simpson. Remember when they took her away for rehabilitation for her Valium habit?' Mrs Simpson had been one of their friends, a top golfer at the club. Her mother had told Jennifer about her 'condition' during one of their recent phone calls. Thank heavens she listened occasionally – that bit of information was coming in handy now that she was being interrogated during the Thanksgiving Day dinner.

'Jennifer, please don't be so flip. I'm only trying to understand the man's situation a little better. Now, how about the child?' Unrelenting, Jennifer thought.

'The child is a darling ten-year-old boy, who plays rugby and tennis and excels in his studies. I'll be able to tell you more in January. He's coming to spend a week with me while Nicholas is in the Middle East.'

An exasperated look crossed her mother's face. 'Oh, Jennifer, you really do ask for trouble sometimes.' A distinct complaint about Jennifer's inability so far to find a single, as in 'never married', childless man.

Everyone else in the family had unanimously agreed that Nicholas was fabulous. Ken liked him very much, thought he was a good, solid 'man's man', as he put it. Susan and her husband enjoyed his company, and Pat thought he was great with the twins. Christie was attracted to his thoughts on photography as a viable means of communication and by his ability to converse about so many different things. So, as usual, no one but Marion had anything but praise for the new man in Jennifer's life.

The Thanksgiving holiday afforded her lots of time to question Jennifer, because Susan and her husband and Jason had gone to visit his parents, Christie had gone to Lake Tahoe to ski and take advantage of an early heavy snow, and Pat was busy with the twins.

Jennifer used her time at home to prepare her Christmas list and plan things to do with Christopher in January. Every time she saw something in a newspaper or magazine that she thought might interest him, she clipped it out and saved it. They could go over them in England and plan their days. Zajac & Callahan had promised that the major part of the work on the apartment would be done by the end of December and since she hadn't needed to use the excuse of buying furniture to go to London, most of the pieces had been purchased in New York and had already been delivered. She was delighted with the results, the apartment looked terrific, and she was excited about Nicholas seeing it. A dramatic change since that hot night in July that seemed like ages ago!

Jennifer was troubled over the holiday by a persistent cough that her father had developed. It wasn't only the cough, he seemed to be a little run down, not quite as sharp and energetic as she always expected him to be. They played tennis on the indoor courts a couple of times, and Jennifer felt that he just didn't have the same drive, the same competitive spirit he had always shown. And the cough was aggravated by any strenuous physical activity.

161

She inquired several times during the weekend if he felt OK.

'Of course, darling, just a persistent tickle in my throat. Nothing for you to worry about.'

Nevertheless she extracted two promises from him. One was that he would have a complete physical, which was long overdue, and the other was that he would come to visit her soon in New York, maybe as early as February. She was anxious to share her life there with him.

She reminded him of both of these things as she kissed him goodbye in front of the house when she left for New York on Sunday night.

18

THE light, wispy snow that had started to fall the day before in the early afternoon had grown heavier during the night and produced an accumulation of about ten inches in the city. Connecticut and some areas of New Jersey had over a foot.

There were only two Saturdays left before Christmas, and Jennifer had chosen to spend this one shopping, trying to find the gifts on her seemingly endless list. She hated to go into the stores at the weekend – they were so noisy and overheated – but it was really the only time she could go from store to store looking for exactly the right thing for everyone. Lunch hours were impossible; people were frantic, and New Yorkers were at their worst, pushing and shoving. She was always concerned about what was happening at the studio, and her head was filled with that night's stories. But not today. Today she had reserved just for purchasing. She had mapped out the route she was going to take, down Madison, across to Bergdorf's and finally up Lexington to Bloomingdale's where she knew she would be able to get some funny, unusual things to take overseas with her.

She looked as if she were dressed for combat. In fact, she had planned her outfit as carefully as her purchases. She needed to eliminate carrying a handbag, so she wore an old leather jacket with lots of inside pockets and zippers to keep credit cards, cash and keys from falling out or, more likely, being pickpocketed. Under this she wore a T-shirt and an old Ballantyne sweater. Her jeans had a small hole in the left knee, so she wore her leg warmers. But she was puzzled and later frustrated when she couldn't find her black Mario Valentino boots. She turned the closets upside down. They were nowhere to be found. When had she last worn them? That's right, in Deauville. They had been last-minute additions when Nicholas had mentioned on the phone that it had rained on several days, and she'd thrown them into the suitcase. She even remembered discussing them with him. He had been looking at them one night in the room and had asked her if they were comfortable. Yes, they were. They were a supple black kid leather in a flat style, and they were her favourites. She'd have to remember to ask him about them when he called. She hoped they hadn't been left behind. She couldn't recall having had them when they had stayed in Paris, either. Oh well, for now the lined black patent ones would have to do. They'd probably be better in the snow anyway. She pulled them on and was out of the door.

The freshly fallen snow which would still be virginally white in the country had already blackened on the Manhattan streets. It was at times like this that Jennifer thanked heaven for her monthly facial treatment. The dirt was incredible!

As she trudged back to the apartment that night through the sludgelike snowy mess, she decided that the day had been a success. Her list was reduced to almost nothing, only the little extra gifts were left. Of course, Nicholas had been the hardest; she supposed that those you wanted to please the most were always difficult, and she felt that men in general were a special shopping challenge. It was only by chance that she had stopped at the Banana Republic across from Bloomingdale's. She was vaguely familiar with the canvas photojournalist's jacket that they made, the one with twenty-seven separate pockets, many of them waterproof. But now, she discovered, they made a leather version which was fast becoming a classic. She was able to get him the last large one. A glorious crocodile belt from Bottega Veneta and a superdeluxe multiband radio from Hammacher Schlemmer on East 57th Street completed her gifts. She was also able to find the world's smallest hand-held television set for Christopher and a set of exotic but useful gardening tools for Jonathan at the same store.

Presents for her family had all been sent directly from the various stores to the house in Wayzata. Bloomingdale's provided the stocking-filler gifts for Anna, Martha and Basil. She was especially pleased with the selection of wild socks she would give Anna to wear with her Reeboks. Basil would love his new, sleek Italian-designed flashlight for the car.

Part of Sunday was spent grocery shopping. All traces of the cosmetic cabinet that the refrigerator had once been were gone, as she stocked it with all kinds of items. She hardly knew her way around the aisles of the neighbourhood Food Emporium, but she managed to fill three baskets with things she thought a ten-year-old might like to eat. Everything, including a newly furnished apartment, was ready for them when they returned from London.

There was only one thing left to select before her departure. That was Sidney's gift. He had been so wonderful during the past year, and it had to be something very special but still appropriate for their relationship.

They planned to have dinner together the night before she left, so she still had a couple more days to think about it. At last, she found it in a window on Madison Avenue as she was walking home on Monday night. Time Will Tell was a tiny hole-in-the-wall shop that had the best selection of antique watches in the entire city. In the vitrine, among the many timepieces on display, her eye was captured by an elegant Audemars Piguet pocket watch. She squeezed in amidst the other shoppers and timidly asked the price, hoping it was not outrageous.

'It is truly one of our most beautiful pieces,' commented the salesgirl. 'It is from 1938, one of the first automatics.' She held it out for her to see. It was expensive, but it was so right for him that she felt good about being a little extravagant.

She was soon doubly glad she had got it for him, for when they dined together later that week, she was astounded by the extravagant present that Sidney had chosen for her. They were seated side by side on the red leather banquettes at La Côte Basque, where he had suggested they have their holiday dinner. Just after they had been served coffee, he casually handed her a rectangular box, about the size and thickness of a hardcover book. At first Jennifer thought that maybe it was a book, which would make her present seem too grand and far too serious. But as she looked down at the beautifully wrapped gift she saw printed in light dove grey on the white glossy background of the paper the discreet interlocking C's, the logo of Cartier. She was immediately relieved. Then her thoughts turned in the other direction. What if it was something extremely valuable? The box was too long and too broad for it to be a watch. Oh well, there was only one way to end the mystery.

She pulled gently on the red ribbon which had been secured with a red wax seal bearing the Cartier stamp and slowly opened the red leather hand-tooled box to reveal a glorious opera-length strand of pearls with a pavé diamond clasp. Each pearl was perfectly matched in size, shape, and colour to the one next to it.

'Oh, Sid, they are truly magnificent,' she said, turning to face him so that she could give him a thank-you kiss.

And they were magnificent. As she lifted them out of the box, carefully, like the precious items they were, their full beauty was revealed. They were deliciously large – her untrained eye saw they were at least nine or ten millimetres each, making the strand not only rare, but extremely valuable.

'They're each between nine-and-a-half and ten in size,' he confirmed as she continued to caress them with her fingertips. They had such an elegant, smooth texture.

She knew better than to suggest that she could not keep them, that they were just too extravagant a present for her to accept. He would have been deeply hurt and offended.

'Well, I certainly don't know what I've done to deserve them, but I love them. Thank you.'

'You've just been you,' he replied. 'And for that you deserve the best of everything.'

Sidney loved his watch, and at the office the next day she noticed the gold link chain leading into the side pocket of his suit pants. He wore it now instead of his usual Piaget polo wristwatch.

He told her that night that he planned to spend Christmas Day with some friends in East Hampton.

'No big deal,' he had said. 'But I am looking forward to skiing in February. That's my real holiday.'

She imagined that the traditional holidays must be terribly hard for him, without any family to share them.

The Channel 7 office Christmas party was especially joyous this year. They had all pitched in together to overcome Stewart's loss, both personally and professionally, and once again they were operating on top. They had managed to retain their increased audience share, and everyone felt confident about the spring season. During the evening, which was held at Nell's popular West 14th Street Club, even Steve came up to Jennifer and wished her a Merry Christmas. He said he hoped that the New Year would enable them to forget their past differences and to be friends.

She said she hoped so, too, knowing full well that it would take more than a new year to change his long-harboured grudge against her.

When Jennifer left the restaurant that night to go on her much-anticipated vacation, she was confident that Steve, who would be filling in for her while she was away, would do a credible, responsible job. Despite her personal feelings about him, she knew he was not foolish enough to perform less than professionally.

The time would be good for her, too. She had thrown herself in headlong, giving 120 per cent to both her new position and her new relationship, and she was looking forward to being away from the one so she could devote her full attention to the other.

*　　*　　*

Jennifer had always loved Manhattan around Christmas time. The tree at Rockefeller Center with the ice skating rink filled with novice as well as professional skaters, the snow-capped evergreen branches covering the ceiling at Saks, making it look like a primeval forest, and the Grand Army Plaza with its trees decorated with hundreds of sparkling white lights at the corner of Fifth Avenue and 59th Street always made her slip immediately into the holiday spirit. She had even come to terms with Donald Trump's controversial snowball, which he had first suspended at the Tiffany and Bergdorf intersection the year that Trump Tower was completed. She loved seeing the schoolchildren lined up at Rumpelmayer's for hot chocolate after they had been to see the 'Nutcracker Suite' at Lincoln Center. Even the hansom cabs, decorated with ribbons and wreaths and forever holding up traffic, held a special appeal for her. New York City at the holidays had always been a happy place.

But as wonderful as that city could be, nothing could compare to the magical quality of London during the third week in December. Walking down Old Bond Street and through Burlington Arcade, Jennifer was fascinated by the variety of the decorations. The atmosphere in the city was distinctly less commercial than New York's, much more traditional and old-fashioned, and she found it extremely charming. As they did their last-minute shopping, Nicholas was constantly having to stop and pull her along. Invariably, some glistening window display caught her eye, or she would stop to listen to the carolers and become distracted, unaware that she had lost him in the crowd.

'But it is so beautiful, just one second, please,' she would plead as he tried to coax her along. She knew she was being childlike, but she was on holiday and so happy to be with Nicholas, she couldn't help herself. And it was glorious, every street held a new treasure.

'I know, darling, but your tales of fancy windows will be no substitute for a present on Christmas morning.' As with most men, Nicholas's forte was not shopping.

'You're so right, sweet,' she would agree until they came upon the next irresistible sight.

The house on Grosvenor Crescent had been transformed into the perfect Christmas place. Even the grumpiest Scrooge would have cracked a smile if he had seen the stockings arranged on the mantel. Nicholas's and Christopher's stockings were hand-knitted with trees and reindeer in seasonal colours. Their names had been woven into the top of the stocking. It looked to her as if they had been made by the same person, Nicholas's mother perhaps. Since Anna and Martha had no family in London, they would be staying in the house and celebrating Christmas, and their stockings were also hung side by side. Jennifer was very touched when she moved closer to examine the fifth green-and-red knitted stocking. A gift tag had been attached to its top, and in a child's printing it said 'Jennifer'. She assumed that Christopher had been home last weekend to help decorate the house, and in an effort to make her feel a part of the family Nicholas had insisted that they put up a stocking for her. Or maybe it had been Christopher's idea. It didn't matter whose it was, it made her very happy.

'I'm so glad you've come for the holiday.' Anna entered the main living room and interrupted her examination of the decorations. 'I hope you enjoy all these things. Mr Tate did everything just for you, and he was in a panic about getting all of the garlands hung and the tree decorated before you arrived. He hasn't put a tree up in, well, you know, since . . .'

'Yes,' Jennifer answered at once.

'But I'm really glad he's back to his former self. You don't know how pleased all of us are.'

'I'm so glad too, and the house does look lovely. It looks like a real old-fashioned Christmas.'

The tree, a ten-foot-tall Norwegian pine, had been placed in the middle of the huge front windows. It was covered with hundreds of ornate Christmas decorations, each one more beautiful than the next. There were many varieties of birds with tails of brightly coloured feathers, miniature English houses with stained glass windows, gingerbread men, and all

169

types of traditional balls. The most spectacular part of the tree, however, was that instead of having electric lights connected to ugly green wires, it was lit with real candles. At the end of each branch was a clip-on silver candleholder, each containing a four-inch-high taper. She couldn't wait until that night when it was lit.

'It must have taken ages to put the tree up. It has more ornaments than I've ever seen.'

'It took Mr Tate and Christopher both nights last weekend. But they wanted it to be perfect for you. I had to serve their dinner in here in order to get them to eat. There was no stopping them. Mr Tate has brought home ornaments from all over the world. He collects them when he's on his trips. Some of them, like these multicoloured glass ones' – she pointed to a hand-blown ball – 'are only made in one factory in the world, just outside of Venice. They are my very favourite.'

Jennifer agreed. 'They're all lovely. And I'm just delighted to be here. Is there anything I can do to help you with dinner?'

'Not a thing, thank you. Your job is to keep Mr Tate happy.'

Jennifer was sure that what Anna meant by that remark wasn't exactly the same as what she had in mind. But the results would be the same. She smiled at the sweet woman and headed up the stairs to do exactly what Anna had suggested.

After dinner that night, Christopher helped his father light each candle on the tree. Even Nicholas agreed that it was spectacular, and he photographed them arranging the gaily wrapped presents under the tree.

'Chris, be careful to keep separate the gifts for Anna and Martha and Basil – so we don't take them with us when we pack the car tomorrow.'

'No problem, Dad. I remember which is which. Especially these two huge ones for Jennifer.' He pointed to the most enormous boxes, so large they each took up a corner of the room. She thought he was kidding.

'That's right. And don't let her near them. She's a sneaky one, and she may try to shake them,' Nicholas teased.

Jennifer added her suitcaseful of gifts to the already substantial collection. She followed Christopher's instructions as he pointed to the pile that would remain in London, versus those that would go tomorrow in the cars to Exbury.

Nicholas surveyed the growing stack of gifts. 'Now I'm certain we'll have to take two cars. Basil can drive you down in the Daimler, Chris. Jenn and I will follow you. Then we can all come back to go to the airport together.'

After everyone had gone to bed, Nicholas pulled shut the panelled doors that separated the living room from the main hall.

'I've been dreaming of making love to you under this tree since we brought it home. I couldn't think of anything else tonight.'

'I was hoping you would share my fantasy,' she said as they lay down in each other's arms on the thick Turkish carpet.

They woke up suddenly after what seemed like hours. They had drifted off, floating away together in their contentment. Jennifer was convinced that it must be almost daybreak, but the candles had not burned down very far, and it was only two a.m.

'We could have destroyed your entire house if we'd slept longer,' she said.

'It would have been worth it,' was his response as they crept naked upstairs to his bedroom, clothes draped over their arms, shoes dangling from their fingers.

Snuggled securely in Nicholas's arms, she dreamt that night about the contents of the large packages downstairs under the beautiful tree.

19

'ARE you sure that's everything, Master Christopher? We don't want anyone to be disappointed on Christmas morn.' Basil was about to close the trunk on the fully loaded TATE I. The car was now low to the ground; it looked as if it were being used as a removal van. The back seat was stuffed with boxes of all shapes, including the large ones with Jennifer's name on them.

'Yes, that's it, Basil. Let's go before we miss the holiday.'

'Drive carefully, Basil. You can't see a thing through the rear window,' warned Nicholas.

'Yes, sir, I will. We'll see you there.' Nicholas climbed in beside Jennifer, whose legs were cramped for space in the TATE II, his honey-coloured Aston Martin DB–6. It could barely hold the overflow of gifts plus their luggage. They had combined their belongings into one suitcase in an effort to accommodate everything, but it was still too much.

As the cars were pulling out of the garage Christopher yelled to his father, 'Did you remember all of the stockings, Dad?'

'Yes I did.'

'Even Jennifer's?'

'Especially hers, yes.'

Nice, Jennifer thought. Maybe her stocking had been Christopher's idea after all.

If London was the perfect, magical city in which to spend the holidays, the village of Exbury was its counterpart in the country.

172

Jonathan and Lisa's estate bordered the extraordinary gardens for which the area was famous. The main house, an imposing stucco and wood structure that was a solid foil for the harsh winds and salt air, sat on a promontory facing the Isle of Wight. It was three storeys high and had ten bedrooms, five bathrooms, and a number of reception rooms, including two libraries. Each room had at least one fireplace and there was one servant whose main function was to keep them all stocked with wood, burning brightly.

Further inland, about half a mile, were the stables. It was the largest private setup that Jennifer had ever seen, and in the afternoon of their first day there, she and Christopher spent hours just walking from stall to stall. He seemed to know everything about each horse: there were thirty-six on the property now, and he was anxious to share his knowledge with her.

'Maybe we'll ride tomorrow, on Christmas Day,' he said with a smile that Jennifer perceived as hiding a secret. 'Would you like that?'

'I'd love it,' she said, not realising it would be unlike any horseback ride she had ever taken.

'Okay, we'll go out right after we open the presents, of course.'

Christmas morning began very early at the Phillipses'. Nicholas pulled her close to him, and whispered, 'Believe it or not, we *have* to get up now.'

She groaned and buried her head against his chest. But the smell of freshly baked sweet rolls and coffee combined with Christopher's insistent knocking on their bedroom door convinced her that he wasn't kidding.

'No dressing or making up,' he yelled to her through the bathroom door. 'This event requires a dressing gown only. Hurry, or I'll eat your bun.'

She scrubbed her face and cheated somewhat by putting on a little mascara and blusher. After all, it was the middle of winter. Pulling on her plaid woollen robe and heavy socks, she hoped she wouldn't be the only one without pyjamas underneath. Not the height of elegance, but perfect for this chilly morning. The fire in their room had been reduced to embers, and she welcomed the warmth of the blaze in the living room downstairs.

They were all waiting for her in front of the tree – Jonathan, Christopher, Nicholas, and Lisa, who was already busy distributing a present to everyone.

'Good morning, Jennifer. You'd better come and sit over here next to your oversized presents. They're too heavy for me to move.'

The cook had prepared plump, luscious scones which she now passed around on a silver tray, followed by the coffee Jennifer had smelled earlier.

Christopher was thrilled with all his things – his mother had sent some new winter clothing, Lisa and Jonathan gave him some rugby gear, and his father got him the latest computer model he had been asking for. The little TV from Jennifer was a big hit, and he immediately tuned in to an early morning station.

'Thank you very much,' he said politely, anxious to get on with things. 'Now open your big one. It's from Dad and me, but it was really my idea.'

She struggled with the wrapping, and Christopher finally had to help her break down the sides of the enormous box. Inside was one of the most extravagant items in the world, an Hermès English riding saddle, in the rich brown known as London. She squealed with delight as Nicholas helped Christopher lift it out of the box. It was a piece of art, hand-made by the few craftsmen in the world who were able to produce such an item. She had always admired the saddles on display in the Paris store, once she had even been given a tour of the atelier on the second floor where some of the work was done, but never had she thought she would have one of her very own.

'Do you like it?' asked Christopher anxiously. She was so overwhelmed she hadn't said a word.

'Do I *like* it? Christopher, it's a dream come true. It's the most beautiful thing in the world. Oh thank you, thank you.' And she hugged both of them.

'There's more,' he continued. 'Hurry and unpack the rest of the boxes so we can ride after breakfast.'

'OK, I'm going as fast as I can,' she said.

Inside the second box were a bridle and girth, of the same leather and workmanship as the saddle.

Lisa handed her two more presents. 'Now that your horse is dressed, here are some things for you. From Jonathan, too.'

'This is really too much. I feel very spoiled.'

'And so you should,' Nicholas joked.

The Pikeur breeches, German made and among the best, fit perfectly, as did the tweed jacket.

'We've almost made a rider out of you,' Nicholas said. 'Just a couple more things, my love.'

Inside the third large box was a pair of Hermès riding boots. They were the simplest, most classic model, all black and skilfully constructed out of a single piece of leather. Nestled next to them in the box were her old Valentino boots she had been frantically searching for last week. The same ones that Nicholas had claimed to have no knowledge of when she had asked him on the phone if he'd remembered seeing them when they were in Deauville.

He grinned at her as she shook her head in amazement.

'I couldn't help it,' he explained. 'I had to take them to give to the shoemakers, otherwise the new ones would never have fitted. Anyway, you've got them back now. Do you forgive me?'

'Of course, sweet. Oh, everything is so luxurious. Thank you all.'

Everyone loved the presents Jennifer had brought for them. Nicholas insisted on wearing his Banana Republic jacket into the breakfast room over his robe.

Christopher was anxious to get out to the stables and prepare the horses.

'Sit still for a few minutes, Chris. You've just had an enormous meal. They will still be there when you arrive. If you go out now, you'll probably be sick,' cautioned his father.

175

Amid much grumbling, the boy managed to stay at the table for another half-hour.

When it was finally time to go, Jennifer put on all of her new things. The boots fit like house slippers, and the breeches were a good style for her long legs.

While Christopher ran on ahead, Nicholas walked with her across the manicured lawn out to the waiting horses. When they were about sixty yards from the entrance to the stalls he suddenly stopped.

'I believe you have forgotten your gloves, m'lady,' he said as he handed her another orange-and-brown Hermès box.

'Oh Nicholas, it really is too much. You made quite a substantial contribution to the French economy this year. Thank you.' She held the box against her chest and continued to walk. She'd wait and put them on inside.

He stopped her after a few feet. 'Please open them here.'

'OK,' and she removed the ribbons. Not surprisingly, inside was a pair of pigskin gloves of remarkable quality.

'See if they fit. You didn't have any gloves to pinch in Deauville.'

The right one went on easily. As she started to put her fingers into the left one, she noticed a resistance in the reinforced area between the ring and little finger. The reinforcement had been made because, when properly placed, the reins rested there. She pushed a little harder, then heard a thump as something fell to the ground. She bent down to pick up the object. Halfway down she realised what it was. In her hands she held a sapphire-and-diamond ring. Two perfect blue stones flanked a steel-white diamond that glistened even under the dreary, fog-laden sky.

He took her by the shoulders. 'The saddle and all that stuff were just extras, so I'd have a reason to give you the gloves. It was the most unexpected way I could think of to ask you to marry me.'

His eyes begged her to respond.

'Oh, Nicholas, this is wonderful, but . . .'

'Yes, my love, I know there are lots of "buts", hundreds of things we haven't even talked about. But I wanted you to have something to think about while you're riding.'

'You've certainly succeeded at that.' She laughed and kissed him passionately. The ring fell to the ground again.

He bent down, picked it up and slipped it on to her finger. 'We'll talk about everything tonight. Now go and don't keep my son waiting any longer.'

She started to walk toward the entrance.

'By the way, if you want to talk with Christopher about it, it's OK. He thinks it's a wonderful idea.'

The two of them rode for hours through the countryside surrounding the Phillipses' property. Jennifer knew that the combination of breaking in her new, very stiff saddle and the fact that she hadn't ridden for quite some time was going to result in her being very sore tomorrow. But she didn't care. She rode with reckless abandon. She wanted to stay out as long as she could, so she could have as much time as possible to think.

Nicholas's proposal had really caught her off guard. She removed her left glove to make sure it hadn't been a dream. But no, the glistening three-stone ring was there, in all its splendour. They had never discussed the future beyond their plans for New Year. Had she assumed that they would just carry on as before? The daily phone calls, the six-thousand-mile trips every few weeks just to spend a couple of days together? She couldn't answer any of these questions. She needed to discuss them with him. That was the whole point. She did need him, and it had been clear to her for a long time that she loved him. But marriage? What about her career? And where would they live? She drove the horse harder and harder. Christopher didn't seem to mind that they had barely spoken since they had left the stable.

When they returned to the house it was late enough to telephone the Martins to wish them a Merry Christmas. Nicholas had agreed that they would not mention her new piece of jewellery or their plans for the future. After all, even they weren't really sure yet what those were.

'Hi, honey.' It was Ken. 'Merry Christmas. We love all of your wonderful presents, especially the ones Nicholas sent.'

'What presents from Nicholas?' She looked at him quizzically, as he held the other phone extension across the room.

'The pictures of you are terrific. Deauville is certainly a pretty spot,' he went on.

She was so pleased with Nicholas's thoughtfulness, and her parents were genuinely touched. She felt even better when her father assured her that his thorough check-up hadn't uncovered any problems and that his nasty cough of the last two weeks had totally disappeared.

After everyone exchanged greetings and they had hung up, Nicholas explained that he had sent two pictures, from the ones he had taken of her on their last trip, in silver frames, one to each of her parents with his belated thanks for a lovely weekend, and best wishes for the holidays. He hoped she didn't mind. She didn't, did she?

How could she?

Jennifer figured that she had slept a grand total of approximately forty-five minutes on Christmas night, between her excitement about Nicholas's proposal, her very real concerns about her career, and her aching derrière, a result of the day's ride. They had stayed up late, sitting in front of the fire in the library, talking about their future together. Nicholas's understanding and compassion regarding her career made her decisions that much more difficult. He said he was willing to do whatever he could, including living in the States for a while, so that she could realise her dream. He thought it would be beneficial for Christopher to spend some time at school there. He did want them to have a child together, but he assured her he wouldn't push her on that subject.

They both cried when early the next morning, finally, she said, 'Yes I will marry you, Nicholas Tate, I love you so very much.' However they both agreed not to make a formal announcement or to tell her parents until after he returned from the Middle East. It would give them both a little more time to find some answers to questions that would inevitably be asked. Somehow they overlooked how difficult it could be to hide a ten-carat ring.

20

*T*HE next five days seemed like five minutes, and now she was packing for the trip home.

She and Christopher had gone riding every day at dawn, and then the three of them would go out together in the late afternoon. They took endless swims, ate hearty home-cooked meals, and left the property only once, on Boxing Day, to go into town to deliver their gifts.

Basil brought the remaining luggage down from London so they could avoid going through town, and he dropped them at Heathrow just in time for their flight to New York at four. Lisa and Jonathan rode with them – the first leg of their flight to Tibet left just an hour later. Their trip would take a little longer than five weeks.

'When did you have the chance to do all this?' Nick sounded incredulous.

They had just arrived at the apartment, and he was seeing the results of Zajac & Callahan's efforts for the very first time.

'Well, I didn't exactly *do* it. I got to play the client for a change. They presented alternatives to me, fabric, paint, furnishings, and I just pointed. Not as easy as it sounds, however.'

'I realise that, but it seems you did very well. The results are superb,' he commented as he examined the bookcases.

Christopher seemed very much at home, but he was anxious to get out and see the city. The first night they went to the Hard Rock Café so he could compare it to the one in

180

London. Jennifer's fame helped them get a table at the always crowded hangout.

'I think ours is more hip,' he commented. 'The kids in London looked like this two years ago.'

Jennifer agreed. 'You're right. London is always way ahead in trends. New York takes the best from California and Europe and this is what you get.'

They asked Christopher what he wanted to do during the next few days, and from that they made their schedule. The World Trade towers, the Empire State Building, and the Hayden Planetarium were at the top of the list. Some things he and Jennifer would save to do after Nicholas left for Beirut. Nicholas decided that visiting the Bronx Zoo in the twenty-degree weather was one of those things.

Jennifer awakened early on the morning of her birthday, eager to get to the studio.

'No breakfast in bed for the birthday girl?' Nicholas offered.

'Not a chance. I'm a working princess. Now please disengage from me and allow me to go out and make a living.' She pushed him off her and headed for the bathroom.

She was dressed and ready to go out the door in less than an hour.

'Have fun today. Think of me slaving away.' She kissed them both goodbye.

'Will we ever see you again?' Nicholas enquired.

'Indeed, even earlier if you tune in at six. I'll be home shortly thereafter. Bye.'

In the taxi she realised he hadn't said anything about tonight's plans. She wondered what the two of them had cooked up. So far their teamwork surprises had been pretty sensational.

Everyone had missed her at the studio; her warm smile, and the professionalism she brought to the broadcast were only two of the reasons why. The crew agreed that Sidney seemed to be in a much better mood, much more agreeable, when she was there.

181

Andrea remembered that it was her birthday, and they celebrated with champagne and a Carvel ice-cream cake right after the show.

She was just the slightest bit light-headed when she opened the door to her apartment.

The first bouquet of red long-stemmed roses was on the new Biedermeier table in the foyer. The second and third dozen were on the side tables in the living room. The flowers were everywhere. They must have bought every red rose in New York City, she thought.

The apartment was filled with the scent of roses. Other aromas poured forth from the kitchen. Nicholas was at work again on another spectacular meal. He hardly noticed her when she entered the kitchen.

'Hello, my love,' she said. 'Is this what house-husbands are all about? I think I like the concept.'

'Yes, this is it. You can only get really good ones in Britain, though, and there are very few available.'

'I'll settle for you then. Where's your offspring?'

'Tied to his bedpost so we can celebrate your birthday doing wild and crazy things.'

'You're wild and crazy. Christopher, where are you?' She started off in search of him.

'He's busy wrapping your present. He'll be out soon. Get changed and come back here. I need you desperately.'

They drank a glass of champagne in the kitchen while Nicholas finished preparing the meal – a prime rib roast with individual Yorkshire puddings, and sautéed green beans with almonds. She hoped there was a birthday cake hidden in the kitchen somewhere.

There was a strange presence in the apartment, something she couldn't put her finger on, but it was nevertheless there. Christopher had been very quiet all night. She hoped he wasn't homesick or, worse yet, changing his mind about her.

They ate as if they were starving, pausing briefly to tell each other about their respective days.

'Time for cake and presents,' Christopher announced just seconds after they had finished eating. 'You promised we could do it right away, Dad.' He seemed very anxious about whatever they had done.

'Okay, Jenn, into the living room. We'll be in shortly.' She did exactly as she was told, no questions asked.

Minutes later, as she sat in her rose-filled, darkened living room, the melodious voices of two of her favourite men resounded throughout the room singing 'Happy Birthday'.

More champagne and a luscious hazelnut cream cake from S'ant Ambroeus on Madison Avenue were consumed. She was just calculating the number of additional situps she would have to do to rid her body of the extravagance when Nicholas got up and crossed the room.

From behind one of the tables flanking the couch, he pulled out a large chocolate-brown alligator portfolio. It measured about four feet high by three feet wide and eight or ten inches in depth. It was the type of thing one saw frequently in New York under the arms of aspiring photographers or models, a showcase carrier for their work. Usually they were made of black plastic, or if the person had enjoyed some success, leather. But never, ever, had she seen one made of alligator.

'Nicholas, this is the *entire* alligator quota for the year. Where did you find it?' She stroked the side of the case to confirm that it was the real McCoy. She couldn't believe it. 'It's gorgeous!'

His smile told her how delighted he was that she was pleased. 'I thought it might be useful for you to house all of your press clippings and announcements. But Chris and I filled it with some other things for you first.'

She unlocked the latch and swung open the heavy front cover. It took about the same strength as opening a door. The inside was lined in leather, and there were ten pages, each one protected by a plastic insert. To fill the portfolio one would slip the photos of articles under the protective plastic sheets. But as she turned the pages, she saw that they were filled not with those things, but each page contained a different colour cashmere sweater. The sweaters had been artfully arranged, their sleeves neatly folded across the front. They had chosen a beautiful array of colours – light pink, seafoam green, royal

183

blue, cocoa, plus a selection of the basics in black, cream, navy and bright red. She flipped back to page three and removed the navy one. It was beautifully made, luxurious triple-ply cashmere, the kind that's heavy enough to wear without a jacket. All were simply styled with a collar only half an inch or so higher than a classic crew neck.

'How did you two ever come up with this idea?'

'Well, we thought it was a little tacky to give an empty case, even though it is alligator,' answered Nicholas. 'We also decided you would look terrific in these on the air, as well as with jeans.'

'That's it then, it's final. I'm keeping you both as my wardrobe consultants.'

'Yuk,' said Christopher. 'Dad, can I give her the real present now, please?'

'Of course, that's what we've been waiting for.'

He dashed off in the direction of the guest bedroom where the door had remained closed since Jennifer came home. When he returned to the living room he was carrying a squirming bundle of blond fur, almost the exact colour of Jennifer's hair. Around its neck they had tied a bright red ribbon. The little creature couldn't weigh more than ten pounds.

Jennifer gasped. So this was the stranger she had felt in the apartment. All she could think of at that moment was responsibility, responsibility, responsibility. Dog walking, vet's bills, boarding him when she went out of town – right then she was really furious with them both. But it was clearly too late now. By the time Christopher had crossed the room and held out the precious animal for her to take, she was forever in love.

'We decided that the only thing missing from your almost completely English-style apartment was a domestic animal.'

'Oh, you did, did you?'

Nicholas heard the irritation in her voice.

'Yes, we did. And we also think we've thought of everything. This beautiful little golden retriever puppy comes with his own dog walker, three times a day for forty minutes each, schedule to be determined by you, plus a year's supply of dog food, a premium blend. Only the best for your little Buster.'

'Buster? Surely you're joking! His name is Buster? In New York, everyone knows Buster as the doorman at Bendel's, not a furry little animal.'

Christopher still held the puppy tightly against his chest, stroking him nonstop. 'But, Jenn, I really wanted to name him before we gave him to you,' he insisted. 'I think Buster is just the right thing to call him.' He hugged the animal even tighter.

'Of course, we *could* change it,' Nicholas offered, 'but he would probably suffer for the whole of his life from an identity problem.'

'Don't be silly,' she agreed. 'Buster it is. Christopher, do I even get to hold him?'

'Oh yeah' – he looked hesitant – 'but only for a minute. They said the first few nights he could be lonely and one person should stay with him and pet him.'

'OK, I'll give him right back. Just let me see if he's as soft as he looks.'

'Oh, he is, I promise,' he assured her, hoping that if she had his word she wouldn't need to take the puppy from him.

'Now what happens to young Buster when I jet off to London for a couple of days?'

Nicholas's smile told her that he had also covered this important detail.

'For out-of-town trips you have two options. Either the trainer will come and stay in the apartment with him, or if you prefer the more social approach, he can be taken to her apartment somewhere in the Fifties, where she lives with two Bernese mountain dogs. Buster will be given top priority, however, because golden retrievers are her favourite breed. She was here this afternoon, too, as they would only say in Manhattan, to "interview" the dog to make sure he was of the calibre she is used to working with. You'll be glad to know that he passed, so she'll pick him up tomorrow at seven. Her name is Esther Hartigan, supposedly one of the city's finest.'

'You are something. You could do a book – *Dog Ownership for the Career-Minded* or *Puppy Sense for the Upwardly Mobile*. It would be a wild success.'

All the time they had been talking, Buster had lain sleeping on Jennifer's lap. Happy to be somewhere soft and warm instead of in his pen at the breeder's, he groaned contentedly. He was a very handsome little puppy, with all the traits of a champion gold retriever – large, boxy head, eyes spaced evenly and not too far apart, and a glorious light colour. His ears indicated the colour he would be when full grown, a warm golden shade without a touch of red. His puppy fur felt like eiderdown.

'How big is this little fella going to get?' she asked, but was fearful of the answer.

'Well, he will be sizable. The breeder showed us his father, who weighs in at 110, pounds not kilos, that is.'

She just smiled and looked down at the adorable twelve-week-old fur ball. 'More champagne, please.'

Christopher was up the next morning at six with the puppy, 'preparing' him, he announced, for the walker. He said he had slept with the cage next to his bed, but Jennifer suggested that Buster may have enjoyed the comfort of the guest bed also.

Esther Hartigan arrived promptly at seven. She was a stern-looking woman who reminded Jennifer of a drill sergeant. She was carrying a leash that seemed more appropriate for a lion than the tiny puppy.

'Is that what you walk him on?' Jennifer tried to sound uneducated, not combative.

'Better he gets used to it at fifteen pounds than to spring it on him when he's over seventy-five, not too long from now,' replied Esther, surveying the tiny puppy.

'Sounds right to me,' she agreed.

And out they went, Buster looking slightly confused.

'Are you sure she's all right? I don't want to send poor Buster off to Central Park with just anyone,' she said to Nicholas.

186

'You're too much. Last night you weren't even sure if you wanted him to stay, now you're acting like a new mother.'

They all laughed. It hadn't taken her very long to become irreversibly attached to the new arrival.

When Jennifer and Nicholas asked Christopher later that morning what he would like to do on New Year's Eve, they were not surprised when he said he wanted to stay home and play with Buster. No fireworks, no trip with millions of the world's crazies in Times Square to see the apple drop? No . . . Buster. He was adamant. They looked at each other and shrugged their shoulders, but inside Jennifer wasn't the least bit disappointed.

Sidney hadn't made any plans for New Year. The holidays were a tough enough time for him anyway, and for the past two years he had stayed home alone, having his own private party to celebrate the end of the season, glad it was over, glad that things would now return to normal, or as near normal as they ever got in Manhattan.

When Jennifer found this out she insisted that he come over and have dinner with them. He refused the meal, but promised to stop by for a drink.

He stayed only a short time, just long enough for him and Nicholas to reacquaint themselves. It had been over ten years since they had met at the Museum. He voiced his approval of the way in which she had done the apartment, and he was sincerely mad about Buster.

'Can't you bring him to the studio?' he asked.

'Sure, Sidney, and the first time he eats one of the day's stories, what would be his fate?' Buster looked over in their direction, knowing he was being discussed.

After Sid left, they did exactly what Christopher had suggested – focused all of their attention on the new addition. Both dog and child were sound asleep, exhausted from the antics, long before midnight.

Jennifer and Nicholas each took a glass of wine and went outside on the terrace. An early evening snow had left a light dusting on the city. Central Park appeared before them as a

187

white wonderland. The lights of Tavern on the Green sparkled in the distance like an enormous jewel.

Linking their arms, they toasted the New Year.

'I hope you're as happy as you look. I've never seen you so beautiful,' Nicholas said.

'It's a lovely feeling for me to know that there's no place else in the world I'd rather be right now than here with you.'

'I do love you so. Let's be married when I return.'

She agreed at once. She was ready now.

They made love for the first time that year, in front of the fireplace, slowly, gently, wanting it to last forever. Now that they had made their lifelong commitment, their desire to please each other in every way possible was heightened. A large quilt was at arm's length in case Christopher should decide that he or Buster needed a midnight drink of water.

Knowing that Nicholas was leaving in the morning, and that they would be separated for several weeks, Jennifer refused to let him rest.

'You can catch up on your sleep on the plane. It will keep you out of trouble.'

'No complaints on this end,' he said as he slid his hands across the flatness of her stomach. She instinctively guided them down further, begging him to please her in the way she'd come to love.

21

CHRISTOPHER spent the first day after his father left for the Middle East with Jennifer's friend Wendy and her son, Sean. The two boys apparently hit it off with each other right away, and Jennifer was surprised when Wendy called the studio to ask if he could spend the night at their apartment. She was delighted and welcomed the opportunity to spend a night alone. She hadn't done that in over two weeks. She could fill the bath with Calèche and really relax.

By her calculations, Nicholas should have arrived in Lebanon almost a full day ago. The plan was to meet the three other members of the team, spend one night in the hotel, and go out from there the next morning.

She hoped he would be able to call them soon. Her fear was that, because of the fighting in the area, the phone lines were probably in no better shape than India's.

But her fear was eliminated that night when the phone rang as she and Christopher were halfway out of the door on their way to the movies.

He was fine, a little tired from the long trip, but everyone had arrived on schedule, and they were ready to head out tomorrow. They wanted to get some aerial shots of the more remote villages outside the city, so a helicopter had been arranged. He estimated it would take two full days of shooting to get the story.

'Sounds a little dangerous. Do you know the pilot?'

'Yes, love, not a thing for you to worry about. He's a fellow Brit who's been doing this kind of flying for years. I've got to hang up soon. Pass me on to the young man I've left behind to look after you. Is he behaving?'

'Very well, and I think he's having a wonderful time. Here, I'll let him tell you himself.' She handed the phone to the anxious little boy who couldn't wait to give his father all his news.

Christopher went on and on about his new friends, about taking Buster to the park in the snow, and about the film they were going to see.

As they sat in the darkness of the Coronet movie theatre on Third Avenue that night Jennifer looked over at Christopher, his face illuminated by the outrageous antics of Spielberg's latest blockbuster. She was so happy that the father of this charming little boy would be coming into her life for ever.

Christopher and his new friend, Sean, had been begging for a chance to go to the studio to watch Jennifer do the news. She had promised and tonight was the night. Wendy delivered them at the end of the day, right before airtime. They'd watch the programme and then go out for a pizza.

The big story that week was the weather. A severe winter storm had dumped more than thirty-one inches of snow in the metropolitan area, a new record for the decade. Airports and schools were closed, the poor and elderly were unable to get out to get food, and the homeless and heatless were freezing to death. For three nights now, the lead story had been the storm. Jennifer knew that they were providing a much needed service to residents of the city, but she couldn't keep her mind from wandering. She longed for the larger viewpoint and international coverage that were handled by the network anchors. Her impatience was growing, and she was anxious to take the next step. How and when would the opportunity arise? She determined to start concentrating to make it happen. As the ratings soared, so had her confidence. As soon as Christopher returned to London, she promised herself that she would begin a campaign to let people in the industry know she would soon be ready for a bigger slot.

*   *   *

The boys loved the studio. They asked hundreds of questions of anyone who had the patience to listen. Kevin gave them each a set of headphones, and they sat with the rest of the crew at the monitors during the broadcast. Andrea brought them Cokes and gave them a tour of the newsroom. Jennifer was sure they'd had enough and after she was off the air suggested a pepperoni-and-extra-cheese pie.

'Can't we stay and watch the tapes?' Christopher pleaded.

Plenty of work waited in her office. 'Of course, come and get me when you're ready to go. I'll be in my office.'

'Great. Thanks, Jennifer. We'll see you later.' And they were off.

A huge stack representing the afternoon's mail greeted her as she sat down at her desk. Halfway through the inter-office memos, requests for her to speak at various functions, and a plethora of junk mail, she looked up to see Sidney standing in the doorway, his hand clutching a telex, the paper still rounded at the edges. He looked terrified, as if he'd seen a ghost. In many ways, he had.

'Sid, what's wrong? You look awful.'

He didn't respond. He only raised the hand holding the just-received message. It was shaking.

'I . . . Jenn, oh, I . . .'

'Sidney, what is it?' She had never seen him react to a news story in this way. Not even the Grand Central disaster had shaken him up so much.

Suddenly fear overtook her. She realised that he was trying to tell her something, something personal. Thoughts of her father ran through her mind, that little cough had been fatal, one of her sisters, or maybe somehow Christopher had hurt himself in the newsroom. The thought that something might have happened to Nicholas never crossed her mind.

'Jenn, it's Nicholas,' he finally managed to say. He held up the telex – but she had already come around from the desk and grabbed it out of his hand.

'Oh, Jenn, I'm . . .' he continued, but she had already started to read it. He put his arm around her while she continued.

191

The paper, now crumpled from Sidney's hand, said:

TO: JENNIFER MARTIN, C/O CHANNEL 7, NYC
FR: THE BRITISH EMBASSY, BEIRUT, LEBANON

SORRY TO INFORM OF ACCIDENT INVOLVING
MR NICHOLAS TATE, PHOTOJOURNALIST
WORKING ON ASSIGNMENT OUTSIDE CITY.
HELICOPTER BROUGHT DOWN BY GUNFIRE.
MISTAKEN AS ENEMY TARGET. PILOT AND
UNIDENTIFIED CREWMEMBER KILLED. TATE IN
CRITICAL CONDITION AT AMERICAN UNIVER-
SITY HOSPITAL HERE. PLEASE CONTACT US
ASAP.

It was signed by the British Ambassador to Lebanon, Andrew
Knightbourne.

She covered the paper with her hands and turned to Sidney
in disbelief.

'Oh God, it's not possible. He was so sure there would be
no problems. We talked about it the other night, last night.'
She was too shocked to cry. She continued to look at him, not
seeing him, not hearing him, thinking only about what she
must do to help Nicholas now.

'Let's get Mr Knightbourne on the phone. I've got to find
out just how badly he's hurt, and what they're doing for him.'

'Jenn, it's four in the morning there. Should we wait a
while?'

'No,' she almost screamed, already on the phone to the
international operator.

An hour later she had Mr Knightbourne on the phone. He
explained that he did not know the extent of Nicholas's
injuries but thought they were quite serious, and he anticipated
going to the hospital to see him some time during the day. He
also said that Nicholas's papers indicated that his next of kin
was Mrs Jonathan Phillips and that in case of emergency, if
Mrs Phillips was unreachable, Jennifer Martin should be
contacted. He hoped he had acted correctly. She thanked him

192

and assured him he had. She also made him promise to call her back with a full report after he visited the hospital.

Suddenly, she remembered Christopher and Sean. She frantically dialled Wendy and explained the situation.

It wouldn't do any good to tell Christopher yet. It would only upset both of them even more. No, she had to wait, and Wendy immediately volunteered to come over and pick them up. Both boys could stay at her apartment that night. Good, that would give her all night to get more information.

Claiming she had a crisis that had to be solved at that very minute, she put Christopher in the car with Wendy and Sean. He thought that was fine, glad to be able to spend another night with his new friend.

Alone in her office, panic engulfed her and she began to cry. What if he was seriously hurt? If the attack had been forceful enough to kill two people, how could he not be seriously injured? She tried to pull herself together while going through her overloaded Rolodex in search of friends, business associates, or mere acquaintances who could be of help to her now. She tried to approach the situation as a professional journalist needing information, but her mind was shattered knowing that the life of the man she loved was in danger. She found the names of two journalists she knew in New York, both of whom had covered the Middle East for a time. Perhaps they could be of help. She pulled out those cards. Next, she needed assistance from the owners of Destinations Unlimited, the travel agency that booked the most unusual trips to exotic destinations. They would be able to help her locate Lisa and Jonathan, wherever they were on their journey through Tibet. It was too late to call them now, so she concentrated on trying to find her reporter friends.

It was after three a.m. when she was startled by the ringing of the phone. It was Andrew Knightbourne with a discouraging, frightening report on Nicholas's condition.

'He has, I'm afraid, incurred some very serious injuries. His left arm was severely crushed, and from the rescue squad's report it appears that he must have suffered a major impact to the left side of his head. He has been comatose since they brought him in two days ago. I strongly recommend that someone, either you or a member of his family, get over here as soon as you possibly can. I don't mean to pry, Miss Martin, but are you related to Mr Tate in any way?'

She swallowed hard and tried to keep her composure. 'I'm his fiancée. We were planning, no, we are going to be married soon.'

'I see,' he replied. 'Well, please keep me informed. I'll be waiting to hear from you about your arrival time. If you let me know in advance, I'll send a car for you.'

'That would be very kind, Mr Knightbourne. I'll telex you as soon as the arrangements are made. Right now I'm trying to locate Mr Tate's sister. She's on holiday with her husband.'

'Yes, I know, Tibet or somewhere. Well, good luck,' he said. And the connection was severed between Jennifer and the only person who had been to see Nicholas lying desperately ill in a hospital bed so far away.

Sidney came in as she was hanging up the phone. He had insisted on staying with her and had been busy trying his own connections, to see if they could contact Lisa.

'I've got a good lead. I remembered that Mary Langston, a friend over at NBC, has been to Tibet several times on her way to attempt Mt Everest. She has a lot of contacts in the country, and I read her Lisa's itinerary. She thinks they're probably pretty far inland by now. If they left Lhasa, the capital city, on schedule, which is rare she said, then they should be fairly close to Jih-k'a-tse, where there's a military airbase. She's going to try to call there and see if she can leave a message for them to get to Beirut at once. She also said she hopes they haven't started down the Brahmaputra yet, because once they've gone out on the river it's practically impossible to get in contact. She'll call us back later, as soon as she has anything. I gave her your number at the apartment also. But right now, young lady, you're going home. There's nothing more either of us can do tonight.'

As tired as she was, sleep eluded Jennifer. At four she went in and took Buster out of his bed in the kitchen. She sat in the

194

living room on the new down sofa, cradling the cuddly animal in her arms and crying so hard that he gave her a frightened look.

'Oh Buster, please let him be all right,' she whispered as she stroked his precious little head.

She must have dozed off for a little while, because the next thing she remembered was being awakened by a wet kiss on her cheek.

Wendy agreed to keep Christopher for another day or for as long as it took Jennifer to arrange their travel plans.

She called Anna at the house in London, who was, of course, badly shaken by the news. They decided that Christopher should return there at once and await the news in his own house. She made a reservation for him on the nine o'clock British Airways flight from JFK that evening.

Her own arrangements were going to be more difficult – it was necessary for any American wanting, for whatever reason, to travel to Lebanon to apply for a visa. There were many restrictions and much delay in getting the paperwork approved. Anyone who applied had to meet individually with the consul general at the Lebanese Consulate on East 76th Street, right around the corner from her apartment. Getting to the building, however, was the only easy part. Appointments were scheduled at the consul's convenience, and expediting the interview was based strictly on who one knew with clout. Again, without hesitation, Sidney intervened and found someone to make the call. When she arrived at the building the next morning, having done her best to disguise her looks – hair pulled back and large sunglasses, the consul was most gracious and ordered the visa to be issued at once. Sidney never revealed how he managed to do all of this. They were just both very happy that the man had not recognised her as the anchorwoman for Channel 7; allowing a US journalist into the country would have been completely out of the question, regardless of the power of Sidney's connections.

She and Christopher rode to the airport in silence. Jennifer had been as gentle as possible when she told him about his father, not wanting to alarm him unduly, but fearful of sugar-coating her description of Nicholas's condition. The British Airways stewardess was compassionate when Jennifer explained the situation, and they both tried to comfort him when he started to cry just as he was ready to board the plane.

'Jennifer,' he sobbed, 'please promise, please, to bring my dad back home soon.'

'I promise to do everything I can. We both love him very much. Now go on, have a nice sleep on the plane, and I'll be calling you and Anna soon.'

'He'll be OK though, won't he?' he asked. Children were unaccustomed to dancing around issues.

'I hope so, sweetie. Your Aunt Lisa and Uncle Jonathan and I are going over to be with him, to make sure he's getting the best care possible.' That was all she could get out before her tears came, and she held him tight against her chest, trying to hide her fear from him.

'Don't forget to give Buster his vitamins and those pills the doctor said he needed.' With that, Nicholas Tate's only child boarded the plane home.

Jennifer's trip was fraught with what seemed like interminable delays. As they flew two hours out of their way to avoid turbulent weather over Europe, she became more and more upset. She had left New York still not knowing whether Mary Langston's efforts to have a message delivered in one of the remotest parts of the world had been successful.

As always, Sidney had been extremely understanding and unbelievably supportive.

'Of course you have to leave as soon as you can get clearance,' he had insisted. 'Don't worry about a thing – Steve's ready to cover for you. You're useless here anyway, I wouldn't chance putting you on in your condition. Please, Jenn, just go and get him out of there and into the best medical facility you can if he's able to be moved, you've got the names of all the doctors in Zurich. They're waiting to hear from you.' Sidney had tracked down the best orthopaedic specialist and top neurosurgeon in Switzerland, anticipating that Nicholas might require surgery once he could be transported.

She spoke briefly with her parents, offering as few details as possible. They shared her concern and made her promise to be very careful. In her conversation with Pat she had divulged more of what she knew about the situation.

'Oh, Jenn, how terrible. I wish I could be there with you.'

'I know, me too,' she admitted. 'It would be so good. I'm so lonely and afraid.'

On the other end, Pat heard her sister trying to hide her sobs.

'Jenn, you've got to pull yourself together. You've got a long, long trip ahead of you, and you're going to need all the strength you can muster. You've got to do it for Nicholas's sake.'

At the sound of his name, her crying became more audible.

'I know. It's just that he is so far away, and no one can really tell me how he is. The hardest part is not being able to talk to him.'

Pat felt so helpless. She tried her hardest to cheer her sister up.

'Jenn, do you remember when we were little, and we really wanted something to happen, we'd all sit on the bed with our legs crossed and hold hands, and pray for whatever we wanted? Do you remember?'

'Yes,' Jennifer sobbed.

'Well, I know it sounds silly, but I'm going to do that tonight. I'll pretend I'm there with you, and . . .'

'Thanks, Pat. You're the best. I know you'll be thinking about me. I love you, and I'll call as soon as I can.'

The ambassador's car was waiting on the tarmac when her plane landed under cloudy, rain-drenched skies. He had arranged for priority customs clearance for her, a nearly impossible feat, for which she was eternally grateful.

The driver spoke only French, and when she answered him

in that language and began asking a myriad of questions about the city and the hospital, he was visibly surprised. He was polite but offered very little information, perhaps out of ignorance or instruction, it was hard to tell.

The route from the airfield to the hospital took them through what was left of downtown Beirut, at one time one of the most fashionable cities in the Middle East, its discos and casinos rivalling those of Monte Carlo or Paris.

But the lunacy of the religious disputes had destroyed all the beauty. What remained were the shells of world-class hotels and office buildings, graffiti madly scribbled on their once-trellised walls of marble and granite.

As the Rover with the Union Jack proudly displayed on the bonnet crawled cautiously through the thronged streets, Jennifer couldn't help but be reminded of the scene at Grand Central on the morning of the bombing. As she looked into the grief-stained faces of the people hurrying from building to building she thought about the madness of the world, the senseless crime, and man's seemingly endless capacity to destroy his fellow man.

But more than anything else, she thought about the changes that had occurred because of her chance meeting with Nicholas on that fateful morning. In that short period they had been together, Nicholas had enriched her life so dramatically, convincing her that she could become all she longed to be, that her extraordinary career goals did not preclude her also being a lover, a wife, and someday, a mother. He had shown her that all was possible and attainable if only she believed in herself. She remembered the night they had celebrated her promotion to anchor. Nicholas's excitement and enthusiasm had seemed to surpass hers. As the car pulled into the hospital entrance, there was not a trace of doubt in her mind that she would trade all her achievements and all her ambition if only she could take Nicholas home to England.

The American University Hospital was obviously not a top-notch medical facility, but it was better than she had expected. It too had suffered from the war. Gaping mortar holes in the outside walls and blown-out windows attested to the reality that nothing was safe from fanatics.

Almost everyone spoke French, so she had no trouble communicating her needs to the nurses and other hospital personnel. She was told that the attending physician was out of the building but would return shortly. That was fine, she responded, but she wanted to see Nicholas now. No, she was informed, that was impossible, the doctor had left specific instructions that she not be admitted before he returned. She pleaded with them, first using verbs she hadn't uttered since her early days in French class and then switching to street slang, the worst she could remember, but after a while she realised it was useless. She waited in the cold, dreary, makeshift waiting area, exhausted and frustrated.

Dr Roland Hix strolled down the hall two hours later. It seemed to Jennifer that she had been waiting an eternity, but it had given her time to regain her emotional strength.

'Hello, Miss Martin, I'm sorry to have kept you waiting. It is a most difficult city in which to move around. One is always delayed.'

He was charming and apparently highly qualified. Roland Hix had been educated at Cambridge and had come to Lebanon for reasons far beyond her understanding or caring. Her only concern was Nicholas's condition.

'He is very, very critically wounded,' the doctor began.

Jennifer sat in his office, listening to his every word and trying her best to be patient.

'When they first brought him in he was conscious but in a great deal of pain. He stayed awake, talking to us long enough for him to indicate where his papers were and whom to call. That's how we got to the British Ambassador and then to you. I think he realised that the two others had been killed. He talked a little more about his son, and then he lapsed into a coma. He's been slipping a little each day, and his temperature has steadily increased.'

'Can I see him now?' Being by his side was all she wanted. The specifics could be dealt with later, one at a time.

He stood up and directed her out of the office and down the hall.

Thanks to the intervention of Ambassador Knightbourne, Nicholas had been given a private room in an area separated from the war's other victims.

Nicholas looked like who he was – a man who had barely survived being shot down out of a helicopter. His head was bandaged, and his arm was in a cast held high over his head by traction wires. IVs were attached to his other arm, and an oxygen tent had been placed nearby. His eyes were closed, and he looked peaceful, not appearing to be experiencing any pain. For a moment, she stood in the doorway, shaking her head, her arms clutched around her waist, refusing to believe that this was the same vigorous, dynamic man she was engaged to marry.

Moving slowly to the side of the bed, she took his hand in hers, caressing the fingers of the man she loved so much. She squeezed them gently; there was no response. It was as if she were holding an inanimate object, a . . . no, she couldn't, wouldn't face that possibility.

'Oh, Nicholas, sweet, it's me, Jennifer. I'm here, darling, and you're going to be fine.'

Dr Hix excused himself, saying that one of the good points about the hospital was that there were no limits on visiting hours. She could stay as long as she pleased, but, because of the curfew imposed on the city, if she stayed past eight she would have to spend the night. She thanked him and told him that she definitely planned to stay the entire night. She would go to the hotel tomorrow, or the next day, or the next, just as soon as Nicholas's condition started improving.

His limp hand in hers, she talked to him throughout the night. With each 'I love you' she prayed for a response, any slight movement that would let her know he could hear her.

For two days, she sat by his bedside, oblivious to the constant stream of doctors and nurses coming in and out to check on him. She was determined to will Nicholas back to health.

When that will began to weaken, when she became so

frustrated that she wanted to beat her fists against his chest and demand that he awaken, that he come back to her, she picked up her bag and walked down the empty green-grey hallways to the vending machine. She had had more Coke in the last three days than in the past three years.

On the fifth day, word came from the Ambassador that he had received a telex from Lisa Phillips. She and Jonathan would be leaving Lhasa for Peking immediately. The next flight would be from Peking to Bahrain and then on to Beirut. If all went on schedule – highly unlikely for China Airlines – they would arrive the day after tomorrow.

Her strength renewed, Jennifer rushed back to Nicholas to tell him, fully expecting to elicit a reaction. But once again, nothing. That night as his temperature climbed to 106 degrees, he tossed and turned fitfully. It *had* to be a good sign, despite Dr Hix's warnings to the contrary.

The following day he returned to his earlier state, but his temperature held steady at 105 degrees.

She estimated by the number of Cokes she had drunk that it must have been about five a.m. when she heard a faint noise coming from his bed. She had been standing at the window watching the first signs of daybreak. He started coughing violently. It was the only sound he had made since her arrival a week ago.

'Nicholas, yes, Nick, I'm here, you're all right, yes, my love . . . take it easy,' she dropped his hand to his side and ran to the doorway to scream for his nurse.

More coughing, and then he eventually grew quiet. Minutes later she saw a flutter of eyelashes, and his glorious blue eyes opened slightly. They looked glassy and distant; he was unable to focus. The lids shut as slowly as they had opened.

'No, darling, keep them open, I'm here, it's Jennifer . . . you're all right, my love, Nicholas . . .'

They opened again. 'Jenn,' he whispered faintly.

'Yes, yes, it's me. Take it easy. Relax. Not too fast, love.'

'Jenn, where's Chris, Chris, where is he?'

'He's in London, darling, waiting for you to come home.

He's fine. He misses you. Anna is taking good care of him. They're all waiting for you.'

'No, Jenn, you don't understand.' He seemed disoriented.

'What is it, darling? What's wrong? Christopher, your son Christopher is fine, he's fine.' She held on to his still listless hand.

Suddenly his eyes widened. 'Jennifer, promise me . . .'

'Yes, what is it? I'll promise you whatever you want. Tell me.'

'Jenn, promise me you won't let Victoria take him. Please. She can't handle it. She's very ill.'

'Yes, Nicholas, I know, but you don't need to worry about that, you're going to be just fine. Lisa and Jonathan are on their way, and we're going to take you home.'

His voice grew stronger. 'Promise me. Please, I love you both so much.'

He waited for her answer.

'Yes, love, I promise.'

And with those final words, his glorious, kind eyes grew bright for a split second. She even thought she felt his hand curl around hers for a brief minute before he died.

It took her several minutes to realise that he was gone. And when she finally did, all the frustration of the past seven days poured out of her. She shook his shoulders and cried out for him.

Dr Hix had been in the room for the last ten minutes, and now he moved forward to try and comfort her, to move her away from the body. She collapsed into his arms and allowed him to lead her from the room. The sound of their shoes on the cold tiled floor resounded in her ears.

The two figures moving toward them from the end of the hallway must be a mirage, everything seemed so dreamlike now. But the pain and horror she saw on Lisa's face awakened Jennifer sharply to the truth.

'You're too late,' she cried. 'Ten minutes earlier, he was talking, he was asking about Christopher, and then suddenly – I'm so sorry, so sorry, I tried so hard, he . . .'

'OK, OK, it's enough,' Jonathan said as they each took one of her arms, releasing her from Dr Hix's grasp.

He left them alone in the cold, heartless hallway, alone with the grief caused by another senseless act of war.

Somehow Jonathan found the strength to make all the arrangements necessary to get the body shipped to London. It was difficult at best. Only the herculean efforts of the Ambassador eased the way.

Knowing that Nicholas's body was in the cargo area of the 727 as they flew toward his final resting ground was somehow very comforting to Jennifer. . . . She stared at the beautiful engagement ring he had given her less than a month ago. The dreams they had shared and the life they had hoped to spend together were symbolised in his gift of love. For ever, each time she looked at it she would see him bending down, rescuing it as it dropped from the glove, and then offering it up to her, his eyes full of hope for their future together.

Christopher's reaction when the three of them sat down to explain Nicholas's death was disbelief that turned quickly to anger toward Jennifer.

'You lied, Jennifer,' he shrieked. 'You lied, you promised me he'd be OK. You said that you were going to bring him home. I hate you, I hate . . .' and the rest of his words were muffled by his sobs. Jonathan held the boy tightly against him, a look of hopelessness on his face.

The funeral was held at a small country church in a London suburb. The burial was to take place immediately afterward in the private cemetery where his parents had been laid to rest over ten years before.

They stood under oversized black umbrellas in the late morning mist, which became heavier as the service continued. By the time Christopher stepped forward, Lisa's hand on top of his, guiding him to place a single flower on the casket, it was pouring.

Jennifer watched the service, standing at Jonathan's side. She felt somehow removed, as if this was still all a very bad nightmare.

Victoria did not attend the funeral. Her doctor advised against it. In fact, he would not allow her to be released from the centre, claiming her condition was far too unstable to handle something so traumatic.

They did not realise until much later what a blessing his judgement had been.

As the priest said his final words, Jennifer's thoughts took her back to the empty hospital room. They had returned later on the day of his death to claim his tattered belongings. The sight of his leather jacket, the one she had been so pleased to give him for Christmas, was more than she could take. With the jacket on her lap, she slowly started to empty the contents of the pockets. Film, keys, chewing gum, more film, mostly unexposed, filled most of the twenty-seven openings. The large left front pocket held a map of the area he had been flying over. She unfolded it and tried to locate the exact spot where he had been shot down. But then she thought, why does it matter? It's not going to change anything. The man she had cared so much for, had committed to spending the rest of her life with, was gone for ever. One more item was still in the pocket, another map she assumed. But when she reached in and took it out, she was surprised to see that Nicholas had been carrying a photograph that he had taken on Christmas morning. They were all there: Lisa, Jonathan and Christopher gathered around her new saddle, smiling faces, coffee cups in their hands; Jennifer smiling most happily of all. She threw the other things away, put the photo in her purse, and left the room, never glancing back at the torn jacket lying on the freshly made bed.

The night of the funeral service everyone stayed in the house on Grosvenor Crescent. Jennifer sat on the Chesterfield couch in the library, reliving the memories of the room until the sky became a lighter shade of grey and it was time for her to return to New York.

Lisa and Jonathan had agreed to begin proceedings at once to obtain custody of Christopher. Their feelings that Victoria was not capable of caring for him were further confirmed

204

after Jennifer told them about Nicholas's last words. They were sure that the courts would remain sympathetic to the mother, but they were willing to try anyway. Victoria's doctor felt it would be at least a few more months before she could be released. Enough time for them to begin legal action. Jennifer would come back to testify if the case went to trial.

Even the Concorde flight seemed to take for ever. Jennifer sat with her eyes shut tightly, summoning up all her strength to will away the pain in her heart. She tried to concentrate on work. She had assured Sid that she would be ready to go back on the air the night of her return, but now she wasn't so sure. In fact, she wasn't too sure of anything now. The past six months had been so joyous, so filled with happiness, and everything had seemed to be falling into place. But nothing was right now; it seemed as if it never would be again.

22

SIDNEY was waiting for her as she emerged from the customs maze at the international arrivals gate.

For the first time in a long while she couldn't respond when the agent asked why she had gone overseas: 'Business or pleasure?' She tried desperately to remember the times when it had been pleasure, and to block out the horrors of the last ten days.

'I didn't think you should have to ride in alone today,' Sidney said. For some reason, it seemed the most natural thing in the world for him to be there for her. They were always there for each other in times of greatest need.

'You're a sweet man,' and she managed a smile. It was important to her that he realise how much she appreciated his coming out to the airport on a blustery January day.

'No, Sid, I don't want to go home yet,' she said when she heard him give the driver instructions to go directly to her apartment. 'Let's just go to the studio. I need to get to work.'

'I understand. We've all missed you.'

She leaned back and rested her head against the seat. Exhausted, and somehow relieved to be home and in the company of her good friend, she fell asleep. Forty minutes later Sidney shook her gently as the car stopped in front of the studio.

'Are you sure you don't want to go home and rest for a while? I'll hold the edit meeting until later this afternoon,' he urged.

'No, no, I'm fine. That little nap did me a world of good. No, I'm ready to go in.'

Everyone welcomed her back warmly. She was the driving force that pulled the station together, and they all shared in her grief. Jennifer had always been a delightful, charming colleague, but no one had failed to notice how much happier she had been recently, how much in love she had been with Nicholas.

She stuck to her decision to go on that night. The make-up man had been put to the test in the afternoon. In stark contrast to the way she had looked recently when he had complimented her complexion, her skin was now sallow and drawn, with deep blue circles under her eyes.

Even she commented on it when they watched the tapes.

'Get some rest, you can't go on like this,' was Sid's advice when he dropped her off that night.

She couldn't bear to walk through the apartment. She threw her luggage down in the foyer, grabbed the mail, and headed for the bath. She hadn't even arranged to pick Buster up from Esther Hartigan. Although she missed the beautiful little animal, he was just one more reminder she wasn't ready to face quite yet.

The luxury of the Calèche bubbles enveloped her, and she began to relax. But she couldn't help staring at the button on the telephone, the one she had pressed a little over six months ago that had released Nicholas Tate's glorious voice into the room. The reality of what had happened struck her like lightning, and she suddenly realised that never again would she hear his voice.

23

FEBRUARY can be the single most depressing month of the year in New York City. The thrill of finding a great clothes bargain at the January clearance sales is long past, and for most people the thought of lying in a bikini under the scorching sun on some Caribbean island is only a distant dream.

But Jennifer had decided that the February blues would not attack her this year. She cancelled Esther's seven a.m. pick-up, and instead ran in Central Park with Buster in the morning. She joined a group of friends for a weekly indoor tennis match, vowed to learn Italian, and accepted Sidney's offer to be his regular companion at the Metropolitan Opera every Wednesday.

It seemed to work. Of course, there were those unavoidable times, almost always unexpected, when something would remind her of him, and she would fall apart completely. Sometimes she allowed herself the tears; other times she would dash out the door to a movie or call a friend for dinner.

None of it was easy. But she forced herself to make plans and keep them. All this was done, however, when she wasn't working, which became more and more rare. The studio was her main focus. Her relationship with the correspondents and feature editors developed to a level where they really depended on her comments and views before finalising a story. They were constantly soliciting her opinion, and she embraced the opportunity for additional input. They talked about what stories they should do, not only next week but next month. She began to take more control of the programme, to be prepared with background materials on big stories that could break soon. Her contributions started to shape the broadcast into a more buttoned-up, slicker operation. No detail was too small, and few escaped her scrutiny. The viewers sensed it, and the ratings continued to climb.

She also took the time to do more writing, and rewrites where necessary. Mostly the rewrites were for style, rarely for content or factual information. She wrote in a unique way that gave her very special imprint to the show.

Over the next several months the broadcast continued to improve, night by night. More and more frequently, they were able to air the prebroadcast run-through.

The audience came to enjoy her own particular manner of delivering the news, and she was convinced that that individual style was what made her so attractive to Walter Updike, the President of USBC. USBC had joined the ranks of ABC, NBC, and CBS as the fourth national network only four years earlier. In that remarkably short period the organisation had achieved a much higher status than anyone had originally predicted. The founders, all ex-CBS employees, had worked together to change and in many ways improve the content of network news in America. They sought the best journalists the country had to offer, and they rewarded them accordingly, both financially and professionally.

Walter Updike called Jennifer and asked her to lunch the first week of April. He suggested the Russian Tea Room. She counter-proposed the King Cole Room in the basement of the St Regis Hotel. It was clear that discretion was not one of his major concerns. At least her choice would give anyone who saw them an option; they could either be discussing business or having an affair or both.

She looked fabulous in a new Saint Laurent spring print shirtdress when she entered the restaurant. Jennifer still carried grief and loneliness with her constantly, but she had regained her exterior glow.

'Mr Updike, what a pleasure, I've been following the progress of your network since its inception. What a terrific story.'

'Thank you, Jennifer, I've – I should say, all the members of our top management have – been following your story pretty closely, too. We think you're exactly right to take over our anchor slot when John Handley moves on to a foreign assignment in July.'

The man certainly wasted no time getting to the point. His lack of bureaucratic nonsense was refreshing and very appealing. He continued, 'I don't need to tell you it's a wonderful opportunity, if it's what you want. Since I don't know anything about you personally, I hope I haven't been presumptuous in assuming that a network anchor is your goal.'

'Not at all,' she replied. Was she interested? It was a dream about to come true. The fact remained that the offer wasn't from one of the big three, but USBC had every chance of knocking one of the old-timers out, and this was a chance to be an integral part of the team that would do it. Wasn't that just as good as, or maybe even better than, going with something safer, something more established? Anyway, it didn't appear that any anchor changes were imminent at the other networks.

'It has been my dream, Mr Updike, for quite some time to become the first woman to anchor a network news programme.'

'Wonderful,' he said, and they toasted to further discussions.

It was almost three when she returned to the studio. She had listened intently to what Walter Updike had to say, and she liked his spirit, his dedication, and his conviction that they would succeed. By the time he had finished, she had formulated a hundred questions, many of which he was not prepared to answer on the spot. But it was clear that they were very interested in her, and a date was set to continue talking early in the following week.

'Can you believe it, Dad, they want me to head their nightly news?' She was practically yelling on the phone that night.

'Of course I believe it, my darling, I've always known you had what it takes, and USBC, I think it's wonderful, what a statement those guys are making. They're one sharp group. I think you'd be proud to be associated with them. And they should be happy to have you, too. You have so much to offer.' Praise that only a father could give, she thought. Ken Martin had been following the USBC story and knew almost as much about it as Jennifer.

'Right, Dad, as if they don't have any other choices.'

'Not as good as you, I'm sure. But there is one thing I would ask you.'

'Sure, anything, you know that.'

'If you decide to take the job, take a little break in between, some time off for yourself. Since, well, you know, since the accident, you've been working far too hard. Your mother and I are worried about you and would enjoy seeing you here for a few days. So would Pat and the twins. They're growing so fast you'll hardly recognise them. And Christie could use a visit . . .'

'OK, OK, I promise. But you don't need to worry about me. Thank heavens my work was there when I needed it. It has really pulled me through.'

'I know, darling, but it's not everything. You've got to start seeing people again.' She could sense that her mother had been hard at work on him.

'I agree, and I do see people, just not anyone special. It's way too early for that. It's going to take some time.'

'We only miss being with you, Jenn, you know that. Now promise me you'll call the minute you make your decision and that you'll be out soon. The garden looks beautiful – the twinflowers I planted for the girls are in full bloom. I want you to see it.'

'I'd like that very much. I miss you both.'

Buster was scratching at the front door, anxious to go on his nightly walk, and as usual she took him out the apartment building and down Madison Avenue for a few blocks. She had avoided thinking about how different she would have felt about the offer if Nicholas were still alive. But in the quiet of their walk, her mind wandered. It would have meant so much to him that she had even been offered the opportunity. Whether or not she would have taken it was another question. Who knew what they would have decided by now? Slowly, day by day, she was learning to live with questions like that, questions that would remain unanswered for all time.

That Wednesday, when they attended a lengthy, boring production of Verdi's *Don Carlos* at the Met, Sidney sensed an uneasiness in Jennifer. Afterwards, as they were leaving Lincoln Center, he asked her what was up.

'I realise that was the worst performance of the entire season, but you're really distant tonight. What's the matter?'

She wasn't prepared to discuss anything with him yet – after all, he was still her employer. USBC hadn't made their final offer, it was due tomorrow, which was one of the reasons her mind was so preoccupied.

'Nothing really, I'm just a little tired. But you're right. The opera was a real yawn.'

She could tell by the way he smiled at her that he didn't believe one word that she had said.

'I wish you wouldn't be so hesitant about discussing the USBC deal with me,' he said casually.

She shook her head in disbelief. How had he known about that? And for how long?

'You don't miss much. In fact, you don't miss anything.'

'Come on, Jenn, you didn't really expect me not to know about it.'

'I guess not,' she admitted. Then she started to laugh. 'The world is pretty small, isn't it?'

'Especially our world. You must remember I've got about fifteen years on you. I know almost everybody in this industry.'

'Why haven't you asked me about it before tonight then? You must know it's almost a done deal.'

'Nothing's done until the ink dries on both signatures. Besides, I was hoping you'd ask me for my thoughts, or at least an opinion on your contract.'

She'd given her lawyer USBC's proposed contract last week. They had met twice since and reviewed his suggested changes, before returning it to the network. She'd considered discussing it with Sid but wasn't sure what his reaction would be. They had such a complex relationship that sometimes it was difficult to predict which emotions would surface.

'Of course, you know I'd value your opinion very much. It's just that, well, I . . .'

'I know, you didn't know what to expect from me, what my reaction would be. I thought you knew me better than that by now, Jenn. You know I've always wanted the best for you. When Walt Updike called me to ask about you it was in early January, right after Nicholas's death. I told him I thought it would be better for him to wait a bit. He wasn't wild about waiting so long. They've been in need of a replacement for that schmuck they've got on now for a long time, but he said he'd take my suggestion and wait. But then I thought that wasn't really fair to you, that maybe the best thing for you, what you really needed, was a challenging spot that you could sink your teeth into. I thought it might be just what the doctor ordered to help you through this tough time. So I called him back a few weeks ago, said I'd rethought it, and then I heard from him again after you two met. Of course he thinks you're exactly what his network needs, and I couldn't agree with him more. He's convinced his board that they should do anything and everything to get you, so I hope you're holding out for whatever you want in the contract.'

'So you've known about this all along,' she said. 'I'm sorry I didn't discuss it with you earlier, but I'm glad Walter called when he did. Now that it's out in the open, I do have several things I'm dying to talk to you about.'

They decided to go to the Four Seasons, the quietest after-theatre, after-opera or after-whatever restaurant they could think of where they could discuss her deal.

'I'm awfully lucky to have you in my life,' she said, taking his arm as they descended the stairs at Lincoln Center and got into his waiting car.

They sat in the Grill Room until they were the last people in the restaurant. Even the Pool Room was empty as they walked past it to go below and claim their coats.

By evening's end they had discussed every point in the contract. They hammered out each section detail by detail. Jennifer's memory was so acute that when she reviewed the papers later at home, she was pleased to see they had covered all of the important areas. Sidney had shared the knowledge he had gained from many years of negotiating contracts and his experience saved her untold numbers of surprises and greatly aided her financially.

She exuded strength and confidence when she spoke with her attorney the next morning, advising him of the two small changes she wanted to make.

The ball was now in USBC's court. It seemed like only a matter of days before her long-held dream would come true and Jennifer Martin would set a precedent for women everywhere.

willing to settle for anything less than the best. Jennifer knew she had made the right decision in joining them.

'I'll leave you all with that thought. Welcome, Jennifer, we'll see you in July.'

With that brief introduction, Jennifer stepped back into the crowd to receive congratulations from the other members of the news team. She was very pleased with the way they had handled the announcement. She had only known about the award for a short time. The Peabody, a programme administered by the University of Georgia's School of Journalism, was the Academy Award of her industry. Winners were notified by phone that they had been selected to be honoured at the annual ceremony held in May in New York. Of course, she immediately realised that Sidney had been responsible for submitting her story. After the morning reception, she was even more thrilled that he had done so. The honour gave her the extra credibility she felt she needed to put her new colleagues at ease. Earlier that day she had arrived looking sensational in a new Donna Karan red suit, the fashionable short skirt accentuating her outstanding long legs, for breakfast with all the board members. She had met only two of them before, and her impressions of the other seven, only one of whom was a woman, were very favourable. They seemed sincerely interested in her opinions concerning the role of the media in delivering a fair, impartial report to the viewers, and their questions only served to reinforce the confidence that Walter Updike had in her. She felt several of the men's admiring glances, she accepted them for just that, for they were paying her far too much money, and had entered into far too serious a contract with her, to view her as anything less than an extremely capable professional.

After their private session, several key members of the media arrived for a short press conference. Most of the questions were fielded by the appropriate members of the board, but when Jennifer was specifically queried about her new role she gave concise answers in keeping with the network's strategy. She heard later through Sidney via Walter that the group had been most pleased with the way she had handled the meeting. It was always a lot easier when you had been in the other person's shoes before, she reminded him.

The cocktail party that evening was handled as well as the breakfast had been. Held in the fifty-eighth floor conference room of USBC's headquarters, invited members of the staff ate delicious hors d'oeuvres prepared by the in-house kitchen and were offered champagne or white wine. The building was on West 55th Street, and one entire side of the room faced south, offering a spectacular view of the Manhattan skyline. On the crystal-clear evening, she could see all the way downtown to the World Trade Center. Once again her confidence in the decision she had made was strengthened.

One of the toughest points of negotiation had been Jennifer's insistence that she be allowed to take several weeks off before the time she left Channel 7 and her first air date at USBC. Sidney had requested that she stay on with him for a month, giving him ample time to find a suitable replacement. He feared that the ratings they had worked so hard to build up would be hurt if there was a long hiatus between one permanent anchor and the next. Of course, there was no question in her mind that she would do whatever he asked to make it a smooth transition. Staying on for four weeks was a small concession.

They had finally agreed to a starting date the first Monday after the Fourth of July, giving her almost five weeks from the time she left until the start of her new assignment. She really felt that she needed to take that time to travel a little, to do some of the things she had been promising to do for a long time, and – even more important – to adjust mentally to the new life she was about to begin.

Her parents had been asking her to come for months, a legitimate request since she hadn't been to visit them since Thanksgiving. At Christopher's request, Jonathan and Lisa had called her a few days before to invite her to London to see him play in his rugby championship game the last week in June. Despite his tragic loss, he had managed to achieve his goal of becoming the team captain this year. It would be a very difficult trip for her, but one she felt she had to make. In addition to all of that, Christie had begged her to fly to Los Angeles for the Fourth of July weekend. So there was certainly no lack of things for her to do during the break.

At the apartment that night, exhausted yet exhilarated by the day's activities, Jennifer allowed her thoughts to wander. So many mixed emotions raced through her – elation that she was literally one step away from realising her long-held dream, sadness that it still seemed incomplete because there was no one special with whom to share the joy. She knew she would make headlines tomorrow, or if not tomorrow then the next day, in a story announcing her achievement as the first woman to be a network solo anchor. Women everywhere would read about her in articles in *Cosmopolitan*, *Elle*, *Self*, and *Working Woman*. At least those were the magazines that had contacted her so far. Surely more would follow. Jennifer Martin was an inspiration to women all over the world who shared a dream of climbing to the top of their profession. Women who wanted to make their own news stories, their own headlines.

Yes, she had done all that, and now there was even more hard work and dedication needed in order to stay on top, to continue her success. By all measures, she should be very happy, very content. Why was it then, that she still felt such a profound emptiness, such a strong feeling that she needed so much more?

25

CHRISTOPHER Tate led his teammates to an 8 to 4 hard-fought victory with all the sportsmanlike conduct his father had taught him was so important, so vital to being a true gentleman. Watching him throughout the match Jennifer thought he bore even more of a resemblance to Nicholas than he had when she first met him in the foyer of the house on Grosvenor Crescent less than a year ago. Christopher had grown up so much, adjusting remarkably well to a new life with his aunt and uncle.

The beautiful white house had been rented out, and Jonathan and Lisa had moved into town so that Christopher could finish the school year among his friends in London. They had taken Anna to live with them.

Jennifer went out alone one afternoon and walked the short distance from the Phillips house on Belgrave Square to Grosvenor Crescent. Standing across the narrow street, gazing up to the shuttered windows on the second floor, she relived the lovely memories of the times they had shared there.

'May I help you? Miss, are you all right?'

She was startled by the woman's voice. Lost in her thoughts, she hadn't noticed a well-dressed woman with a small child walk up the street and turn to enter No. 18.

'No, no, I'm fine,' she replied weakly.

'Are you sure?' she asked again, leaving the little girl at the front door and crossing the street to speak with Jennifer.

'You look as if you're about to faint. May I offer you a cup of tea? You're welcome to come in for a moment.'

The thought of going inside Nicholas's house made Jennifer's entire body weak.

'No, no, thank you. I must be going now.' She attempted to sound gracious.

'Are you looking for someone on the street?' the woman continued. 'I don't know everyone. We only moved here last month. But you're welcome to call from my home if you want.'

'You're very kind,' Jennifer offered. 'But I really must be going. I just wanted to see Nicholas's house once more.'

'Oh, I'm so sorry. You must've known the owner. He certainly must've been a lovely man, such a tragedy. The house was so beautifully kept, and the kitchen, my heavens, what a joy!'

Jennifer could almost hear Nicholas singing as he put the finishing touches on the exquisite meal he had prepared for her, Anna's shocked voice as she surveyed the extraordinary mess he had created.

She tried her hardest to smile. 'I really must be going now,' she said. Turning sharply and allowing no time for the woman to respond, she hurried down the street. It still hurt – almost more than she could bear – but it was over now, and to the extent she could, she was ready to close this chapter of her life and begin a new one, starting next week.

Tomorrow she would fly from London over the pole to Los Angeles to spend the holiday weekend with Christie. Knowing her sister, she would have every minute planned with one activity or another, allowing no time for Jennifer's mind to wander.

Her prediction had been absolutely accurate, for when she boarded the plane for New York on Sunday, after three days on the West Coast, she was exhausted from the tennis, the shopping and the parties that went on until all hours. Christie's social schedule was as rigorous and demanding as her work schedule, so they were constantly changing outfits and rushing off in her new bright red Porsche 944 Turbo to someone's house tucked away in the Hollywood Hills or Beverly Hills for another poolside lunch or dinner.

Christie had made every effort to guarantee that Jennifer had a good time. She introduced her to all her friends. It was obvious that Christie was very proud of her, for she had told them all about her achievements, as well as her new position. Jennifer fitted right into the LA scene. People who didn't know her well often suggested that she looked like a typical California girl. Just yesterday, someone had asked her how she managed to keep her healthy good looks living in a city like New York. They insisted that it took the California climate to maintain such glowing beauty. She smiled distantly at the comment, recalling what Nick had once said about California women.

At the parties they went to, she was always surrounded by men, many of whom found her very attractive. Nothing could have been further from her thoughts than dating or becoming interested in any of them. That's why she was so astounded when Christie yelled to her while she was in the pool one afternoon that the telephone was for her.

'Who is it?' she yelled back, not wanting to move one inch from the comfort of the raft.

'It's Eric Diamond. Hurry up, he's calling from the hospital.'

'Who?'

'Eric Diamond,' she yelled again, her voice an octave higher. 'You remember the guy you met at Jeremy and Sheila's last night? I think he wants to ask you out.'

She vaguely remembered being introduced to someone by that name.

'Tell him I'm not here.'

'Are you crazy?' Christie had now come outside and was standing by the edge of the pool, glaring down at her older sister. 'Have you lost your senses? It's Eric and he wants you to go to dinner with him. Now get out of the pool right now and talk to him.'

'No,' Jennifer said. 'I don't care if it's Jack Nicholson, I'm

221

not interested. Now please, Christie, tell him I'm not here.' And with that she turned herself over on the raft and paddled into a sunny area. In the distance, she heard Christie slam the sliding glass door after her.

Minutes later she was back. 'Now please explain why you are not at all receptive to the idea of having an innocent dinner with Eric Diamond.'

Jennifer rolled over on her back.

'First of all, I hardly remember who he is.'

'Who he is?' Christie was amazed. 'He's only the most handsome, most charming and most gifted plastic surgeon at UCLA. The nurses faint in the halls when he arrives for surgery.'

'Sounds a little soap operaish to me,' Jennifer said. 'Is he the blond sort of big guy who came with two other men?'

'Oh, you know damned well that's exactly who he is. Should I call him back and tell him you've come to your senses?'

'No, Christie, please. Remember, I'm the one who never dated much to begin with, and now it's even harder.'

'Oh, I suppose, but he's only asking you for dinner. It's not as if he's asking you to marry him.' The second the words left her mouth, Christie regretted them. She saw the pain flood Jennifer's face, and she felt terrible.

'Oh, Jenn, I didn't mean it. I'm so sorry. It's just that . . .' Christie tried desperately to apologise.

'It's OK, really. I only wish everyone wouldn't try to be so helpful. I'm not ready to see anyone yet. Not even for a casual date. It's still too painful. All I really want to do is get back to New York and get to work.'

'I understand, and I'm really sorry I pushed you so hard. So, now that you don't have a hot date tonight, what would you like to do?'

'How about a trip to Tower Records followed by some powerful margaritas and real Mexican food, not the kind they try to pass off on us back East?'

'I'm starving already. Hurry up and get dried off.'

26

'*GET* up and go show them how it's done,' said the familiar voice over the phone.

'I'm already up, dressed, and ready to go. The question is what are *you* doing awake and speaking at this hour?' she asked Sid.

'I set my alarm so I wouldn't miss you before you left. I tried you until late last night, but you must have taken the red eye.'

'No, I took the three o'clock, but with all of the holiday traffic, it was well after one by the time I got home. How are you? What's the news from the past few weeks? They went so fast, it's hard to believe today's the day.'

'Not much new. I'll bring you up to date later on. How about you, are you nervous?'

'Are you kidding? I've been up talking with Buster since dawn. He's giving me the last-minute encouragement I need.'

'That's good. I know you'll be fine. If you need me, I'll be at the studio all day, and probably most of the night. It's tough without you. I didn't realise how much extra work you did around here.'

'It's good to hear. I miss you too. Let's talk after my premiere,' she laughed. 'I hope I won't be shaking before the entire nation.'

'You'll be great. Call me later if you need a last-minute pep-talk.'

'You're the best,' she said before she hung up, really meaning it.

Regardless of the position, from secretary to president, the first day of any new job is always a trying experience. Jennifer concentrated, listening carefully, wanting to learn everything about the new studio as fast as she could, but it was still overwhelming. By the time they were ready to tape the run-through that afternoon, she was exhausted. The monitors were in a different place from where she was accustomed to, the set and the area where she kept her papers were totally different, and her earpiece kept falling out. She took Sidney up on his offer of a last-minute call.

'Hold on, Jennifer,' Cindy said, 'he's around here somewhere. He asked me to find him if you called. I'm gonna put you on hold, I'll be right back. I sure wish you were still here, he's been a super-grump ever since you left.'

Jennifer laughed. 'Thanks, Cindy. It's good to know I have a place to go back to if I screw up tonight.'

'Oh God, that's right, you start tonight. Wait, I'll go get him right now. Good luck. We'll all be watching you over here. Hold on.'

Sidney's reassuring words did pep her up, and she went back into the newsroom with renewed energy. If she was able to get through tonight's programme without going on live, she would be over a big hurdle. To her astonishment they were able to air the second run-through, and later on when they reviewed the tape, the crew clapped and congratulated her on the success of her first night.

'I don't know what you were worried about. You did brilliantly,' Sidney told her later that night.

She had gone straight home after the broadcast and was almost asleep when the phone rang.

'Thank you, thank you. Not bad for a girl, huh?'

He laughed.

'It's all a credit to one of my visiting journalism professors. He taught me everything I know.'

'He must be some crackerjack guy! But I really believe it was the pearls you were wearing. I've heard they guarantee a flawless broadcast.'

She had worn her Christmas present from him with the

fancy diamond clasp turned to the back so she wouldn't appear too glitzy, too sophisticated for the middle-American viewers.

They teased each other some more and she was aware of how good it felt to really laugh again.

'There's a lot to be said for performance under pressure. I wonder if every night were opening night, could one continue to give a super broadcast?'

'You'll be even better once you can relax and inject your own personality into the programme, exactly like you did at Channel 7.'

'That reminds me, it was selfish of me not to ask sooner, how's Carl doing?' Carl was her replacement on the six o'clock news.

'He's fine. Not of your calibre of course, but he'll do fine. I'm comfortable enough with him that I've finally scheduled my long overdue visit to some of the other affiliates. I'm set to leave next week. I'll be gone for two, maybe two-and-a-half weeks, depending on how it goes.'

Suddenly she became anxious thinking about his being out of town for so long. A weekend or a few days, OK, but somehow two weeks sounded like an eternity.

'Where are you going?' she asked, trying to hide the anxiety in her voice.

'A selection of garden spots such as Detroit and Cleveland. But the second week takes a turn for the better – I'll be in LA and San Francisco. I'll try to spend the weekend there. What are the new hot spots?'

'In San Francisco, how would I know?'

'Weren't you out there last week?'

'Yes, but only in LA.'

'I'm very surprised at you. You were all the way out there and didn't even go up for a day? I thought you loved it.'

'I do, it's one of my favourite cities, but I was with Christie, and she had planned so many things for us to do that there wasn't any time left. Now that we're talking about it, I'm sorry I didn't go, it's always such a relief to be there this time

225

of year. The city is so cool and refreshing in August after the Eastern triple H days.'

'Triple H?'

'Don't you listen to the meteorologists? They're always sliding that into the forecasts – hazy, hot and humid.'

'Remarkably interesting. Well, I've got an idea. Since you missed it last week, why not come out and join me for the weekend?'

She hesitated.

'Jenn, come on, say yes, or at least say you'll think about it. It's still three weeks away. By that time you'll have USBC down pat. You'll probably even know where your Tele-Prompter is.'

'You wise ass, I was wondering when you'd say something.'

There was a split second during that night's programme, discernible only to those in the business, when Jennifer had been confused about the position of her TelePrompter. It had changed because of the position of the photograph on the screen behind her.

'I can't let you get away thinking there's no room for improvement. You'd be impossible to deal with!'

'You're right,' she agreed.

'So, promise to think about coming out? It will be fun.'

'I promise.'

27

THE difference between being a local affiliate anchor-person and a national network anchor was tantamount to the difference between playing a casual game of tennis at the local club and competing on centre court at Wimbledon. The rules of the game were basically the same, but the difference in the audience was overwhelming. When Jennifer reviewed the ratings, studied the numbers, and realised that each evening she was reaching tens of millions of Americans with the broadcast, she was astounded.

Almost overnight she had become a media celebrity. Her great looks, her recognised talent as a reporter, and the fact that she was the first woman to hold the position made her a primary target for the media. She was hounded constantly to do interviews, speak at various functions, and appear on a myriad of television chat shows.

She wanted to accommodate as many of the requests as her schedule allowed, but she was careful only to accept those where she could control the topics of discussion. She was generous with her extra time when it benefited charities or causes which interested her, like AIDS or Alzheimer's disease, or the New York City Ballet.

One chat show hostess, Nancy Demarchellier, was particularly aggressive. Her show, *Women on Top*, which she had started only two seasons ago, was one of the most popular, widely watched new programmes. The show's objective was to interview women who were presidents or CEOs of companies, or women such as Jennifer who had set precedents in their field. A former political reporter, Nancy's questions were always hard hitting, and sometimes vicious. She often tried to find the dark side or the hidden past of a woman's rise to the top. Even though Jennifer had nothing to hide on either her professional or personal side, she was afraid that Nancy would uncover her tragic experience with Nicholas, and would end up making that the focus of the interview. The possibility that that could happen was still too painful for her to contemplate. When she accepted Nancy's invitation to lunch to discuss her appearance on the show, Jennifer tried her hardest to decline graciously.

'Nancy, the time isn't right now,' she insisted. They had only been served the salad course of their meal at Le Cirque, and already Nancy had started to insist on her appearance. It was going to be a long lunch.

'Jennifer, I simply *must* have you on the show, and the sooner the better, both for you and me,' replied the expensively yet atrociously dressed woman. Nancy leaned even closer to her on the plush upholstered banquettes, looking as if she were about to reveal one of the secrets of the universe. 'My viewers are craving to hear from you about you. You are news, news, news! Not only do you deliver it, you *are* it,' and she laughed a little too loudly for the conservative atmosphere of the elegant restaurant.

'Nancy, please,' Jennifer continued, but was immediately interrupted.

'No please. Look, you know as well as I do the overwhelming success my show has been. Your appearance will skyrocket your ratings even higher than they are now. Besides, the personal press for you is fantastic. Who knows what you're going to want to do next, after you've come this far? You're not about to stop now, if I know you.'

The woman was really revolting, and Jennifer prayed that they would bring the rest of the meal at once. She knew, however, that Nancy was also right in many respects. And she was far too smart to burn bridges with this powerful, vociferous animal.

The lunch dragged on. Nancy would allow only brief

switches in the conversation from her main objective. Two sentences later, she was back to talking about the show.

'OK, OK,' Jennifer agreed as Nancy was paying the bill, 'I will appear on your show.'

Immediately Nancy's face broke into a celebratory grin.

'But not right now,' she continued. 'I want some time, I'm not certain how long, to really get settled at USBC. It's a world of difference from a local station, and in a few months I'll have a lot more to tell your viewers. Believe me, it will be a much more powerful piece if I've really had a chance not just to get my feet wet, which is the case now, but to have been totally submerged.'

'How much time?' Nancy demanded. Jennifer was sure that she had only heard her first sentence, none of the supporting logic that had followed.

'I don't know, a couple of months, maybe after the fall season.'

'Not very definite, I must say,' she complained. 'But I'm going to hold you to your word.'

The air outside on 65th Street was refreshing.

'Thank you for lunch,' Jennifer said. It was after two, way past time for her to be back at the studio.

'I'll be calling you. Don't forget your promise to me,' Nancy said.

As Jennifer hailed a cab on Park Avenue, she thought there were very few things in life a person could count on. Federal Express service was one of them. Nancy's call was another.

28

JENNIFER faithfully kept her promise to Sid, and three weeks later, right after the Friday night news, she left for the City by the Bay.

She always found that San Francisco was a city that from year to year, visit to visit, changed very little. The Transamerica pyramid and the majestic Colt Tower continued to dominate the skyline, despite the recent construction surge in the financial and Embarcadero districts.

She and Jeffrey used to fly out fairly often from Kansas City to spend long weekends. They craved the sophistication, the cool evening breeze, the superb restaurants, and the unparalleled views. He would sometimes combine the trip with his attendance at one of the numerous medical conventions the city attracted. She felt she knew the city pretty well; certainly she was familiar with the locations of all the smart boutiques and top hotels, which was why she was so surprised when Sid gave her the address of the hotel where they would be staying.

'Are you sure?' she asked. 'That address sounds very residential, somewhere out in Pacific Heights or Cow Hollow,' as the area just up from the Marina, around the Union Street bars and cafés, was called.

'Trust me on this one, Jennifer. It's wonderful,' he insisted. 'I'll be sure a car is waiting for you when you arrive. Can't wait to see you.'

True to his word, Sidney had arranged for the hotel to pick her up in one of their vintage cars. The white Vanden Plas limo was attracting the attention of many arriving passengers outside the terminal building. She rode in comfort to her destination.

The Sherman House, located as Jennifer had predicted in a residential area, was one of the most charming small hotels she had ever seen, far surpassing anything else in the States, and on a par with the finest relais in Europe. Built in 1876, it was originally the residence of Leander Sherman, founder of the Sherman Clay Music Company. After many hard-fought battles for planning permission, it had been lovingly renovated to create a fifteen-room luxury hotel. It was all sparkling white, in elegant contrast to some of its Victorian neighbours whose gingerbread trim had been painted in a multitude of colours. The reception area was extremely understated, only a small desk manned by a well-dressed gentleman, who handed out large brass keys with a heavy metal ball attached, a gentle reminder that guests should leave their keys with him when they weren't in their rooms. But there was no reason to leave the luxury of the beautifully decorated rooms, each with its own fireplace, and many with a terrace facing the San Francisco Bay and the Golden Gate Bridge.

Sidney had reserved a room for her on the floor directly below his. When the bellman opened the door and stepped aside to allow her to enter, she was immediately reminded of one of the many charmingly decorated guest bedrooms in Lisa and Jonathan's house in the country. The oversized couch and chairs were covered in yellow-and-white striped silk, and fragrant plates of potpourri had been placed on the brass-bound Regency-style tables. The four-poster canopy bed draped in rich Stroheim & Romann fabrics was as inviting and elegant as any she had ever seen. When she sat on it she was amazed to find that the entire mattress was made of down which enveloped her totally. Not terrific for a bad back, she assumed, but for two nights she couldn't have been happier.

In stark contrast to the old English look of the bedroom, the bathroom was sleek, very high-tech, and all detailed in highly polished black granite with mirror-covered walls. It was extremely luxurious: double sinks, a bidet, a Jacuzzi and steam cabinet in the combined bath and shower. Thick white towels of all sizes, from face cloths to giant bath sheets, were stacked up on the brass towel rails. A robe of the same soft terry hung on the back of the door. All the amenities, ample supplies of shampoo, conditioner, shower gel, and body lotion were neatly displayed in flat wicker baskets. And they were all from Hermès, Calèche for the woman and Equipage for men. When she saw them she thought about the many Christmas boxes embossed with the Hermès logo and all of the other wonderful things she had been given from there. Surprisingly, this time the memories weren't as painful, and she smiled to herself. Maybe, as so many people had suggested, time really was a cure, and just maybe, maybe, she was nearing the point where her memories wouldn't keep her from wanting to love again.

Sidney's note said he would be working until about seven, so she unpacked, took a leisurely whirlpool bath, and then dressed in navy gabardine Saint Laurent pleated pants and one of the luscious cashmere sweaters Nicholas had given her. It felt great to wear something other than cotton or linen in August, and Jennifer's outfit was perfect for the San Francisco weather, crystal clear skies with temperatures in the sixties that would drop dramatically into the low fifties as the early evening fog rolled in across the bay.

Downstairs in the small drinks lounge on the second floor, the guests were gathering. Some were just coming in from a day of sightseeing or shopping. Others were already dressed, ready to have drinks at one of the ten tables in the charming dining room overlooking the bay.

The hotel was fabulous, and she told Sidney so when he arrived a few minutes later and found her sitting quietly, listening to the piano player.

'I told you to trust me. When have I ever led you astray?' He smiled, kissing her warmly on both cheeks.

'Not recently that I can recall, but I'm sure you must have at some point.'

'Not likely. Anyway, how do you like your room? I made them show me every available one. Each one is different, all very special, but I picked the one you're in because of the terrace; thought you might enjoy it. You're right below me.'

'It's perfect. It seems as if we're in Europe rather than San Francisco. I couldn't be happier you asked me to come.'

They toasted to a wonderful weekend.

Their evening that night was marred by slow, impertinent service and mediocre food in an Italian restaurant on Telegraph Hill that they had both remembered as being very good.

They were disappointed but made the best of it with sparkling conversation and a game they had devised years ago where they guessed the occupation and favourite sexual fantasy of other diners in the restaurant. They laughed so hard that they barely noticed that the coffee they had ordered was delayed half an hour in getting to their table. Jennifer had always known Sidney was as fascinating a man as she had ever met. Tonight he seemed more amusing and entertaining than ever.

In the peaceful, darkened hallway on the hotel's second floor, Sidney kissed her gently on the cheek and said good night.

The feather bed engulfed her, but she lay awake, unable to sleep. She watched the fire that had been built by the porter while they were out die down to bright red embers. But still she was wide awake, despite the three-hour time difference, which now made it four in the morning in New York, and the bottle of Barola they had shared.

Suddenly she was drawn to the terrace, the need to breathe the cool moist air was overwhelming. Wrapped snugly in the hotel's terry robe, she opened the French windows and stepped out into the night. Still burning lights of Sausalito and Tiburon were barely visible across the blackness of the bay. The fog surrounding the Golden Gate Bridge was so thick that only the aeroplane warning lights occasionally flashed through. The watch tower on Alcatraz Island appeared like a surrealistic demon through the dense greyness.

'It shouldn't be so hard to sleep. You've had a long day.' Sidney's voice from the terrace above startled her, but she welcomed the interruption.

'I know, I don't have any excuses to offer. What's yours?' she asked, tilting her head back to look up at him, her arms clutched around her, trying to keep warm in the damp air.

'Thinking about you,' he answered.

She continued to stand in the darkness, smiling up at him. There were foghorns bleating in the distance.

'Come upstairs to me, Jenn.'

Slowly she climbed the outside staircase that connected the terraces, not knowing exactly why she was going, but aware that it was something she wanted very much to do. As he had so many times before, he held her in his arms, sheltering her from the cold. But this time his touch was different, now more than the embrace of a friend, it was the caress of a lover. They stood together for a long while, long enough for Jennifer's stick-straight hair to begin to curl from the humidity.

Inside his room, he loosened the belt of her robe and slid it off her shoulders. She stood perfectly still in her pale peach silk nightgown. The only light in the room came from the newly fuelled fire.

'You are so beautiful, Jenn. As beautiful as I've always dreamed you'd be.'

She had never felt so strange. They knew each other so well, and had known each other in so many intimate ways for so long, but they had never shared a physical intimacy. The thought of it was now very exciting to her.

'Come to bed with me.'

Sidney was a skilful yet hesitant lover. She sensed his nervousness and tried to comfort him, to relax him with gentleness. She stroked his wonderfully firm body, his long slender legs, and his enormous hardness. His movements became frenzied and she guided him slowly into her wetness. He could not contain the orgasm he had thought about so often in years past.

234

'Oh, Jenn, I love you so very much, for so long I've loved you.' And he allowed his tears to fall as he had once before, only this time they were tears of bliss.

She slept soundly for a while, but was awakened a short time later by a much more confident lover, eager to please her in every way imaginable.

'OK, OK, I give up,' she giggled after her fourth or fifth climax. 'You'd better give me some sustenance, or you'll be up on criminal charges.'

'Are you begging me to stop?' he asked hopefully. 'Have I satisfied your every need?'

'For the moment, yes,' she answered.

And he had satisfied her, not only physically but emotionally as well. She didn't allow herself to make comparisons with Nicholas or Jeffrey or anyone else. As far as she was concerned, they were the past, a past not to be forgotten, but cherished for its lovely memories. Sidney was her future.

'Good.' He was so pleased. 'Now you can eat.'

It was after four when they finally left the room that day.

29

THEY spent their remaining day and a half in San Francisco wandering around the city, visiting art galleries, and exploring the shops in Chinatown. They even went into a porno shop in North Beach, laughing at most of the items, genuinely puzzled by others. They acted like two children, and they were not ashamed or embarrassed by their behaviour, for they both realised what was happening to them. After so many years, after sharing such a variety of experiences, they had discovered a wonderful new dimension in their relationship, and they were enjoying every second of it.

They decided to extend their weekend for as long as possible, and they changed their flight reservations from the three o'clock departure to the red eye, which left at ten that night. Knowing that the next day would be endless, Jennifer tried to sleep on the way home. She succeeded in doing that until Sidney gently awakened her several hours after they had departed San Francisco. He leaned over and kissed her softly. She opened her eyes slowly, taking a second or two to remember where she was. The light in the first-class section had been dimmed, and most of the passengers had donned eyeshades and were sleeping soundly.

She smiled drowsily up at him.

'Marry me, Jenn,' were his only words.

This time there was no hesitation in her answer. She had thought he would ask her, maybe not this soon, but eventually. She had already decided on her response.

'Yes, Sid, yes, I will,' and they embraced each other tightly.

Lulled back to sleep by the humming of the engines, they awakened when the captain announced they were about to land at Kennedy.

'Do you think that since I asked you to marry me while we were flying over Wayzata I've eliminated the need to ask your father for your hand?' Sid asked in the car on the way in to Manhattan.

'Absolutely not,' she retorted. 'Besides, how did you know where we were?'

'I asked the pilot to let me know. Told him it was extremely important that the stewardess advise me when we were in that position. And she did it. Actually, we were a little north of Minnesota, but it was the thought that counted in this case.'

'You're too much, but you'll still have to go there.' She hesitated. 'No, I've got a better idea. We'll invite them to New York for the wedding. At that point, it'll be too late for protest. You'll be stuck with me.'

'Great,' he said, pulling her next to him, 'it's what I've wanted for so long.'

The same week that she agreed to marry Sidney Lachman, Jennifer reported on the first anniversary of the Grand Central bombing. It was hard to believe that only one year ago the madness of Richard Collier had changed the fate of so many families, made twelve women widows overnight and left so many children to grow up without fathers, all of this in addition to the trauma it inflicted on the financial community. His life sentence seemed small recompense for such a far-reaching crime.

It was also the day on which Nicholas Tate had entered her life.

Alone with her thoughts that evening twelve months later, she saw his face clearly as he looked down on her, his bag of film supporting her head. She could feel his kind eyes gaze into hers, and hear his lovely, comforting, English voice, 'Hello there, pretty lady. How are you feeling?'

237

She took Buster for a long walk down Fifth Avenue and across Central Park. She was oblivious to the people who stared at her as the tears rolled down her face. She cried briefly for his memory, but the tears were also for the future, and her new life with Sid. She was so blessed to have so much love in her life now, so much happiness despite the pain of the past.

30

JENNIFER Carolyn Martin and Sidney Alan Lachman planned to be wed on December 9th in a simple ceremony at the Hotel Plaza Athénée in New York. They had decided to make it a small, intimate celebration and invite only their closest family and friends.

Sidney had been married in a very formal ceremony many years ago, and Jennifer refused to attempt to create an enormous event like the one she had once dreamed of, once planned to have with Nicholas. No, this was their wedding, and it was unfair to both of them to dwell on the past.

Marion and Ken had arrived a week earlier to help her with the final details. They had been overwhelmingly pleased for her, and even her mother had accepted Sidney as a welcome member of their family. Not once did she make a negative comment about his age or his previous marriage. For that Jennifer was enormously thankful, and she felt closer to her mother than at any time in the past. Ken, of course, was supportive of anything that was going to add to his oldest daughter's happiness.

The day of the wedding was cold and blustery, but crystal clear, with temperatures in the forties. Jennifer walked down Madison Avenue to Tiffany's early in the morning to pick up some last-minute Christmas gifts. Her attire, jeans and a heavy red turtleneck sweater with her fisher coat thrown over her shoulders, was most unbridelike. But she still had many hours before the four o'clock ceremony to make the transformation into bridal splendour.

The Plaza Athénée had been home to her for the last three weeks. She had sold her apartment to a lovely couple from Atlanta who she hoped would be very happy there. On the night before the closing, she had gone up to take a last look. Except for the built-in bookcases, it was just as empty as it had been on the night she had brought Nicholas here for the first time. Standing on the terrace in the freezing cold, she looked out and saw the light dusting of snow that had fallen earlier in the day. It was the same view she had shared with Nicholas almost a year ago on New Year's Eve. She relived the evening, Christopher and Buster asleep in the small bedroom, and she and Nicholas lying entwined in each other's arms, spent from the very last time they would ever make love together. She remained on the terrace and allowed herself tears for the past. After what seemed a very long time, she walked slowly through the apartment, shutting off the lights, and then gently closing the front door behind her. She left her set of keys with Alberto, hugged him, and promised to stop by when she was in the neighbourhood. The wind was harsh and drying against her tear-stained face, but she held her head high as she walked down Park Avenue on her way back to the hotel.

She and Sid had purchased a new duplex penthouse on the corner of Park Avenue at 68th Street. It was extraordinarily spacious, in true pre-war style, with three bedrooms and three full bathrooms upstairs. On the lower floor there was an enormous living room, a mahogany-panelled library, and a formal dining room. The maids' quarters were off the kitchen. The apartment faced south to midtown Manhattan, and east to the river. Its wide terrace surrounded both sides, providing Buster with much-needed outdoor access, and them with beautiful views. They had purchased the co-op in September, and the very next week Zajac & Callahan had begun renovation. They promised it would be complete and ready to move into when Jennifer and Sidney returned from their honeymoon in Tuscany two weeks later. She loved the apartment, but she loved even more the idea of being able to start their new life together in a home unburdened by history.

'Christie, don't do that, I look like a teenager,' Jennifer protested.

'You look fabulous. It just softens your face a bit,' she insisted.

'I am not used to having little tendrils hanging down the sides of my face. Now comb it back. This is no time to change hairstyles.'

Jennifer's suite looked like a sorority house on a Saturday night. All her sisters had decided it would be fun to dress together in her room. There were stockings, shoes, and clothing everywhere. The bathroom resembled the Lauder counter at Bloomingdale's after a heavy day of promoting. Make-up brushes, compacts, eye shadows, and cans of mousse, hair gels, and sprays were lined up and ready for action. Before they could catch him, Jason had sneaked in and decorated the mirror with various colours of eye crayons and assorted lipsticks.

Jennifer had managed to keep her entire outfit separate from the rest of their things, and she was completely dressed and ready to go. Christie was trying to finish her hair.

'Give me the brush, Chris,' Jennifer requested. 'You've been an enormous help,' she teased.

Marion knocked and entered the room, looking sensational in a raspberry-silk Bill Blass dress. Ken was right behind her.

'Well, I'm sure this appears much less organised than it really is,' she commented, observing the tornadolike scene. 'Jennifer, it is five to four.'

'I realise that, and I'm ready. Let's go, everybody. Out. Now go.' She kissed Pat and Susan, patted Christie on the back and hugged her mother. 'Dad and I will see you in a minute.'

They all left; Jennifer and her father were alone in the room.

The beautiful off-white Ungaro wool crepe dress with long sleeves and shirring at the waistline accentuated her glorious figure. She had never looked more beautiful.

Ken observed her putting on a last touch of lip gloss.

'I'm so proud of you in so many ways, darling. I wish you every happiness.'

'Thank you, Dad. We're going to be very good together. I'm sure of it.'

The guests drank to their happiness with champagne and feasted on caviar immediately after the short ceremony. By midnight that evening they had changed into casual clothes and were halfway across the ocean on their way to Italy.

31

SEVERAL weeks after their return, Jennifer received an envelope containing two letters, one from Lisa and Jonathan, and another from Christopher. She had written them from Italy to tell them of her marriage and to wish them the best of holidays and new year.

Lisa's reply was warm and caring, a reflection of the good friendship she and Jennifer had always enjoyed. It was beautifully written on crisp white stationery with her monogram, LTP, in navy blue. They were all fine and the best news was that they had won Christopher's custody case. Unfortunately the decision had been handed down as a result of Victoria's attempted suicide while she was on a weekend pass from the rehabilitation centre. Jennifer was saddened to read about Victoria, but she was relieved that Christopher had been spared the trauma of a long, ugly custody trial in the courts. It would have been too much for any of them to bear. The note went on to wish her lots of love and joy in her new situation. They hoped to visit New York some time in the spring and wanted very much to meet Sidney.

Christopher's letter, written on lined notepaper, its edges ragged from being torn out of the spiral binder, brought her up to date on his school and athletic activities. He had been elected team captain for the second year, and they were looking forward to a winning season. His penmanship was excellent – all the letters were equal in size, and it was very neat for a young boy. It reminded her of all the sweet notes she had received from Nicholas. He closed his letter by saying, 'Lisa told me you got married last week. I hope you are very happy. We all still wish it had been to my dad. We miss you both very much. Love & kisses, Christopher. P.S. Your saddle is waiting in the stable when you want to come riding with me again. I hope it is soon. Maybe you can bring Buster with you. I'm sure he would like it here.'

32

JENNIFER had never been so thankful that she anchored the evening news instead of the morning edition. She would never have made it during the first three months, when not a day passed without the plague of first-trimester nausea. But now that she was in her fourth month, the much-revered glow of pregnancy had made her look more beautiful than ever. Sidney was on a constant high; in five short months he would be a father for the first time in his forty-eight years.

USBC had climbed to number three in the ratings, knocking out one of the old-timers, becoming a new role model for broadcasting in the eighties.

Jennifer was firmly entrenched in her position, having endeared herself to those with whom she worked, and having created a team that pulled hard together to be the best. In spite of her new marriage, her new home, and the approaching birth of her first child, she was as involved and tenacious about her career as she had been on her very first day.

That was why, when her secretary buzzed her one afternoon as she was deeply involved in doing a rewrite of a story for that night, she drew a total blank.

'Jennifer, it's Nancy Demarchellier on line two. She's called seven times this week. I've got it in the records. She says it's really important. She asked me to remind you that you had given her your word on something.'

For the life of her, Jennifer could not recall the name. She only knew it wasn't one of her correspondents or editors.

'Who?' she demanded of Ellen, her ever-patient, ever-loyal secretary.

'You know, Nancy Demarchellier, Channel 12, she has that show called *On Top*, or *At the Top*, or something like that. It's about important, successful women; you know, women like you,' she teased. 'Women who have it all. You remember now?' she asked.

'Yes, yes, OK, now I remember,' she smiled to herself. Lunch at Le Cirque, it seemed so long ago. Nancy's insistence that she appear on her show.

'Yes, Ellen, OK,' she said into the speaker.

She picked up the phone. The time was right to fulfil her promise.